Praise for *If You Give a Rake a Ruby*

"Galen expertly entwines espionage-flavored intrigue with sizzling passion."

—*Booklist*

"Galen is at the top of her game... Galen is a grand mistress of the action/adventure subgenre."

—*RT Book Reviews*, 4½ Stars,
Top Pick of the Month

"Engrossing and fun. Shana Galen is known for her fast-pasted Regencies, and she scores again with *If You Give a Rake a Ruby*."

—*Historical Novel Review*

"Sensual and sexy..."

—*Publishers Weekly*

"Passionate, exciting, and dazzling... A lighthearted read that is plenty of fun, but it is also an emotional journey that will captivate you completely."

—*The Romance Reviews*

"The writing is excellent and the characters are captivating. Ms. Galen delivers a steamy romance."

—*Night Owl Reviews*, 5 Stars, Reviewer Top Pick

"Full of daring and danger, this Regency romance sizzles with sexual tension, brims with subtle humor, and entertains with characters that sweep the reader into a whirlwind of high-risk action and euphoric love."

—*Long and Short Reviews*

"When Shana Galen writes about spies, everything clicks into place... a grand romance."

—*The Royal Reviews*

"Filled with intrigue, blazing romance, and wit, this book will keep your interest from cover to cover."

—*RomFan Reviews*

"A great story with plenty of sass, humor, and spice. Do not miss it!"

—*Romance Junkies*

"With these fiery characters and steady plot, you will fly through this book."

—Reading Between the Wines Book Club

"This series just gets better and better."

—*My House of Books*

"I know I can always turn to Shana Galen for fast-paced, sexy, adventurous romances and this is exactly what this book delivers!"

—*Rogues Under the Covers*

"I absolutely love what Shana Galen does for historical romance... The characters are fresh and enticing."

—*Books a al Mode*

"Historical romance at its best. It's intriguing, exciting, mysterious, sexy, and carries us to a romantic happily ever after."

—*Unwrapping Romance*

Also by Shana Galen

SAPPHIRES ARE AN EARL'S BEST FRIEND

SHANA GALEN

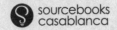

sourcebooks
casablanca

Published by Sourcebooks Casablanca, an imprint of Sourcebooks,
Inc.
P.O. Box 4410, Naperville, Illinois 60567-4410
(630) 961-3900
Fax: (630) 961-2168
www.sourcebooks.com

Printed and bound in The United States of America.
QW 10 9 8 7 6 5 4 3 2 1

For my daughter, who loves twirly dresses and long bedtime stories and the color blue.

Better a diamond with a flaw than a pebble without.

—Confucius

One

"ONCE UPON A TIME, THERE WAS A LITTLE GIRL named Lily."

Lily snuggled under her covers and listened to her mother's singsong voice. She heard the rain pattering outside on the roof and the clip-clop of horses' hooves as a hackney passed her family's modest home in London. On the floor below her, the low rumble of her father's voice reverberated as he spoke to the man who'd arrived shortly after supper. Her father entertained more and more unexpected visitors of late. When she pressed her ear to the door to listen, she heard names like Napoleon and Fishguard and *La Légion Noire* whispered in furtive voices. Until Mamma told her to come away.

Sometimes she was scared, even though she didn't know what she was scared of. But here in her cozy room with the low-sloped ceiling, lying in her soft bed with her baby doll and her mamma beside her, she felt safe. Lily yawned. "What about the little girl, Mamma?"

"She was in possession of several very special dresses.

There was a green dress that glittered with emeralds, and when she wore the green dress, she could fly."

Lily closed her eyes, imagining flying.

"There was a purple dress with a velvet bodice and ruffles on the skirt, and when she wore the purple dress, she was a princess. There was a pink dress covered with spangles, and when she wore the pink dress, she could dance like a ballerina. There was a red dress that radiated with rubies, and when she wore the red dress, she was *so* strong."

"As strong as Papa?"

"Yes. That strong. Now, close your eyes and listen."

But Lily knew her favorite dress was coming, and it was so hard not to bounce with excitement.

"There was a white dress that dazzled with diamonds, and when she wore the white dress, she could swim like a fish. And there was a blue dress, and that was her favorite because it sparkled with sapphires. When she wore the blue dress, she was invisible."

"And no one could see her."

"That's right, Lily Bea."

Her name was Lillian Beatrice Dawson, and sometimes her mother called her Lily Bea. Mamma had pet names for all of her children—names like Robert Bear for her big brother and Lottie for Charlotte, who was only a year older than Lily—but Lily liked her special name best.

Mamma tucked the coverlet in snugly, and Lily yawned again. "Lily," her mother asked, "why do you like the blue dress best? Is it because blue is your favorite color?"

"No." Green was her favorite color, but it was all

right that Mamma didn't remember that. She had a lot to remember. "It's because I want to be inbisible."

"In*vis*ible? Why?"

"Like Papa. He says his job is to be in-vis-i-ble."

"Hmm." Her mother huffed, and Lily opened her eyes to see Mamma's expression. Sometimes Lily said things that made her mother unhappy. Usually they were statements related to Papa. Mamma smoothed Lily's hair off her brow, and Lily closed her eyes again.

"And lastly there was a black dress," Mamma said, "as long and black as midnight, and when she wore the black dress, she could sleep for hours and hours. So let's put on our black dress, and go to sleep."

"Good night, Mamma."

"Good night. Sweet dreams."

Lily closed her eyes and dreamed of jewels and ball gowns.

అలో

London, last weeks of the 1816 Season

Lily was of the opinion that any lady who possessed a modicum of intelligence should be on good terms with her modiste. This was even truer for women, like herself, who were not ladies. Lily had no name or reputation to fall back on. There was only her ability to stun and impress. And when Lily needed to impress, as she did tonight, she called on Madam Durand.

Madam Durand was, in Lily's estimation, the best modiste in London. This was not because the woman was the most expensive modiste, though she was, or because she was the most innovative, which she was. It was, in Lily's judgment, because she had an eye for what styles and colors would complement a woman, and she dressed each woman accordingly. It did not matter what the latest fashion might be in Paris. If said fashion did not look well on a lady—or, in Lily's case, on the courtesan—Madam Durand would not dress her in it.

"No, no, no!" Madam Durand said in her heavily accented English as soon as Lily walked through the shop's door. "I do not comprehend why you insist on defying me."

The seamstresses in the shop, as well as the young girl who must have had the appointment directly before Lily's, turned their heads in Lily's direction. Lily merely smiled and curtsied. So much for slipping in unobtrusively.

"Everyone is wearing high waists," she said, kissing Madam Durand on both cheeks. "My gown is perfectly fashionable."

"And everyone is jumping off bridges!" the modiste replied. "Will you jump too?"

"I think what you mean to say is—"

"Bah!" Madam Durand waved a hand. "Have a seat and a cup of tea. I will be with you in a moment, and then we will discuss the waist that looks best on your figure!"

Lily perched herself on the red damask chair and accepted a cup of tea from one of Madam Durand's seamstresses. She knew how the discussion with Madam would go. Madam would tell her she had a tiny waist and must wear gowns to flaunt it, and

Lily would acquiesce and buy another gown with an unfashionably low waist. She would look stunning—Madam Durand could guarantee that—but her style would not be emulated as Juliette and Fallon's had been. She seemed doomed to live in the shadows, despite her efforts to stun.

Drat, she thought, sipping her tea. But it couldn't be helped. At the moment she had tasks more important than setting fashion trends—more was the pity. She had an extremely important man to attract.

Madam Durand finished with the young lady ahead of Lily, and the girl's mother ushered her child out. As Lily finished her tea, she heard the chit—who must have been all of sixteen—whisper, "Who is that, Mama?"

"Shh! Do not look at her. Keep walking."

"But who—?"

"I shall tell you in the carriage."

"I doubt that very much," Lily muttered and rose. Madam Durand did not wait for Lily to enter the workroom before she waved Lily's note about.

"What is this, Countess? A red gown? With your hair? *C'est impossible!*"

"I know," Lily said, touching her tightly coiled auburn hair. It was, thankfully, a dark auburn. "But there is a gentleman."

Madam Durand rolled her eyes.

"And he is said to prefer red. Ruby red."

Madam Durand studied her for a long moment. "I might have known a gentleman would be involved. Fortunately for you, I am a genius."

"I have every faith in you, Madam," Lily answered,

stepping on the dais and raising her arms so Madam's assistants might remove her dress.

Madam clapped her hands. "Phillipa! Fetch the Countess of Charm's gown."

When the offending gown had been removed and Lily stood in her petticoats, the assistant presented Madam Durand's gown. Lily's brow winged upward. "Pink?" she asked. "I am not a debutante, though I thank you for the compliment."

Madam Durand waved her hand. "Men like a woman in pastels. It reminds them of innocence." The gown was sarcenet with a thin crimson gauze overlay on the skirts. The overlay was beaded with delicate ruby beads, which formed pretty floral patterns, while the bodice was a pale, pale pink ornamented with flowers formed of those same crimson beads. Lily knew immediately the gown was going to cost her. The materials, the beading—it was some of Madam Durand's finest. She prayed she would not like it when she put it on. That would save her finances.

But when the seamstresses helped her don it, and pinned and taped it into place, Lily peered into the looking glass and sighed. It was perfect. It was exquisite. She had to have it. She could not fail to be noticed in this.

"Madam…" Lily breathed, but she could not find the words. The modiste was smiling, having seen the pleasure on Lily's face already.

"A few adjustments, I think." The women went to work pinning and measuring, and Lily stood still and allowed herself to be prodded and poked. She did not mind, especially when she was wearing such a stunning gown. The duke was going to be smitten.

At least he'd better be. The bill was going to be astronomical. Lily could not have afforded it without Fitzhugh's assistance. She complimented Madam Durand several more times before the gown was taken away for its last alterations. "It will be ready for the ball this evening?" Lily asked.

Madam Durand gave her a look that indicated she did not like to be questioned.

"I apologize, Madam," Lily said, gathering her reticule and her parasol. "Of course it shall be ready."

"I will have it sent to your town house."

"Very good, Madam." Lily would need to pay the delivery man at that point. And that meant it was time to speak to Fitzhugh. She exited Madam Durand's shop and waved to her coachman. He rushed to speak with her. "Yes, Countess?"

"I am going to walk, Franklin. The day is lovely. You may return home."

"Are you certain you do not wish me to follow you?"

"Quite certain." She was a notorious courtesan, but that did not mean she wanted to be seen arriving at the home of her friend's betrothed. She would be far less likely to be noted if she arrived on foot. And she preferred to avoid notice if at all possible—not simply because Fallon was engaged to Fitzhugh. Fallon knew Lily was not carrying on with Fitzhugh. But there were others who might be watching and whom Lily did not want to connect her with the leader of the Diamonds in the Rough.

She set out amongst the hustle and bustle of peers,

their servants, and shopkeepers. The sounds of the city were unmistakable—the clash of hawkers' voices, horses' hooves, church bells, harness bells. She loved the busyness of London. She felt alive here.

She did not love the poverty she encountered on London's streets. She noted a thin young woman hunched in a doorway with her hand out. The beggar did not meet the eyes of those who passed her, noses in the air. Any moment now, the shopkeeper would spot her and order her to move. Lily stopped, dug in her reticule, and pulled out what few coins she had with her. "Here," she said, placing them in the woman's hand.

The woman's defeated gaze met Lily's for a brief moment. "Thank you, my lady." Then she closed her hand on the coins and scurried away.

Lily watched her. "I'm no lady," she murmured to herself. "There but for the grace of God—and the Earl of Sin—go I."

Lily walked on at a leisurely pace, reminding herself to breathe in the last of the spring air and admire the azure sky and the fluffy white clouds floating in it. Of course, the air smelled more of manure than flowers, and the sky had a black haze from coal fires, but she would not allow any of that to bother her today. Dirt and grime could not touch her when she wore this yellow gown—with the extremely high waist Madam Durand had chastised her for—and carried its matching yellow parasol with the pretty white-and-yellow ruffles. She felt pretty, and the admiring looks from the men she passed told her she looked the way she felt. This was Mayfair, so she had few worries about any of them accosting her, but she had her mission on her mind and tried to stay alert.

Perhaps that extra measure of cautiousness was what led her to notice she was being followed. Perhaps the man following her was not a very good shadow. Or perhaps she had simply been lucky. But two blocks from Fitzhugh's town house, Lily spotted her tail. She told herself she was simply paranoid or overly cautious. She stopped in front of a window and pretended to admire a display of ugly hats. The man stopped as well, studying a shop that sold women's shoes.

Lily sighed and considered, momentarily, just ignoring him. But no, she had to take action. She looked down at her gown, knowing it would be the inevitable casualty of this encounter. It was so pretty, but she supposed Madam Durand was correct—it didn't suit her. The loss would not be so great, though it still pained her to cause damage to anything beautiful. Gritting her teeth, Lily dropped her reticule. When she bent to lift it, she caught a finger in one of her flounces and deliberately tore it. The ripping sound it made rent her heart. She pretended not to notice the damage and continued on until she had almost reached an alley. And then she made a production of looking down, spotting the tear and looking shocked and horrified. She peered about, as though making sure no one saw the embarrassing condition of her gown, and stepped around the corner and into the alley.

Once out of sight, she sprinted down the length of the alley, passing several dark doorways, the rear entrances to the shops she'd browsed earlier, until she found one that was narrow but deep. She shot into it and flattened herself against the wall, lifting her parasol and rubbing her fingers over the polished ivory handle.

And then she waited.

Her shadow would think she had stepped off the street to repair her gown. When she did not return to the street in a few moments, he would come looking for her. Lily was not the patient sort. In fact, if she were ever asked to make a list of what she detested most, waiting would be at the very top. Every time she had to wait, she needed the privy, even if she had just used it. It was all in her mind, she knew, but she had to cross her legs anyway.

She tried singing in her head part of an aria she'd heard at the opera last week, but she had forgotten the words. She was never very good at Italian. And then she heard a splash and froze. Finally! She would perish from boredom if forced to wait much longer. Lily pushed her spine against the wall and made certain no part of her gown was peeking out. She heard the man's footfalls approaching. He would be confused now, wondering where she'd gone and not believing she would have ventured this far into the alley. She wondered who he worked for. Ravenscroft? Lucifer? Or perhaps it was one of her own checking on her.

She sensed more than saw the man draw nearer, and she held her breath, sinking into the shadows. The man stepped into her line of sight, and Lily watched as he slinked carefully forward. He had not yet seen the doorway where she hid. Idiot. He was looking forward, not even thinking that she might have stepped to the side and now lay in wait. And she supposed that was to her advantage, but still, this was going to be far too easy. Hardly worth her time. He took another step, and she moved into position, rose on tiptoes, and slammed the parasol on the back of his neck. Fortunately, he had not been a tall man, or she would never have been able to achieve the right angle. As it was, she hit him perfectly, and he crumpled to the ground.

"Simple," she muttered and knelt beside him. Her hem trailed in a muddy puddle, and when she'd pounced, she'd caught her sleeve on a sliver of wood poking out from the door. She now had two tears in her gown, and it was soiled with God knew what. Most vexing. She rifled her pursuer's pockets and found only a few shillings, a cheap pocket watch, and a moldy bit of cheese.

It was disappointing, to say the least. If she'd had the time and resources, she could have tied him up, questioned him, forced him to answer her questions. That was her true talent—charming people. It was why the prince regent had given her the sobriquet Countess of Charm. Little did everyone know it was a talent she'd had to acquire. She'd grown up shy and reticent, not charming at all.

Lily studied the tall fence marking the edge of the alley. She would have rather walked out the way she'd come in, but she supposed she had better take precautions. If one man was following her, there might be another. And the next time, she might not spot the shadow.

Lily shook her head. "And the day began with such promise," she muttered. She couldn't possibly scale the wall with the parasol in hand, so she abandoned it in the doorway where she'd hidden. It had been a pretty parasol, but it was irreparably bent now, and she wouldn't need it anymore, since she was disposing of this dress when she arrived home. In truth, she suspected one reason she wore this gown, even though she knew it didn't particularly flatter her, was because she liked the accompanying parasol so much.

Lily took a step back, studied the wall, then tied up her skirts. She loved working for the Foreign Office, but she could have done without the physical aspects of her position—at least those that forced her to soil pretty gowns. Lily ran forward, gaining momentum, jumped, and reached the top of the wall. She scrambled over with a groan and lowered herself to the ground. She looked down at her gown. Streaks of dirt marred the expensive muslin. Now she was glad she was taking a circuitous route to Fitzhugh's. She didn't relish her disheveled clothing becoming the topic of the scandal rags.

She arrived at Fitzhugh's town house and knocked on the servants' entrance. One of Fitzhugh's under maids opened the door, and her eyes widened when she recognized Lily. "Hello!" Lily waved as though her presence here was unremarkable. "Is Mr. Fitzhugh at home?"

The maid blinked at her, and Lily supposed the poor girl was beyond scandalized. Not only was a notorious courtesan knocking on the servants' entrance of her employer's home, she was requesting to see the master. A single woman, unchaperoned, calling on a man at his home. Such a thing was not done. Lily did not care. She was used to causing scandals. She'd been doing so since she was sixteen. What was one more at this point?

"I—I—" the maid mumbled.

"Never mind," Lily said, pushing past her and into the kitchens. "I shall find him myself."

"H-he's with his betrothed," the maid whispered.

"Fallon is here?" Lily brightened. "Splendid! Where are they?"

"Taking tea," she squeaked.

"In the drawing room?" Lily was already on the stairs. "No matter. I'll find them." They were not in the drawing room, but she found them in a small parlor adjacent to Fitzhugh's library. She was not surprised to find that "taking tea" involved Fallon sitting on Fitzhugh's lap in a rather warm embrace. Lily cleared her throat.

"Out, Pressly," Fitzhugh growled.

"It's not Pressly," Lily said. Fallon jumped up, and Fitzhugh scowled at her.

"What happened to you?" He rose and crossed to her, his eyebrows coming together in an expression of concern.

"I had a small incident," Lily said, closing the door on the curious servants pretending to dust just outside.

"Are you well?" Fallon asked, taking Lily's hands. "Your dress is ruined!"

"You should see my parasol."

"Oh, no! That was your favorite parasol."

"Yes, the parasol is a tragedy," Fitzhugh drawled, "but might you enlighten us as to how it was damaged?"

"It is past damaged," Lily said, allowing Fallon to lead her to a chair and pour her a cup of tea. "It is ruined. But I suppose it's for the best. Madam Durand says this gown does not suit me, and the only reason I continue to wear it is because I adore that parasol."

"Then perhaps it's best the source of temptation has been removed," Fallon remarked.

"That was my thought, and wait until you see the gown Madam Durand—"

"Miss Dawson!" Fitzhugh barked. Lily jumped, sloshing tea onto the saucer. "Could you and Fallon speak of fashion later and tell me what happened to leave you in this state?"

Fallon put her hands on her hips. "There's no need to shout."

Fitzhugh sighed. Loudly. Then looked pointedly at Lily.

She gave him a sweet smile. "I was leaving Madam Durand's shop," she began, "when I noticed I was being followed."

"Are you certain?"

Lily raised a brow.

Fitzhugh held his hands up defensively. "My apologies. I did not mean to question your skills. Do go on."

"As I was on my way here to collect payment, I did not want to be followed. I ducked into an alley, and the man followed."

"Forgive me," Fitzhugh said, taking the seat across from Lily. "What payment?"

"For my gown," Lily said, looking exasperated. "The Foreign Office cannot expect me to take full responsibility for financing the seduction of the Duke of Ravenscroft."

"Now I am confused," Fallon said. "Why on earth would you seduce that lecher?"

"Because we suspect the duke is the man who wants to see the Diamonds in the Rough assassinated," Fitzhugh told his intended. "He is in possession of some rather large rubies."

"Rubies he was using to hire assassins to kill our best spies..." Fallon's wide eyes narrowed. "Why was I not informed of this danger to you?"

"It didn't concern you," Fitzhugh answered. Lily winced. She glanced at Fallon, who was rising slowly from her seat, daggers shooting from her eyes. Lily jumped to her feet.

"Before you two progress any further in this discussion," she said, "could I have the blunt? Madam Durand is sending the gown this afternoon, and I'd like to go home and burn *this* dress."

"I'll send for your coachman." Fallon rose and left the room.

Fitzhugh steepled his hands. "How much?"

Lily told him.

"Is this a gown or a town house?"

"It's an exquisite gown. Ravenscroft will not be able to keep his eyes off me."

Fitzhugh raked a hand through his hair. "I don't have to tell you to be careful. You know the latest intelligence?"

"Artemis? Do you believe we've found him?"

"I think much of the evidence points to the duke."

"I'll find out the truth." Lily sank into her seat again, impossibly weary. She would need all of her skills tonight to convince those at the ball she was lively and charming. She would much rather go to bed and sleep.

How perfectly tedious.

"I don't like this," Fitzhugh said. "Artemis is aptly named. He hunted and killed several of our best during the war. I don't like putting you in jeopardy."

She felt her belly knot at his words. This mission was unlike most of the others she was assigned. If Ravenscroft was Artemis, she would be risking her life to uncover his secret. She could very well end up with her throat slit, her body thrown in an unmarked grave somewhere in Nottinghamshire.

But she could not show her fear to Fitzhugh. Any other agent sent in would be much more at risk than she. She did not want to be responsible for anyone's death because she was a coward. Lily gave Fitzhugh a shrug and waved her hand dismissively. "Why would Ravenscroft suspect me of being anything other than a courtesan? In which case, the only thing in jeopardy is my virtue, and that is but a distant memory."

Fitzhugh didn't smile at her jest. "If he attempts to force himself on you—"

"I am perfectly capable of handling that sort of thing," Lily said, forcing herself to sound confident. "You have nothing to worry about. Plan your wedding and watch your back. I will obtain the information you need."

"My mother is planning the wedding, and Fallon's brute of a butler has my back. You'll have to forgive me if I have little to do but worry over my agents."

"You should be in hiding."

"I plan to seclude myself and my wife for weeks after the wedding."

Lily rolled her eyes. The door opened, and Fallon stepped inside. "I sent a messenger, but it may be some time before the coach arrives. In the meantime, let me show you to a room. At the very least, you may splash water on your face."

Fallon knew Lily well enough to realize when she was weary she craved peace and solitude.

"I'll have your funds ready before you depart," Fitzhugh said.

"Again, thank you."

She followed Fallon to a small bedchamber. A maid was just finishing building a fire in the hearth, while another poured water from a jug into a basin. Both curtsied and retired. Lily washed her hands and face and pressed the cool cloth to her eyes. When she opened them, Fallon was watching her. "Are you looking forward to the wedding?" Lily asked.

Fallon shrugged. "I am looking forward to the marriage."

"He is lucky to have you," she said, running the cloth over her neck.

"He seems to think so." The awe in her voice told Lily Fallon still wasn't quite certain she deserved real love. "Lily, there's something I wanted to speak to you about."

Lily smiled. "Is it about the wedding night? You see, my dear, when a man and woman love each other…"

Fallon rolled her eyes. "It is not about the wedding night, and you know it. It's something else. Someone, actually."

Lily's pulse kicked at the grave look on Fallon's face. "What's wrong?"

"Darlington is back in Town."

Lily tensed but pretended to be uninterested. "I saw him when he was last in Town. He seemed a bit surly. I won't seek him out again."

"But he will seek you out. He's come to see you."

Lily willed her heart to stop thundering in her chest. *Her?* Not possible. She was invisible to him. Lily could hear Fallon still speaking, but her voice sounded far away and muted under the thrum of blood pounding in Lily's ears. Without waiting for her friend to finish, Lily interrupted, "Why would he want to see me?"

"According to Juliette, he 'will not allow that harlot to soil the memory of his mother or the hallowed ground of Ravenscroft Castle.'"

Juliette. Lily's fists clenched. Of course. "Hallowed ground?"

Fallon shrugged. "It was something like that. I only told you because I thought you should be aware."

Lily nodded, unable to speak.

"Lily," Fallon said, placing her hand on Lily's arm. "Darlington may be your biggest impediment."

Two

LATER, WHILE SHE SAT AND PRETENDED TO READ AS HER lady's maid styled her hair for the night, Lily thought about Fallon's words. Lily had difficulty imagining the amiable, good-natured Earl of Darlington as any sort of impediment. He might not be overjoyed when his father became her protector, but he would laugh it off.

At least she thought he would. The last time she had seen him, in Hyde Park a few weeks ago, he had seemed severe and unapproachable. Her efforts to tease him into smiling hadn't been successful. She attributed his foul mood to two recent events. Firstly, his mother had died quite suddenly in a tragic carriage accident. Darlington appeared to be the only member of the family mourning the late Duchess of Ravenscroft. The duke had been in Town for weeks playing the libertine. Even some of the more debauched members of Society had raised their brows at the duke's blatant disregard for any sort of show of mourning his late wife and the mother of his three children.

Secondly, the Duchess of Dalliance was married. She was newly wed to the Duke of Pelham. It had not been a secret that Darlington had been in love with Juliette since the moment The Three Diamonds made their debut in Society. This was before they were The Three Diamonds. That sobriquet came later, when the courtesans had suitably dazzled. But Darlington had been there from the beginning.

Lily remembered, because the first time she'd seen him, she'd fallen in love with him.

And he'd fallen in love with Juliette.

She would have recovered from her infatuation with Darlington more quickly if Juliette had loved him back. Then Lily would not have been able to hold out hope he might eventually give up on the Duchess of Dalliance and notice her. But Juliette all but ignored the man. Lily supposed this was because her friend did not want to encourage his attentions, but the snubs only made Darlington more determined.

Lily could hardly blame the man for being slightly cross when he'd lost both his mother and the woman he fancied himself in love with within weeks of each other. But she did not think Darlington was the type of man to hold on to anger. That was why she liked him so much. He was lively and charming—the part she also played. And he was safe. He was not too dark or deep. If they were ever to fall into bed together, she would not have to share much of herself with him. And she preferred it that way.

Her maid helped her don the gown Madam Durand had sent, and Lily admired herself in the looking glass before dismissing the servant. When the door was closed, she went to her escritoire and unlocked a small center drawer. There, she withdrew a delicate pistol with a pretty silver handle inlaid with sapphires. It had been a gift from the Countess of Sinclair when Lily had said she intended to continue her work with the Foreign Office. She had never yet had to use it, though she certainly knew how. She rarely ever took it anywhere with her, and certainly never to a ball.

But this ball was not for pleasure. It was deadly serious. Someone had to stop the man trying to murder the Diamonds in the Rough. Someone had to discover to whom Lucifer had sold the Diamonds' identities. If Ravenscroft was that man, Lily intended to find out.

And then she had to stay alive long enough to stop him.

&

The Earl of Darlington watched the men and women of the *ton* dance across the ballroom and made no attempt to stifle the scowl on his face. Had he once found amusements like this… amusing? He did not now. He found them tedious and grating. He would not be here tonight if not for his father.

Slowly and with dread, he turned in his father's direction. The man was surrounded by painted women covered in jewels and little else. The old duke swatted one woman on the bottom. She threw back her black hair, and her red mouth, ornamented with a black spangled beauty mark, broke into a wide grin. Andrew gritted his teeth. His mother might not have been a beauty or the kind of woman men sought out at soirees, but she had been a good duchess and a good mother. She'd been calm and quiet and serene, and she'd loved her children. She'd certainly looked past her son's flaws often enough.

The late Duchess of Ravenscroft deserved some measure of respect.

Andrew had already spoken with his father and been ceremoniously rebuffed. Actually, he'd been told something to the effect of: you won't be the only one having fun anymore. Andrew had squared his shoulders and bit back his retort. If his father believed he still had wild oats to sow, Andrew was not the man to censure him. After all, he'd done his share of carousing and been quite the gallant at one time.

But that was over now. The idea that he might share a bed with a woman who had also shared his father's attentions disgusted him. He wanted no part of it.

A commotion erupted in the vestibule, near the door where Andrew had stationed himself. The butler, who had been announcing the guests, stepped away and returned a moment later with a woman who could only be described as delicious.

Andrew's gaze traveled from her tiny waist to her rounded breasts to the pale, porcelain skin of her cheek. Ruby earrings dangled from small shell-shaped ears, reflecting light on the curved slope of a delicate neck. Green eyes flashed at him, and a sensual mouth smiled. He felt his blood warm and begin to pump faster as she gave him a saucy wink.

"The Countess of Charm!" the butler announced, and the drone of voices rose again.

Andrew shook his head. Lily? *That* was Lily? He watched her glide through the ballroom, seemingly unaware of the attention she created. No wonder there had been a dispute when she'd arrived. Not only was she a notorious courtesan, but she had reportedly caught the attention of—who else?—the Duke of Ravenscroft. Otherwise known as Andrew's father.

And that was why Andrew was here. He'd wanted no part of London and had been about to return home when he'd heard the rumors—the Duke of Ravenscroft intended to seduce the Countess of Charm and then make her his wife. For the woman who, it was rumored, had ruined the Prince of Wales for other women, no enticement but that of the title of *duchess* might tempt her into the old duke's bed. And here she was, probably hoping to lay her claim to that title.

Andrew would make certain she did not.

He'd intended to waylay her before she could rendezvous with his father, but she had obviously bewitched him in some form or fashion. Why hadn't he recognized her? He'd known her for years. She was making her way toward the duke, and Andrew started after her, catching up with her easily as she was stopped by every eligible gentleman—and a few that weren't—in the room. He came up behind her, took her elbow. "Lily, I need to speak with you."

She glanced at him over her shoulder, her gaze traveling down to her imprisoned elbow and then back to his face. She'd never given him such a cold reception before, and without thinking, he released her. She turned back to her companion and laughed at some inane comment the fop made. Andrew waited. He knew how to play this game. Courtesans liked to feel as though they were important enough to merit a man's time and attention. He would play, for the moment, and wait while she finished her conversation.

But when she was through, instead of turning to him, she glided away. Devil take her, because that was where she was going when he was through with her. Andrew went after her, and this time he grasped her upper arm and turned her to face him. "I want to speak with you."

She flicked a distasteful glance at his hand on her flesh. "Unhand me."

Who was this woman? Lily had never spoken to him like that. He almost complied. "After we've spoken."

"It should be obvious that I have nothing to say to you." She attempted to tug her arm from his grasp, but he held on. Even through his gloves, he could feel how warm her skin was, how soft.

"But I have something to say to you. Either come with me now or I say it in front of two hundred of our closest friends."

She glared at him, her green eyes hard as emeralds. He'd always thought her hair her best feature, but now he saw she could use her eyes to her advantage as well. "Make it quick," she said and muttered something about *impediments*.

Andrew clenched his jaw and led her to the spot he'd decided on before she'd arrived. It was a small parlor adjacent to the ballroom. He opened the door and interrupted a man and woman in an embrace. "Out," he said when they dashed apart and stared at him with flaming faces.

Without protest, the couple fled.

"Ever the romantic," Lily said, gliding into the room and turning to face him. The rubies on her gown glinted in the light from the brace of candles set on a table.

"Interesting criticism, coming from a courtesan," he shot back. He closed the door behind him, though being seen with him was no danger to her reputation. He couldn't ruin her. Her reputation was ruined beyond repair.

Lily's brow arched. "You never seemed to mind associating with the Fashionable Impures before. Perhaps you are bitter because your favorite Cyprian has chosen another."

Andrew balled his hands. He did not want to think of Juliette, married to his so-called friend, the Duke of Pelham. Juliette was the least of his worries at the moment. He had his father and the harlot before him to consider. "I don't remember you ever being deliberately cruel," Andrew said, knowing his words were crueler than hers.

Her face fell into an expression of regret. "You are correct. I apologize. That was unkind of me. And now would you give me the courtesy of saying what this is about so I might return to the ball?"

"Return to my father."

She nodded. "I have promised Ravenscroft a dance."

Andrew shuddered at the image of his portly father dancing, his arm about Lily's waist. "You will find someone else to dance with."

She merely looked at him. "Will I?"

"As a favor to me, you will turn your attentions elsewhere."

She tilted her head, studying him. "I don't owe you any favors."

Anger swept through him, and he closed in on her until he towered over her and glared down into her sparkling green eyes. "What do you want? Blunt?" He pulled a handful of quid from his coat and tossed it at her. "There. Meet me at Threadneedle Street in the morning. I shall have my banker draw up a draft for more funds."

Her eyes hardened and went dull. "I don't want your money, Darlington."

She pushed past him, stepping on the notes. He grabbed her elbow. "Five hundred pounds."

"Release me." She did not look at him.

"One thousand, and that is my final offer."

"You insult me, my lord. Release me now."

"So it's the title you want, then. You won't have it. I'll never consent to a marriage, and my father is no fool like Pelham. He won't marry a slut."

The slap rang out in the empty room, and his cheek stung. He would have a hand print, no doubt.

"Unhand me, or I shall scream."

Andrew blinked at her. He had not thought she would be so difficult to persuade. Of The Three Diamonds, Lily had always been the sweetest, the... most charming. Even her sobriquet, the Countess of Charm, told of her amiable personality. Why was she being so deliberately difficult now?

"I have tried to reason with you," he began.

With a petulant look, she opened her mouth and screamed. "Help! He—"

He kissed her. Andrew couldn't think what else

to do to make her stop causing that infernal racket. The last thing he needed was to be booted out of a ball, or for his father to realize he was attempting to manipulate the old duke's liaisons. And so he kissed her, not thinking of anything but shutting her up. But when his lips touched hers, all of that changed. He hadn't expected her lips to feel so soft, her mouth to be so ripe, taste so sweet. He hadn't expected his arms to wrap around her and pull her close, crushing her breasts against his chest.

And he hadn't expected to like the feel of her body molded against his. Hadn't expected the urge to explore her curves and to find the places that made her sigh and moan.

He tried to control himself, remind himself of who she was. She was not beautiful, golden Juliette. Lily's eyes were not blue, her hair not pale blond, her form not tall and regal. That was the sort of woman Darlington preferred. He could see the appeal of a woman like Fallon. She was dark and voluptuous. What man wouldn't want her in his bed for a night or two? But Lily? She was pretty, if one liked that sort of thing. He didn't care for her red hair, though it was striking. He didn't care for the sprinkle of freckles across her nose. He didn't care for all the smiling she did. She reminded him of his younger sister, who had always followed him around and attempted to attract his attention.

And if he disliked her so much, why was he still kissing her?

He broke the kiss and caught her hand just inches from his face. "I deserve to be slapped for that," he said, "but you've already doled out my punishment."

"Let me go, or I will be forced to employ stronger methods of resistance." Her voice was breathy and low. Andrew considered that she might have been more affected by the kiss than she allowed him to see. He released her, not because he worried overmuch about her "stronger methods of resistance." He was certain she had them. One did not survive as a courtesan without learning how to fend men off. But he did not think her methods would prove all that successful if he truly intended to take her against her will. Fortunately for her, he didn't want her.

Much.

"Think about what I said," he said, releasing her. "Stay away from my father, or I will make your life very, very inconvenient."

"No!" She inhaled a sharp breath and put a hand over her heart in mock distress. "Not *inconvenient*."

He scowled at her, and she moved closer to him, poking his chest with a gloved finger. "Think about this, Lord Darlington. If you continue to threaten and harass me, *I* will make *your* life *inconvenient*. You know I can." She opened the parlor door, and the orchestra's strings swelled into the room. She shut the door with a bang behind her and was gone.

To his father, he supposed.

Andrew ran a hand through his hair. That had not gone as expected. Normally, he would have gone to ask Pelham or Fitzhugh's advice, but both were involved with the closest friends of his new mortal enemy. He could not rely on them. He had other friends. But those friends were not what one might call sensible, and he could certainly not rely on them to give him any advice over and above which bawdy house offered the best girls or which gaming hell had the best odds.

He opened the parlor door, stepped into the ballroom, and his gaze sought his father. There was Lily, standing at his side, making his father laugh with something she said. She looked over at him, said something more, and the circle of men and women around them laughed heartily.

Andrew's face flamed. How dare she presume to make him the subject of some jest? He would make her pay for this. He stomped out of the ballroom and called for his carriage.

He thought of going to his club, but he knew his father and the Countess of Charm would be all the talk there. Instead, he directed his coachman to take him to a seedy part of Town. A place where he could wallow, undisturbed. He had his coachman stop on the outskirts of Seven Dials and ordered him home again. Then, walking stick at the ready, Andrew made his way into the bowels of the decrepit section of London until he reached The Horse and Crown.

It was a favorite haunt when he had been younger and wanted to prowl the rookeries. Now he came to drink. He had been drinking quite a lot since his mother's death and Juliette's marriage. He found gin dulled the pain.

He made his way to a back table and nodded to the gentleman seated there. The man nodded back. Flynn was not dressed in evening clothes, but he still looked the nobleman—the debauched nobleman. His coat was soiled, his hair had come loose from its queue, and his cravat spilled down his linen shirt. He had a drink before him and several empty cups on the table in front of him.

"Darlington," he said. He never slurred his words, though Andrew knew he must be drunk at times. He'd sat with the man and drank half what Flynn consumed and could barely walk home. "You look rather pretty tonight."

Andrew sat, and a buxom barmaid brought him a gin. She kissed his cheek and attempted to sit on his lap, but he picked her up and shooed her away. He could still taste Lily on his lips, and he didn't want the barmaid tarnishing the memory.

Which was a completely irrational thought. Which was why he needed the gin.

"Ball tonight," Andrew said and took a swallow of gin.

"Ah, yes. Did you stop the nefarious woman from implementing her plan and luring your poor, innocent father into a marriage based on lust and money alone?"

"How did you know all that?"

Flynn indicated the glass of gin. "You talk when you drink."

"You make it sound ridiculous," Andrew said.

Flynn shrugged. "To each his own. My life has its own foibles."

Flynn never talked when he drank. Andrew knew almost nothing about the man except that he was heir to a title and he had done something horrible and did not deserve it. Andrew had thought about telling the man that if titles were deserved rather than inherited, his father would not be the Duke of Ravenscroft. But the man seemed content to wallow in drink and a Byronic malaise.

"I haven't stopped her yet," Andrew said. "But I will."

"How gallant of you to do all of this in honor of your mother. The sole motivation for me is desire for a woman."

"I have no interest in Lily." Andrew drank again. "She reminds me of my sister."

Flynn's brows rose. "You will have to introduce me to your sister."

Andrew narrowed his eyes. Flynn would not be allowed within five miles of his sister. "Not in appearance, in my feelings for her. The Countess of Charm has always struck me as the kind of woman I want to pat on the head and tell to run along and play."

"Has she, now?"

"I have never thought of her in any sort of carnal fashion."

"Haven't you?"

Andrew drank again, surprised his glass was empty so quickly. "I suppose I might have thought of her carnally once or twice. She *is* a woman."

"An attractive woman and a courtesan. She's said to be a favorite of the prince."

Andrew clenched his fists. He had always detested that rumor. "That is simply rubbish. She would never share the prince's bed."

"Wouldn't she?"

Andrew slammed his glass on the table. "Stop questioning me."

"Questioning you? Why, I believe every word you've spoken, old boy."

"No, you don't."

Flynn drained his own glass. "You're right. I think you are lying through your teeth."

Andrew would have thrown his gin in Flynn's face, if he'd had any remaining.

"Don't look so Friday-faced, Darlington. I *want* to believe you. Trouble is, you're not all that convincing."

"You can go to hell."

"Oh, I will. No doubt on that score. But since I am already damned, let me offer you some advice."

"*You* are going to offer *me* advice?"

Flynn nodded and signaled for another round. "I understand completely if you do not take it to heart." Two more glasses arrived, courtesy of the barmaid, and Andrew drank immediately. He was going to need a great quantity of gin to listen to this.

"First of all, Juliette was never going to fall in love with you."

"She doesn't concern me any longer."

"Yes, she does, and I'm telling you to forget her. I didn't know her, but our paths crossed. I've met the Duke of Pelham a few times as well. If Pelham is the sort of man she likes, you had no chance. You two couldn't be more different."

"I shall take that as a compliment."

"You should. I could never drink with a man like Pelham. He would annoy me in less than a quarter of an hour. Secondly, you and the Countess of Charm would suit."

"Lily and me? How far in your cups are you?"

"Have you ever looked at the chit? Have you ever noticed the way she watches you?"

"We are discussing Lily, correct? She has no such feelings for me. In fact, tonight she was rather cool."

"That's because you were being a horse's ass, which, by the way, you have been ever since you returned to Town."

Andrew shook his head. "I don't have to listen to this."

"No, you don't." But Flynn was the one who rose. "You've annoyed me enough for one night. It took you three-quarters of an hour, which is better than Pelham."

"At least I have that consolation."

Flynn grinned and swayed.

"You had better sit before you topple over," Andrew told him.

Flynn waved a hand. "I'm going to hail a hackney and tell the driver to surprise me." He lurched out.

"Good luck finding a hackney in this hellhole!" he called. The tavern's other patrons quieted and gave him stony looks. Andrew grinned. "No offense, of course." He pushed his gin away. He had better be able to walk out on his own. Flynn wasn't really going to hire a cab and tell the jarvey to simply drive. Was he?

And the more Andrew pondered the idea, the more he liked it.

Three

THE EVENING HAD GONE WELL, DESPITE DARLINGTON'S best efforts, Lily thought the next morning as she broke her fast. She sipped chocolate in bed and skimmed over the Cytherian Intelligence column. Her liaison with Ravenscroft was not mentioned in this morning's edition, but it would be before the end of the week. She had made progress at the ball. Not only had Ravenscroft danced with her three times—three miserable times— he'd attempted to seduce her and asked if she would accompany him to the theater tonight.

Lily was glad it was one of the Shakespearean tragedies she had agreed to attend. She could never stay awake through the opera, and she would need all her powers of observation to study and learn what she could about the Duke of Ravenscroft. Thus far, he did not strike her as a man who wanted to kill the group of agents the Crown held responsible for the ultimate defeat of Napoleon. But then, traitors rarely wore signs proclaiming themselves as such. Still, nothing the duke had said or done had struck her as suspicious. Her instincts did not tell her she needed to fear him.

Only one event from the evening stayed with her—and it took the employment of all of her willpower not to think about him.

She'd dreamed about the kiss, of course. She was exceedingly weak-willed in her dreams. She'd dreamed of Darlington's mouth on hers, his hands moving over her flesh, the delicious weight of his body hard and solid on top of hers…

Lily drank more chocolate. How had Fallon known Darlington would be such an impediment? He'd never so much as looked at her before! And now he would not leave her alone. It pained her to treat him so coldly, but she had no other choice. Her mission was paramount. And perhaps she hadn't needed to be quite so cold. But it galled that when she was finally over her infatuation with him, that was the moment he chose to kiss her.

How she would have killed for that kiss months ago.

She lay back on her pillows and searched for something in her room to distract her. She'd had her room done in white lace and robin's egg blue. Compared to Juliette and Fallon's bedchambers, hers was a little girl's room, but she sometimes felt her childhood had ended too soon. Her innocence taken before she was ready. She wondered what the gallants of the *ton* would think if she actually admitted a few to her bedchamber. Would they be surprised it was not exotic and lush as Fallon's was or full of silk and splendor as Juliette's?

Not that she suspected Fallon or Juliette had admitted many, if any, men to their bedchambers. Once all three girls had lived under the Earl of Sinclair's roof.

She'd missed that closeness when they had moved into separate town houses. She'd always been part of a large family, and it felt strange to live alone. Now she was the only one still living alone.

Once she had dreamed of sharing, if not her life, at least her bed with Darlington. She remembered when she first met him. He'd taken her breath away—and not simply because he frequently wore extremely tight breeches. He had curly brown hair she had never seen tamed into any sort of proper style. It was the kind of hair that made a woman want to run her hands through it, watch the curls twine about her fingers. He had thick eyebrows that offset large, dark eyes. His eyes were heavy-lidded and almost always looked as though he'd just been wakened. He had a sleepy quality about him that made Lily think of tousled beds and twisted sheets. But his mouth was his best feature. It was full and pouty and boyish. He had lips made for kissing. She could have feasted on those lips.

And if his good looks hadn't been enough, he had the best taste in fashion save for Beau Brummell— better than Brummell to Lily's mind. She felt that icon of fashion dressed too plainly. Darlington added a bit of flair to his choices. Darlington was too good-natured, too witty to wear sober garb. And yet he'd always dressed in a manner that befitted an earl who would one day be a powerful duke. Except, of course, for those sinfully snug breeches.

Lily had loved him—or at least lusted after him— from the moment she saw him. But he'd never looked twice at her. He'd walked right past her, his gaze fastened on Juliette and never wavering. Even when

Juliette had introduced her, he hadn't taken his eyes from the Duchess of Dalliance. Over the years, Lily had tried to tell Darlington that Juliette was a lost cause. She'd hinted and even been quite bold on one occasion when she'd had too many glasses of champagne. But Darlington had never listened. And while other men flocked around her, offering her jewels, houses, thoroughbreds—anything for access to her bedchamber—Darlington, the only man she wanted, had happily ignored her.

Until last night.

But even last night he had not wanted her. He wanted a way to be rid of her. She didn't blame him for resenting his father's lecherous behavior so soon after the Duchess of Ravenscroft's death, but she did not appreciate the implication that she was some sort of grasping woman who was only after money and a title. Didn't Darlington know her better than that?

Apparently not. And perhaps his judgment hurt most of all. She could not reveal her mission to him, but she would have liked him to at least question her interest in his father. Perhaps wonder at it. He seemed compelled to think the worst of her almost immediately. She would have to be certain to avoid him from now on.

Lily stretched and supposed she should ready herself for the day. She was at-home today and would undoubtedly have callers soon. And then she had the theater and work tonight. She rang for her maid and left her bed for her dressing room. The perfect day gown would make her feel better.

She had a dozen or more lovely gowns. As a

courtesan, she was expected to dress fashionably. The Earl of Sin provided her with a small but steady allowance for these luxuries, which was supplemented by admirers who hoped to gain her favor by presenting her with gifts—everything from jewels to horseflesh. She loved jewels, but horses were much easier to sell. After all, a girl had to eat.

Now she chose a green-and-white striped muslin gown with sheer gauze sleeves for the afternoon, and later changed into a sapphire-blue silk gown with silver embroidery for evening. She wore her favorite sapphire necklace and sapphire earrings to match. She felt quite beautiful and only regretted her companion for the evening was the Duke of Ravenscroft. He had offered to escort her in his coach, but Lily did not relish being trapped inside a small space with the man. The countess had warned her long ago that unless she fancied fighting off her escort for a quarter hour, she should always take her own conveyance. That way Lily could leave when she wanted, especially if the evening did not go well.

She left her town house, giving her servants the rest of the evening off. She gave her coachman instructions and sat back in her seat, trying to prepare herself for the task ahead. The more time she spent with Ravenscroft, the more he would grow to trust her, and the more he would reveal. Most men, she had learned, were lonely and wanted someone to talk to. Lily was an exceptionally good listener.

Suddenly the coach lurched to a stop, and she heard a commotion. There were shouts and curses and what sounded like a scuffle in the coachman's box. The

carriage rocked, and she wondered why the coachman would have jumped down. Not waiting for an
explanation, Lily reached under her seat for her pistol
and parted the closed carriage curtains. She saw a blur
of movement and then a man's face pressed to the
window. She jumped and slammed the curtains closed.

"Idiot!" she chided herself. "You have a pistol!" But
before she could open the curtains again, there was
pounding on both sides of the carriage. It took Lily
a moment to realize what she was hearing. Someone
on the outside was nailing boards across the doors,
trapping her inside. "No!" She pushed at the doors,
tried to force them open, but they were quickly sealed
closed. The carriage began to move, and she threw the
curtains open and tried to lower the window. But that
had been sealed shut as well.

She pounded on the windows, hoping someone
would see, but the carriage was streaming past
the other conveyances. She pounded on the roof,
demanded the driver stop. The carriage continued
on at a breakneck pace. Lily knew when to bide her
time. She could waste her energy now, when fighting
was futile, or she could save her resources for when
the carriage stopped. Gradually, the sounds of the city
faded, and she realized they were leaving London. Her
abductors could be taking her anywhere, and the plank
in front of the window prevented her from seeing
clearly where she was headed.

Wherever it was, her fashionable matched Norfolk
Trotters would tire soon, and the drivers would either
have to stop for the night or pause to change horses.
If they stopped at a posting house, she would alert the

grooms there. If they stopped somewhere remote for the night...

Lily clenched her pistol and waited.

&

Macbeth was as gloomy as ever. Darlington hated tragedies. Even with Kean playing the lead role, the production did nothing to alleviate the melancholy Andrew had felt since his mother's death. He needed a good comedy or a humorous opera—something by Mozart. Or perhaps what he really needed was an evening with an opera singer...

He smiled as the actors departed the stage for a brief intermission. Andrew had been watching his father's box throughout the play, but he glanced at it now and saw the Countess of Charm had still not made an appearance. Good. His father looked annoyed. Perhaps this would be the end of the duke's interest in the courtesan. And Lily never need know that Andrew engineered her little side trip.

He exited his box and made his way along the corridor, pausing when he saw a familiar flash of silvery blond hair. He inhaled sharply.

It was Juliette. No doubt Pelham would be with her. Andrew wished to avoid both of them. He turned to go back the way he'd come, when he saw a disheveled servant break through the men holding him back and call out to the Duchess of Pelham. Andrew paused, wondering what had possessed the man. He would be arrested for certain. But Juliette, always the most gracious of women, held up a hand to ward off the men who might restrain the servant. From where Andrew stood, he could see the man more clearly now, and he noted the man wore sapphire livery. Where had he seen that livery before? It was not Pelham's.

Andrew edged closer, in time to hear the man tell the duke and duchess he feared for his mistress's life.

"Where is your mistress now?" Pelham asked, his voice cool and composed.

"I don't know, Your Grace. When I came to, the carriage was gone."

"Wait a moment," Andrew muttered. He knew who the man was now. It was one of Lily's servants— probably her coachman. He was the man who would have had to be replaced to keep Lily from attending the theater tonight. But why was his clothing torn and his face battered and bruised? Fear seized Andrew's chest like a fist. He'd specified no one was to be hurt. Lily's coachman and outriders were to be replaced and her carriage diverted. He had instructed the men he'd hired to drive her around for several hours and then bring her to the theater. Andrew pulled out his pocket watch and checked the time. He hadn't realized how late it was. Lily should have been here by now... unless she'd just gone home. That was the more likely possibility.

"Darlington!"

Andrew's head jerked up. He knew that voice. Juliette was looking right at him with those light blue eyes that made him feel as though she could see into his soul. Could she see his complicity in Lily's disappearance? He went to her, his feet moving without his mind's permission. But when Juliette called, he had no choice but to obey.

"Darlington," she said again. "Have you seen or heard from Lily? Her coachman was accosted and two of her outriders seriously injured."

Injured? Damn it! No one was to have been harmed! He glanced at Pelham, but the duke appeared stoic as always. "I haven't seen her," Andrew said. He half-expected Juliette to call him a liar, but despite his fears, she couldn't see his thoughts. And even if she had been able to, there was nothing to worry about. Lily was probably home right now, sipping tea. "I'm certain there was some misunderstanding," he said. "She's undoubtedly at her town house."

"Undoubtedly?" Pelham said, raising a brow.

"Lord Darlington," Juliette said, placing her gloved hand on the arm of his coat. "Would you please go to Lily's home and see for yourself? I would feel so much better."

Andrew looked down at her hand and then up at Pelham. Pelham stared at her hand on his arm as well—and scowled. How could he refuse Juliette? He would have rather stayed and spent more time with her, but Pelham did not look as though he favored that idea. Darlington bowed. "Anything for you, Duchess."

Pelham stepped between them, removing Juliette's hand from his arm. "Send a note when you have found her, Darlington."

"Of course." And so Andrew found himself searching for the Countess of Charm—the very woman he had paid to make disappear for the night. He would find her at her town house, pen a note to Juliette, then head to the opera. If he hurried, he could call on his favorite opera singer in her dressing room.

But Lily was not at her town house. In fact, the lone servant in residence had not seen her or heard from her. Andrew checked his pocket watch again. She should have been returned by now. Perhaps the thugs he'd hired had mistakenly taken her to his town house? He traveled home, which was in St. James, and back across Town. She was not there either. And now it was very late, indeed. Too late for opera singers. Too late for Lily not to have arrived home.

But not too late for Andrew to realize he had made a grave error.

❧

The carriage slowed to a stop, and Lily jolted awake. Drat! She'd been trying to stay awake, but a steady diet of too little sleep, coupled by the sway of the carriage for what seemed hours and hours, lulled her into a light slumber. She was still holding her pistol, cradled in her arms, and now she hurried to prime it. She might have time to fire only one shot, but that would be one less man to fight. She heard the scrape of metal against the board sealing the door of her carriage and pushed herself into the darkest recesses of the interior. She was thankful she'd worn the sapphire gown. It was dark and hid her well.

When the door opened, she calmly aimed and fired. The pistol jerked back, the sound deafening her, and the force of the explosion making her arm sting. A man screamed, and the carriage door slammed shut again.

"She's got a pistol!"

That's right. Lily's hand was shaking, but she immediately bent to prime her weapon again. It was difficult with her hand shaking and powder falling on her skirts, but she would show these men she was no easy target. She could hear them whispering outside the conveyance. Their voices were farther away, and then all was quiet. She held the pistol in her hand, poised to fire again. When she heard the banging, she jumped. They were nailing the doors shut again. Good. She was not safe yet. But it bought her some time.

Quite a lot of time, as it turned out. She tried to remain vigilant, but she was tired and hungry, and her eyes glazed over when the black of the carriage began to fade to a subtle gray light. Suddenly, she snapped to attention. She looked around, disoriented.

"Up here, little girl."

Lily looked up and cursed under her breath. She'd forgotten the hatch. It wasn't large enough for a man to fit through, but a man was peering down at her now, a pistol in his hand and aimed at her heart. He grinned. His front teeth were black, and one of his incisors was missing. His scrubby beard and stringy brown hair framed a gaunt face marred with old scars and fresher wounds.

"Now, do as I say, and no one gets hurt."

"I rather doubt I will not be hurt."

He grinned wider. "My way, you have a fighting chance."

Not much of a chance, but she had to take it.

"Hand me yer pistol." He narrowed his eyes. "And no tricks." He shifted his body and pushed his hand into the carriage. Lily looked at her pistol and looked at the hand. It was grimy, dirt under the blunt fingernails, the ratty wool coat dirty and stained. "I'm goin' t'count to three, and then I'm goin' t'shoot you. Somewhere painful where it won't kill you."

Lily blew out a breath and slapped the pistol into his hand.

"Got it!" he said, raising his prize triumphantly. When he moved, she could see the streak of light in the sky behind him. It was just past dawn.

As soon as the man spoke, his companions went to work removing the board from the door again. It came off easily, and the door was thrown open. Lily stared at three grinning men—the man from the hatch and two others who looked just liked him. All three were thin and dirty—and leering.

If the other door hadn't been sealed shut, she would have escaped that way, but as it was, there was one entrance and one exit. The men studied Lily, and she stared back. Her fear warned her to run, to try and escape. She ignored the instinct and waited. Let them strike first.

It didn't take long. A man with matted red hair reached for her, and Lily kicked out, striking him in the jaw. He fell back and came up roaring. Wildly, he reached for her again, and she easily evaded him, managing another kick at his chest. But the third time she was not so fortunate. He caught her foot and dragged her off the squabs. She landed unceremoniously on the floor of the carriage, and the men caught hold of her legs and dragged her out.

Lily went limp, allowing them to think she'd given

up or fainted. As soon as she hit the grass outside the carriage, the men released her and stepped back.

"I'm first," one of them said.

"I got her out."

"I got her pistol. I'm first."

Lily rolled, cutting her foot across the knees of the man who had spoken. He wobbled and went down as Lily jumped to her feet. She threw soil in the face of one of the men gaping at her and slammed her elbow into the face of the man kneeling before her. With a quick swipe, she had her pistol back. She held the pistol straight out, trying to keep her arms from shaking. "Now who's first?" As she spoke, she assessed her surroundings. There was an abandoned cottage behind the men and a copse of sparse trees lining the road behind her. The trees would provide just enough cover that she couldn't expect anyone traveling past them to see her, especially since the sky was still pewter gray.

The boy with the red hair sneered at her. "You have one shot. Kill one of us, and there's still two more to take revenge."

The man kneeling wobbled to his feet and extracted his pistol from his belt.

"Shoot her and be done with it," the third man said. He was the shortest and looked barely one and twenty.

"Idiot," the man with the pistol said. "She's worth more alive than dead. We could ransom her. That gentry cove thought she was worth something."

"Or you could return me to London," Lily suggested, "and we forget all of this happened."

"I don't think so," the redhead said.

Lily shrugged. It was worth a try. "Fine. Then my original query still stands. Who wants to be first?" Without waiting for the men to respond or react, she swiveled to the biggest threat—the man with the pistol—and fired. The shot went a little wide, and the ball hit his shoulder instead of his chest. The force was enough to push him backward and to grab the attention of his companions. Lily took advantage of the distraction, hurled her pistol at the men, lifted her skirts, and ran for the road in the distance.

She was wearing a ball gown and slippers. Even if she were an extremely fast runner, she wouldn't outrun the men coming after her. Her only hope was to flag down another conveyance traveling this road. She emerged through the small brush of trees and ran for what she hoped was London. She could hear footsteps behind her, but was it her imagination or did she hear hoofbeats ahead?

Please. Please. Please.

Suddenly a coach was upon her. The horses reared, and Lily raised a hand and threw herself out of the way. She tumbled off the road, tasting blood and dirt in her mouth. When she looked up, the coach had stopped. The rising sun was behind it, blinding her and making everything in front of the carriage appear dark. The carriage door flew open, and a man in black boots stepped out, his black opera cape swirling around him, his tall hat hiding his face. This man was wealthy—a gentleman if his dress was any indication. She squinted into the light, but she couldn't make out any distinct features. Two of her abductors were on the road, but they'd slowed now, as the man stood before her, hands on his hips. "What is the meaning of this?" He gestured to her.

Lily shook her head and tried to rise. Her ears were ringing.

"It's the rich nob from London," one of the men said. Lily's heart faltered. She was not saved after all. This man was in collusion with the other two.

"I paid you to delay her, not to abduct and assault her."

"You wanted her out of the way. She's out of the way," the red-haired man said.

"I am not pleased," the gentleman said and gestured to his outriders. The last thing Lily saw before she closed her eyes were her abductors running for their lives and men in what looked very much like the Duke of Ravenscroft's livery in pursuit.

Four

"That's enough," Andrew said to his outriders. "Enough!"

His men stepped back, straightening their coats. The three men who'd abducted Lily were lying on the ground. One had been wounded from a pistol ball, but the wound did not appear fatal. The other two probably wished they had been shot. But Andrew left them alive with minor injuries that would heal after a few days. That was more courtesy than they would have shown Lily.

"If I ever see you—any of you—in Town again, I won't stop my men from ripping you apart." He walked away, back toward the carriage. In his hand, he held a small, feminine pistol inlaid with sapphires. It had to be Lily's, but he would never have expected her to carry such a weapon. If Fallon had a pistol or twenty, he would not be surprised. But Lily... would she even know what to do with a pistol? Had she actually shot that thug, or had there been some sort of misfiring accident? His coachman met him in front of his conveyance, concern on his face.

"How is she?" Andrew asked without preamble.

"I put her in the coach, my lord. She was able to walk unassisted."

"Good. Then she is unharmed?"

"Yes, my lord."

Andrew started for his coach again but paused when his coachman cleared his throat. "She seems a little… perturbed, my lord."

"I can imagine." Andrew continued walking.

"At you, my lord."

"Well, that seems monstrously unfair." And it was just like a woman. She had probably wanted to rescue herself, or some nonsense like that.

"Yes, my lord."

Andrew paused at the carriage door. "As soon as the men are ready, we hie back to London. Have one of the grooms take the lady's carriage horses back. Slowly." He opened the door and found Lily immediately. She was sitting, arms crossed, on the seat opposite him.

"Countess." He tipped his hat.

"Don't call me that."

"Very well. Good morning, Lily."

"How is it you possess the gall to speak to me? You are despicable."

"I assume you blame me for the events of the evening." He climbed inside and closed the door. He did not wish for his servants to overhear the exchange.

She drummed her fingers on her arms, and he noticed she'd removed her gloves, and her elbows and forearms were scraped and bloody.

"Are you not the one responsible for my abduction?"

"I wouldn't call it an abduction…" At least her face was not marred. Her dress was beyond repair, though. Should he offer to replace it? One look at her stony expression decided him against such a course of action. "I did not intend for events to progress as they did."

"Yes, that is the problem with criminals," Lily said drily. "They are not very good at following the rules."

"In my defense, I did come to save you."

"Save me!" she screamed. "Is that what you think you did?"

The sound of his men returning and climbing to their positions hopefully drowned out some of her tirade.

"Well, you couldn't think you had much chance of outrunning them." Although she had more speed than he would have given her credit for. When the carriage had topped the rise and he'd seen her coming toward them, her red hair flying out behind her like ribbons of flame, he'd thought he was dreaming and she was some sort of fallen angel or demon come to pursue and punish him for his misdeeds. He had not felt much better when he'd realized it was Lily. There was relief he was in time to save her, and anger he had put her in this position.

The coachman called to the horses, and the carriage began to move, turning slowly back toward Town.

"You are impossible," she said, her voice filled with disgust. "When we return to London, you are never to speak to me again. I will cut you directly."

"Whatever will I do?" he drawled.

"Is that my pistol?" she asked, pointing to the weapon he still held.

"Yes." He handed it to her before he thought better of it. But she didn't point it at him, as he half-expected her to do. Instead, she tucked it into her skirts, closed her eyes, and turned away from him as much as was possible in a carriage where they faced each other.

"None of this would have happened," he said, "if you had agreed to stay away from my father."

Her eyes flicked open, the deep green vibrant and flashing. "So this is my fault?"

There did not seem a right answer to that question, and before he could respond, she leaned forward and pointed a finger in his face. "Andrew, you are a spoiled child, and I am sorry I was ever in love with you. I only hope I am there to see it when you are forced to grow up."

Andrew gaped at her, certain he had not heard correctly. Lily had been in love with him? When? Why? How had he not known? But she did not elaborate. Instead, she closed her eyes and did not speak another word.

⤛⤜

Lily nodded to her maid, who listed the items she would pack for the Duke of Ravenscroft's house party, and then consulted her own list. "How many pairs of gloves did you say, Anna?"

"Ten, madam. I planned to purchase two additional pairs today."

"Oh, that's right. You told me. And what about—" She turned as a knock sounded on the door and it creaked open to reveal the Countess of Sinclair. Lily blinked in surprise and hastily rose and curtsied.

The countess waved a hand. "What formalities! They are not necessary, I assure you. Girl, be off with you!" she said to the maid. Anna all but ran from the room.

"I wasn't expecting you," Lily said, offering the countess a cushioned armchair. The older woman leaned heavily on her cane as she made her way to it. "I thought you had left Town for the summer."

"You did not think I would call first? All the papers are full of the news. You have overthrown my husband for the Duke of Ravenscroft."

Lily rolled her eyes. "Poor Sin. First Juliette, then Fallon, now me. Soon we will have to begin referring to him as a saint."

The countess gave her a wry smile. "These rumors do tarnish his lecherous reputation. Say they are not so."

Lily sighed, lifted a hat box from the chaise longue, and seated herself on the velvet cushion. "I cannot. As you see, I *am* traveling to Ravenscroft's lair for a house party."

"I do not wish to embarrass you, but neither can I keep quiet," the countess said. Lily almost smiled. The countess had never kept quiet, whether her words embarrassed others or not. "Is it a financial matter? If you are in need of funds—"

"No. I do not need blunt, and you have been more than generous."

"You cannot possibly be infatuated with the duke. He is old and was ugly even when I was a young girl. And I know you care nothing for his title." The countess tapped her walking stick and studied Lily.

"Might this have something to do with your father and the skills you inherited from him?"

Lily didn't speak, allowing the countess to come to her own conclusions.

"I see. Then might I give you a piece of advice?"

Now Lily did smile. "You are *asking* me?"

"Tut, girl. I do not know why everyone thinks you are charming." But she was smiling. Lily caught an image of the countess as a young woman. Her wrinkles faded and her eyes brightened, her white hair darkened, and she was truly lovely. And then the smile faded. "I do not claim to know Ravenscroft well," Lady Sinclair said, "but I have watched him over the years. He seems harmless. Even foolish. In truth, he is dangerous. He is not a man to be trusted or a man to turn your back on. I do not like to think of you sleeping under his roof."

"There will be other guests."

"Who will care nothing for you. If I am not mistaken, you go alone. If something should go wrong, who is there to help you?"

It was true. She would be somewhat isolated, with only the post to rely on if she needed assistance. By the time a letter reached London, it might be too late. But she had made her decision. "I know how to keep a man at arm's length."

"Yes, when you are in London and when you can retreat to your home or that of one of your friends. But you will be under Ravenscroft's roof, and if he wants you—"

Lily glanced down at her hands, willing her fingers to unclench. She would not allow fear to get the better of her.

"And I have not even mentioned what we both know—you have another purpose entirely, one at odds with that of the duke's."

Lily did not want to hear more. She could not speak on that subject, not even to Lady Sinclair, in any case. "Knowing all of this, what is your advice?" Lily asked.

"Stay home," the countess said. Lily frowned at her, and the countess leaned forward and grasped Lily's hand in her thin, fragile one. "Be careful whom you trust."

"I always am." Lily squeezed the countess's hand, almost afraid of crushing the birdlike bones.

Lady Sinclair grasped the silver handle of her walking stick and rose. "You do know the duke's estate is in Nottinghamshire, do you not?"

"I do." It seemed one of life's little ironies.

"Stay away from *the boy*. There has never been a time when it was more imperative that you keep your secrets. Those you have now and those from your past."

The long drive from London to Nottinghamshire and Ravenscroft Hall was a familiar one for Lily, though it had been years since she'd made it. And she had never made it in such comfort. The duke had provided her with his personal coach for the journey, and she was pleased to find the conveyance well sprung, the matched pair of Cleveland Bays quick and lively, and the coachman quite solicitous. They made good time, but when she arrived at Ravenscroft Hall, she was eager for a comfortable bed and a bath. She would be obliged to forgo dinner to have either. It was dusk as they entered the estate's grounds, and she knew the family and the guests who preceded her would be sitting down to eat. Country hours demanded early meals.

"Anna, when we arrive, set out a dinner gown and order a bath. Then retire for a few hours," she told her maid. She was not certain what the accommodations for the servants had been like at the inn the night before, but Anna looked weary.

"But, madam, I should unpack and press your gown for tomorrow."

Lily waved a hand. "You can do it later, or I shall do it myself. I'm perfectly capable." She had not grown up with servants, other than a cook and a maid of all work. She had pressed many, many gowns—her own and her elder sister's. But this evening she needed rest. She would need all her wits about her if she hoped to deal with the duke. He would expect more than a perfunctory kiss on the cheek from her. In turn, she needed access to his library and bedchamber. Gaining that access without actually sharing his bed would be a careful negotiation.

And then there was the Earl of Darlington to think of. She had not thought of him often since he'd left her at the door of her town house the morning after her abduction. When she had thought of him, it had been with pain or anger. She could not afford either sentiment at the moment. She hoped, quite sincerely, he was still in Town.

As the carriage topped the last rise, the estate came into view. Anna gasped, and even Lily could not suppress a smile. It was lovely—everything a ducal estate should be. She knew next to nothing about architecture, but this was the sort of house she thought others would describe as *stately*. And she had listened to enough talk to know the house was built in the Elizabethan style. There was a high central hall surrounded by four towers, and all of them had pretty decorations and spires on top. She was certain they had a more technical term, but she did not know it. It was a large house, and the setting sun glinted on the limestone, making it look almost greenish blue. Strange, she thought, and beautiful. Had Darlington grown up here? Had he climbed the trees in the park, run down the drive with his playfellows, looked out of the windows when he should have been concentrating on his studies?

And why was she still thinking of him? He had tried to have her killed. If that did not snuff out her affection for him, then nothing could. She pushed thoughts of him away and straightened her shoulders as the carriage slowed and approached the house's entrance. Several servants waited, their green livery seeming part of the house itself in this lighting. The carriage stopped, and Lily took a deep breath. When the door opened, she stepped out, once again the Countess of Charm.

❧

Andrew turned away from the window when Lily disappeared inside the house. A courtesan in Ravenscroft Hall. His ancestors would have turned in their graves. Actually, if the stories he'd heard had any truth to them, they probably would not have batted an eyelash. And Lily was not the first woman of easy virtue to visit here. There were several of far looser morals in the dining room at this moment. His mother would have been horrified had she been alive to see this. For the first time, he was glad she was not.

If Andrew listened closely, he could hear the commotion the servants made over settling this new visitor. *Does madam wish to change and be shown to the dining room?*

He could not hear her response, but apparently it was negative. He had declined to dine with his father and his guests as well. After the debacle of Lily's abduction, he had retreated to Ravenscroft Hall, only to find his brooding solitude interrupted by the arrival of his father and some of the duke's "friends." He had thought about leaving, but it occurred to him the estate would one day be his. He might be better served by staying and ensuring his father did not lose it in a game of whist or billiards.

And now Lily was here. Her words still rang in his ears.

I am sorry I was ever in love with you.

She'd loved him. Now that he knew it, he could see it. She'd always teased him, smiled at him, made him feel welcome and at ease. But was that love or was she grasping for the title of duchess even then?

Something moved in the shadows, and he spun around, eliciting a small scream from the girl standing on the far side of room, almost hidden amongst the tapestries. "Emma?"

"I'm sorry. I did not wish to disturb you. I was looking for a quiet place to read, and I did not think Father's guests would seek out the tapestry room." She moved forward, her manner apologetic. He was struck by how much she looked like their mother. She had the same tall, willowy form—a form which, at fifteen, she had not yet grown into—the same curly brown hair, the same gentle brown eyes. She was quiet and unobtrusive, so he often went days without seeing or thinking of her. He supposed he still thought of her as a child, though she would not be one for long. Had his father even considered what was to be done for her first Season?

Unlikely, as his father had thought of little but his own desires of late. Andrew wanted to groan. He supposed the task would fall to him, and what did he know of Seasons and court presentations and the like?

"Stay," Andrew said. "I was leaving." He started for the door, wondering how, in a house this large, he could think of nowhere to retreat.

"Is she beautiful?" Emma asked, and Andrew stopped short of the door.

"Who?"

"I heard one of The Three Diamonds arrived, the Countess of Charm. Is she beautiful?"

Andrew frowned at his little sister. She was dressed in black, out of respect for his mother's recent death, and the color made her look small and pale. "What do you know about The Three Diamonds?"

"Even here in Nottinghamshire, we receive the London papers," she said with a smile. "I read."

"You shouldn't be reading about women like her."

"And you shouldn't be consorting with them, but I have seen your name mentioned with theirs. Were you really in love with the Duchess of Dalliance? The one who married the Duke of Pelham?"

"Was I… what?"

"Wasn't it romantic? How they fell in love and married?"

"What's romantic about a courtesan as the sixth Duchess of Pelham?" he said with some rancor. But, of course, Juliette would be a perfect duchess. He'd wanted her for his duchess.

"But the way the papers describe The Three Diamonds, they are the height of fashion and elegance. They are the most beautiful women of the *ton*. Women imitate their fashion, and all the men seek their favors."

Andrew blinked, attempted to speak, then ran a hand through his hair. This was why she needed a mother. What was he supposed to say to his little sister—hadn't she been a wobbly, chubby-cheeked child clinging to his leg just yesterday?—about the illicit world of London Society? Especially when he was part of that world?

Finally, out of frustration, he said, "This isn't an appropriate topic of conversation."

"Why?"

"Because young ladies—even older ladies—do not speak of courtesans." He started for the door again. Escape, at this point, seemed his only option.

"But why? Have the papers misrepresented the facts?"

Andrew blew out a breath. The door, and his

escape, seemed so far away. "No, but it is one thing to read about someone like the Countess of Charm and quite another to discuss her."

Emma pondered this, and Andrew sidled closer to the door.

"So I may read about her, but I mustn't speak of her?"

"Correct. You probably shouldn't even read about her." He reached for the door handle. "So glad we sorted everything out…"

"But why can *I* not merely read about her, when *you* know her personally?"

"Because I am a man, and the rules are different for me."

"But you are my brother. Surely I can speak to my brother about these matters. Besides, all I asked was whether or not the Countess of Charm was beautiful. The papers never compliment her appearance like they do the other two."

"What do they compliment?"

"Her charming personality, of course."

"Hmm. The writers do not know her as well as I do, in that case." Andrew turned to leave again, and even had the door open before he paused. He was the heir to the title and would one day be head of the family. He'd been so preoccupied with his own grief and anger at his father, he hadn't really considered his younger sister. His sister Katherine, seven years Emma's senior, had been at the estate, and he'd left her to console their younger sister. But now she had returned to her husband and children. Emma had been very much on her own.

Andrew turned back and found her standing at the

window, looking out on the darkening sky. He should say... something. He was much better at teasing and making his sisters laugh than at anything of a serious nature. "Emma?"

She turned, looking surprised to see him still there. "Yes, my lord?"

Now it was his turn to laugh from surprise. "When did I become *my lord*? You used to call me Drew."

Her nose scrunched up. "That was when I was a baby."

She still seemed like a baby to him. "I think I'd prefer it if you called me Andrew. It occurred to me"—he stepped back in the room, committed now, and closed the door behind him—"I have not asked how you fare since Katherine returned home."

A look of sadness crossed her features. She was young to look so forlorn. "I am well. I miss her."

He missed her too—their beautiful mother. She had loved him, never made him feel inadequate, and always saw through his attempts to pretend his father's indifference did not matter.

"She is in a better place now," Emma said, her gaze on his face. He still grieved her. He had always thought she would be his advisor when he became duke. How would he carry on without her?

"Yes." He should say something more comforting, but he did not know what.

"My lord—Andrew, I know you are vexed with our father because of his recent behavior."

Andrew raised his brows. It had not been a secret, but he did not know how much of his father's recent behavior she had read about. He did not want to enlighten her.

"But you know that mother and father never loved each other. They married for duty, as I suppose you will. So if he seeks someone to love now, in his declining years, we can hardly judge him."

Andrew stared at her. He could judge very well, thank you. But he was not so bitter he did not see logic. When had Emma become so wise? And how did she know so much about their parents' relationship? They had not loved each other? He had never even imagined their courtship or their wedding. Had they married for duty? He supposed that was what dukes did. Was that what he would do? He would have to marry—there was no question of that. He had always thought he would marry for love. He'd chided his friend Pelham for his pronouncements that dukes did not fall in love. But perhaps Pelham had the right of it after all. Perhaps duty was all there was.

"How do you know?" he heard himself asking. "How can you be certain they didn't love each other?"

"Because I saw them together every day. They didn't even *like* each other. He was civil to her, but not kind or solicitous. He trod lightly when she was near, as though he feared something."

"*Feared* her? Emma, your imagination has the better of you."

"Perhaps, but she doted on you, Andrew. Katherine and I…" She shuddered. Andrew frowned. She actually shuddered, as though she'd feared their mother. Fanciful girl. But her view of his parents' marriage was not wholly Emma's fancy. He could easily see his parents' relationship through her eyes. He had never looked at them as a married couple. They were the duke and duchess first, and his mother and father second. Even when he'd been a child, his mother had been more duchess than mother to him. "Why didn't I see this?"

"You were at school and home only on holidays. We lived here every day. You did not see what she was really like, Andrew. She could be cold and, well, frightening."

More fanciful notions, though it was true, of course, that he had not often been home. His sisters had been tutored at home by their governess. He had gone to Eton and then Oxford. Being away at school so often made him feel like an outsider, but even as an outsider, he knew there were certain topics better left untouched. His mother did not discuss his father. His father spoke of his mother only in well-rehearsed phrases of praise.

The sound of laughter, loud and raucous, floated up from the dining room. "His Grace's guests are a rather... varied lot. It occurs to me I should send you to stay with Katherine for the duration of the house party."

Emma's face fell. "No! Please. This is my home. I want to stay."

Andrew shook his head. Why had he not thought of this before? His sister should not be sleeping under the same roof as the notorious Countess of Charm. "I will write to her immediately."

Emma all but ran to him and clutched his arm. Now this was the little girl he remembered. "No, Andrew. Please. I will stay out of the way. I will keep to myself. Do not send me from my home. Miss Peevy will keep an eye on me."

Andrew assumed Miss Peevy was her governess.

"All I want is to be able to observe—from my window—the hats and dresses and wraps," she pleaded.

He could remember hearing his sisters and their governess discuss lace and muslin for hours when he'd been younger. Emma must feel the lack of female companionship keenly now that her mother and sister were gone. "Very well."

"Thank you!" She hopped up and down excitedly.

"But I will speak with Miss Peevy myself. You are not, under any circumstances, to fraternize with the guests."

"They will not even know I exist."

Walking away from the tapestry room, Andrew felt very much the older, wiser brother. Well, he was older, anyway. And he would speak with Emma's governess now, before he reverted to his usual ways and forgot completely. He might have gone to search for her, but as he had only a vague notion of what she even looked like, he decided to have the housekeeper send for her. He made his way to the first floor, where the kitchens were located. Now that dinner was over, the servants were not quite so harried. As he came down the steps, those who spotted him gaped. Many were gathered at a table, which was set for dinner. They rose hastily, and the butler bowed. "My lord, how may we be of service?"

Andrew knew he was intruding. The servants had so little time to themselves. He should have remembered they would be at dinner now. "Please, sit and eat. I didn't mean to interrupt you."

No one moved.

"I am looking for Mrs. Hemmings."

"Ah! Here I am, my lord."

He turned and saw the housekeeper emerging from one of the back closets. Behind her stood the Countess of Charm.

Five

LILY SUCKED IN A BREATH. SHE DIDN'T HAVE TO wonder anymore. Darlington was in residence. He was standing before her looking more handsome than he had any right to look, considering she detested him. Why did he have to be gifted with broad shoulders and slim hips and those long legs? The man would turn heads in sackcloth, but when he wore an expensive wool coat, an emerald-green waistcoat, and those terribly distracting tight breeches, he stole her breath.

"What are you doing here?"

She held up the needle and thread she'd borrowed. "My lace was torn."

He gave her an odd look, which she supposed was reasonable. The housekeeper had given her much the same look when she'd requested the items after unpacking her gowns. She supposed Anna had her needle and thread somewhere, but Lily could not find them, and she did not want to trouble the girl. She could repair her own lace and give Anna a few hours' rest.

"I thought you would be with the others." He sneered when he said it, and Lily took a moment to wonder whom exactly the duke had invited to this house party.

"And I thought you would be in London, but we do not always have our fondest wishes granted." She turned to the housekeeper, whose mouth was agape at the two of them. "Thank you, Mrs. Hemmings, for the needle and thread. I shall have my maid, Anna, return them."

"Of course, madam."

Lily started for the stairs. Behind her, she heard the housekeeper ask, "May I be of assistance, my lord?"

"Yes—er, no. One moment."

Footfalls sounded behind her, and she almost swore. Why was he coming after her? She had been clear she wanted nothing to do with him after he'd had her abducted and almost killed not even a fortnight ago.

"Countess!" he called.

She continued up the stairs. He was quickly gaining, and Lily cursed her cumbersome skirts. She reached the landing, and he grabbed her elbow, pulling her aside so a footman carrying a tureen could pass. Darlington opened a door and ducked into a storeroom filled with tablecloths, candlesticks, and serving trays. He tugged her in, closing the door and leaning on it. "What do you want?" she asked. "I thought I was clear on the occasion of our last conversation. I want nothing to do with you. Move aside."

"That is a wish I can grant," he said. He was still holding her elbow, and she found his touch disconcerting. It was one thing to hate him from a distance, quite another to hate him when his warm hand wrapped around her arm and his deep brown eyes gazed down at her. "You do not need to worry about me. I will stay out of your way."

"Will you also refrain from hiring thugs to abduct me and attempt to rape and ransom me?"

"That was never my plan," he said. "And I did come to your rescue."

"I suppose I should be grateful. Forgive me if I am not." She pulled away from him. "Now, if you will excuse me." When he did not move, she had to quell the urge to stomp her foot. "Step away from the door."

"Is it the title?" he asked. "Is that the attraction?"

Oh, would he never allow her to pass? "It does not concern you."

"My father is smitten with you. That concerns me."

"Then address the matter with him."

"Is it money?"

"Perhaps it is love. Maybe I'm in love with him." She crossed her arms.

He snorted. "You courtesans don't fall in love."

She raised her brows. "Juliette fell in love."

His face darkened. He was still in love with her, stupid ass. He was always going to be in love with Juliette. And, Lily reminded herself, she did not care. She detested him now.

"If it's money, remember I will pay you to go away."

Lily shook her head. "Do you insult everyone again and again in this manner, or am I especially privileged?"

"I am not trying to insult you. I am trying to understand."

"You are trying to be rid of me! And, I assure you, sir, I want what you want. Please remove yourself from the door."

"On one condition."

Lily gritted her teeth and attempted to remain patient. "You cannot keep me here forever."

"You may go, but I want your promise first."

"What good is the word of a courtesan?" she asked. "We are all liars and schemers, are we not?"

"Let me worry about that. I want your promise that if my father asks you to marry him, you will refuse."

Lily sighed. She had no intention of marrying his father, but she could not tell Darlington as much. She did not think Ravenscroft had much intention of marrying her either. But she might have to resort to that tactic to give herself more time to investigate and keep him out of her bedchamber. It had worked for Anne Boleyn, hadn't it?

"Your claim to the title is not in jeopardy," she said. "Even if your father married again and produced more children, you are still the heir."

Darlington turned slightly green. "So you are not against marrying him."

"He has not asked, so there is no point in discussing—"

He grabbed her arms, cutting her off. "You cannot possibly think of tying yourself to him. Allowing him to paw you, leer at you, rut with you nightly."

"So *that* is what marriage involves! Thank you for enlightening me. Well, in that case, I will return home immediately. Move aside." She gave him a little push.

"Lily…"

"*Andrew*. I told you the matter did not concern you. Let me pass."

Light footfalls sounded, and he turned to listen.

"Someone is coming," she chided him. "The servants must need this room. We should go."

He nodded his assent, and then his eyes narrowed. "Not so quickly. I rather like being in here with you."

She frowned at him. "Why?" The steps grew closer. She did not want it reported to the duke that she'd been closeted with his son. Her gaze flicked to Darlington. But that was exactly what the earl wanted. "Out of my way," she ordered, pushing him aside.

"Why, Lily," he said, looking down at her hands on his chest. "I had no idea you felt this way." His arms went around her, and he pulled her hard against him.

"No." She pushed against his chest to no avail. "Let me go."

"I can't," he whispered as his mouth descended on hers.

She wanted to fight him. She wanted to kick his shin or bite his lip or knee him somewhere tender and vulnerable. But she didn't. His lips pressed against hers, and she forgot how much she hated him. She forgot that he'd tried to have her killed, that he'd insulted her, that he was only using her. She forgot everything but the feel of his mouth moving against hers, the pressure of his hands on her back, the hardness of his chest pressing against her breasts, the warmth of his leg where it met her thigh.

She closed her eyes, and her world swirled and tilted. When his tongue touched her lips, she clutched his shirt to keep from falling. Lily couldn't stop a moan. She couldn't stop her lips from opening to him; she couldn't stop herself from kissing him back. And now his hands dug into her back, pulling her closer, while his mouth took possession, kissing her deeply. She'd never been kissed like this, with such intensity. It was a kiss that demanded her surrender, and she found herself giving in.

Heat swirled through her, pooling in her belly with a delicious heaviness. Her body began to throb and ache and reach for... something. Needs, long neglected, bubbled uncontrollably from their depths, and she remembered this feeling. Desire. Arousal. Yearning. But it had never been painful before. It had never been desperate and clawing and frantic. She spread her hands on his chest, feeling the solid heat of him through his clothing. His heart pounded against her palm, and his knee parted her thighs, pressing against her lightly. *Oh, yes. Please.*

He pulled back suddenly, and Lily stumbled and gasped in a shallow breath. Her vision was unfocused, but she would have sworn he looked flushed and as bewildered as she. He raked a hand through his hair, disordering it. "What are you doing to me?" he rasped.

"*You* kissed *me.*" She could barely speak. Her voice was weak and shaky.

He shook his head in denial. "You kissed me back," he accused.

"I told you to let me go." She was very aware that she was still standing in the circle of his arms, still flush against his chest. "Let go."

"That's not possible. Not now that I've tasted you." He bent to kiss her again, and she found some semblance of willpower and leaned back.

"Stop kissing me."

"Lily." He cupped her face. "I cannot." And

his mouth, sweet and persuasive this time, claimed hers again. She wanted to fight him. She wanted to question his cryptic statements. She wanted to escape before they were discovered, which was surely his plan all along, but she simply stood there and melted against him. She let his mouth overtake her, his arms hold her, his body warm her.

"What is—?"

Lily sprang away from Darlington, bumping her head against a low shelf. Through the sharp cloud of pain, she saw it was the butler who had interrupted them. Her cheeks flamed.

"Oh! I'm terribly—" the man said, hand to his open mouth. "I thought you were someone else."

She knew what he thought. He'd thought they were servants, and he had opened the door to discipline them. But now he had seen her, and he had seen Darlington, and certainly the duke was going to learn of this.

Lily closed her eyes, wondering what Fitzhugh and the Foreign Office would say when they learned what a muddle she had made of everything. And then she felt Darlington's frame stiffen. She opened her eyes and found herself staring at a young, female version of Darlington. The girl looked suitably shocked, and the woman with her quickly took her by the elbow.

"My apologies," the butler said, making to close the door again.

"No need." Darlington put a hand out, stopping the door from closing. Lily wished he would just let it shut. Then they could end the scene and sneak away when everyone had dispersed. "This was all a misunderstanding."

Lily wanted to roll her eyes. Did he really think anyone would believe what they'd seen was something other than what it had been? And who was the girl? Darlington's sister? What was she doing here?

"Of course, my lord," the butler said, sounding less than convinced. "I beg your leave."

"Yes, yes, please attend to your duties."

The girl made a sound of distress, turned, and ran.

"Emma!"

The governess gave him a stern look over her shoulder, and it was Lily who clapped a hand on his arm to stop him this time. "Let her go."

"I have to explain." He was still watching the girl.

"Oh, really? And what is your explanation going to be? You see, Lady Emma, sometimes when you are trapped in a closet with a courtesan, you cannot help yourself and—"

"All right. You made your point."

"Her governess will make any necessary explanations. You would do best to pretend it did not happen."

His gaze collided with hers. "I cannot do that."

She clenched her jaw. "You wanted us to be found. Wanted your father to be angry with me. It won't turn out that way, I promise you." She couldn't allow that. She had to make certain she remained in the duke's good graces. "The governess will instruct your sister— she is your sister?"

He gave a curt nod.

"Your sister will be told not to mention this to anyone. Unless I am mistaken and she and your father are unusually close, she will not betray you."

"And what do you know about young girls?"

She simply waited for the words to sink in, and when his mouth turned down, she said, "I wasn't always a courtesan. I was innocent and full of questions and wonder once."

He stared at her as though he didn't quite believe it. She almost didn't believe it herself. That was another lifetime. Another girl. "If you instruct the butler and governess to keep quiet, they will. You are the next duke. They know where to place their loyalties at this point."

"We'll see." His gaze was on her, making her self-conscious. Her cheeks felt warm, and she imagined they were red and rosy. That was the problem with being a redhead. She freckled and blushed easily. Not for the first time, she wished she had Fallon's complexion or Juliette's composure. She couldn't imagine either of them being caught by a butler while kissing a man in a storage closet. It was something a green girl did. She'd probably done it when she'd been younger. This was no way to catch Ravenscroft.

She bent to retrieve her needle and thread, both of which had fallen on the floor at some point during the kiss. The action served to hide her face and to give him a moment to open the door and depart. Which he did without even taking his leave. Horrid man. If he would only stop kissing her, she could hate him properly. For a man who supposedly hated her, he could not seem to leave her alone. Not that this surprised her. Men could profess to love one moment and fall out of love when the emotion became inconvenient. Darlington was no better or worse. He was the heir to a dukedom and could afford to be capricious. She could not. She'd made that mistake once and would never make it again.

Lily hurried back to her rooms, stumbling upon them rather than finding them. The house was large and well laid out, but her head was spinning and her thoughts jumbled. Anna was waiting for her, and she handed her maid the needle and thread. "I will repair the lace on the green gown later. Now I should hurry down. I'll wear the black and silver." It wasn't the best gown for her complexion. It didn't make her look sallow and sick like orange did, or greenish and putrid like yellow, but it didn't brighten her coloring either. Her face was already flushed, though, and she could use toning down. This was the one night she welcomed looking pale and colorless.

When she was dressed and her hair repaired, she rushed down to the drawing room where the ladies had retired after dinner. The men were at billiards, and she knew they would not be long in joining the women now. She was rather surprised they had been this long at their port and cigars. Lily walked into the drawing room and stopped short.

Oh, no.

It was not the room that unnerved her. The room was beautifully appointed. The late duchess had obviously possessed exquisite taste. The carpets were thick and plush. She was not knowledgeable enough to know if they were Turkey or Aubusson or something else, but she felt her slippers sink comfortably into the rug. The walls were covered with elegant papers depicting Grecian urns and motifs. Portraits of the ancestral family were hung here and there, and she had enough of an eye to see that the painters had been talented. The ceilings were high and heavily molded, creating the effect of sumptuousness and openness, something the room needed, as the paneling and papers were quite dark.

The furnishings were upholstered in damasks and silks and arranged in small pairings so as to allow several groups to converse at once. A fire lit the hearth, and a large chandelier brightened the room, which glowed from the light of several lamps. The room was to Lily's liking. The company was not.

She'd expected an assortment of widows and actresses, perhaps an opera singer or two. There was an opera singer and two widows, but there were also four other courtesans. She hesitated even to call them courtesans. They were so free with their favors as to be more akin to prostitutes. The widows, Mrs. Compton and Lady Euglin, were known as relentless seducers of young men. When a new buck arrived in Town, they were the first to sidle up to him at his inaugural ball. The opera singer, a woman whose name Lily did not remember—in the future, she would really need to stay awake during the opera—was the most chaste of all of them.

And that was saying something.

"Well," one of the courtesans, a Mrs. Arbuckle, said upon seeing her. "If it isn't the Countess of Copulation." Lily knew the other courtesans of the *ton* had less than complimentary names for Juliette, Fallon, and her. The Countess of Copulation was one of the better ones. It was at a level with The Conjugal Countess. Some of the other C-words were not so polite. "Where are your friends, *Countess*?"

"Why, Mrs. Arbuckle." Lily forced her feet to move forward, forced herself to step into the room. "I thought *you* were my friend."

The courtesan smiled thinly. "Oh, I am."

The other courtesans, by no means friendly with Mrs. Arbuckle either, tittered. No one in this room was her friend. When one's livelihood depended on snaring a man, one could not afford to befriend other women. Juliette, Fallon, and Lily had been the exceptions. But then they were not typical courtesans.

"Are you looking for a new protector?" a courtesan with brassy blond hair, too much rouge, and several beauty marks asked. "The Earl of Sin not satisfied with just one of you in his bed?"

It was a less than subtle jab at her. The rumors had long circulated that The Three Diamonds pleasured Sinclair and one another for his enjoyment. Now that Juliette and Fallon had retired, everyone speculated that Sinclair was in search of another crop of young girls. None of it was true, but she allowed the speculation because it served her purposes. "Worried I might steal someone you have your eye on, Mrs. Fisher?"

"Not at all, Mrs. Dawson."

Lily clenched her hands, which were hidden in her silk skirts. She hated being referred to by her surname. She always imagined her father hiding his face in shame when she, a notorious courtesan, used his family name. He had tried so very hard to distance himself from her. *Dawson* was a common enough name. She might have told him the effort was unnecessary.

Lily made her way across the room. She was tired and edgy, and the decanter of Madeira looked inviting. She might have preferred something stronger. Several of the women were drinking spirits, but she had a feeling the duke might be put off by that. He saw her as young and sweet. He wanted a girl to seduce. He certainly knew the rumors about her, but he either chose to ignore them or thought they would serve his purpose. After all, most men wanted a virgin in the drawing room and a tigress in the bedroom. She hoped she did not have to play the tigress.

"We all thought the Marquess of Cholmondeley would take you under his wing."

Lily was aware of that rumor as well. Cholmondeley and she were friends, and she knew speculation that there was more between them followed her, but he was devoted to his wife. He was sort of an uncle to her—a man from whom she asked advice. She wished he were here now so she could ask his advice on the subject of the Earl of Darlington. But the man named Lord Steward of the Household, the first dignitary of the court, would never have consorted with this lot. And that was a very bad sign indeed. What did Ravenscroft have planned for this week? How much debauchery was to be expected? And how could she avoid it?

She heard voices and turned as the butler opened the drawing-room doors, admitting the duke and his friends. She caught the butler's eye for one moment, but he looked quickly away. His look told her nothing, and she shifted nervously, hoping Ravenscroft had not yet heard about her mishap with his son. The duke entered, looking ruddy and unsteady. He was heavily in his cups, if his slanting walk was any indication. His friends followed, a motley group of libertines and old roués. Lily forced herself to take a slow breath and exhale it. These were the sort of men she always had to evade. They had nimble hands and slow minds, and they thought their titles and money, what little they hadn't gambled away, entitled them to take whatever they wanted.

She could handle most of them, but the sight of Lord Kwirley gave her pause. He'd been pursuing Fallon, but she had rejected him in such a manner as to earn his ill will. Now he hated The Three Diamonds, and when he saw her, he smiled ominously.

Fortunately, the duke was making his way to her. "Lily, my dear! You have arrived. Finally!" He attempted to execute a bow and almost fell into her. She caught him, steadying him, and he wrapped his arm about her shoulders. She was hauled against his rather substantial girth and could smell the port oozing out of his skin. He was very, very foxed.

"I am so sorry to have missed dinner." Lily was aware of the other women glaring at her. She was used to it and did not find ignoring them difficult. And now that her target was present, she was wholly focused on her mission.

"Did you have something to eat?" the duke asked.

"You'll give her something to eat, won't you, Ravenscroft?" Kwirley said, laughing loudly at his own joke. "And if you can't satisfy her appetite, I'm sure I can."

Lily smiled thinly. "I have not eaten, Lord Kwirley, and I fear I am hungry for more than your little snack."

The room erupted in laughter, and the duke patted

her behind. She had won his favor but at the cost of Kwirley's animosity. She would have to be careful of both men. "This is a lovely house," she said, turning the subject. "I do hope your steward will give me a tour at some point."

"I'll give you an abbreviated tour of the most important room tonight," Ravenscroft said. He leaned close, slobbering in her ear. "Would you like that?"

"I cannot wait," she said. "But first a drink, perhaps?" The key now would be to make certain the duke was too intoxicated to take advantage of her presence in his bedchamber. That would give her the opportunity to have a look about. She knew what she was looking for—anything to tie the duke to the recent attempts on the lives of her fellow agents for the Crown.

Lily signaled to a footman with a tray of champagne. She took a glass and turned to Ravenscroft. "What would you like, darling?"

His gaze roved boldly over her body, making her itch. "I am not thirsty for spirits."

"Perhaps some port, then?" she said to the footman. "You will need fortification," she told Ravenscroft.

"Oh, ho! Will I, then?"

Lily smiled, listening to more of his innuendos and double entendres and trying not to appear bored. She had heard all of them at some point or another. Men thought they were being clever, and her task was to ensure they continued to think that way. When she was annoyed and tired, as she was now, she tried to remember the Countess of Sinclair's advice. The countess was not a courtesan by any stretch of the imagination, but when she'd taken Juliette, Fallon, and Lily in, she'd been married for quite a number of years. She knew the male mind well enough to tutor three girls who had few options other than becoming courtesans.

Make a man feel like he is the most charming, most handsome, most amazing lover you have ever known. Do that, and he will worship you forever.

The earl certainly worshipped his wife—despite rumors to the contrary—so Lily could only assume the countess knew what she was talking about.

Suddenly, the duke's brow furrowed, and he stared across the room. "What the deuce is he doing here?"

Lily followed the duke's gaze and spotted Darlington at the far side of the room. He'd been cornered by the opera singer, and he looked as though he did not mind overly much. She snorted. And he had the nerve to disparage *her* reputation. The man had his own reputation. Everyone knew he'd never met an opera singer he didn't like.

Lily put a hand on the duke's arm. "He isn't hurting anything. Tell me more about your stables."

"Give him time," the duke said, narrowing his bloodshot eyes. "He has become a boorish lout. Doesn't approve of my friends, you know."

"Doesn't he?" Lily looked over her shoulder and caught the earl watching her. It was strange to see the father and son in close proximity. They did not resemble each other at all. Darlington and his sister must take after their mother. Where the earl had dark hair and eyes, a tall, muscular frame, and an inborn grace of movement, his father was pale and ruddy, short and stocky, and lumbered rather than walked. "I am certain he only misses his mother."

"I don't know why you defend him," the duke said. "He protested quite loudly over my inviting you here."

"That does not surprise me. He and I have not been on good terms of late." It occurred to her that now was as good a time as any to lay the groundwork should she need to defend herself from accusations made by the butler or governess regarding what they saw earlier. "He is still in love with my friend Juliette, you see. In fact, shortly after I arrived today, he cornered me and asked after her rather forcefully. I do not think he has yet accepted the fact that she is well and truly married to the Duke of Pelham."

The duke's face reddened further. Lily actually became alarmed at how close to purple the man's complexion had become. "I hope he did not hurt you."

Lily waved a hand, eager to reassure the duke before he expired on the spot. "No, no. A puppy like him? I can snap my fingers and put him in his place."

"And who is this puppy you speak of?" she heard a familiar voice ask behind her. She stiffened, knowing it was Darlington and cursing her inattention. If she had not been so concerned about the duke, she would have seen his son crossing the room and chosen her words accordingly.

She turned to Darlington. "No one you know, my lord."

"Are you certain?" His brow lifted, giving him a cynical, bored look. But she saw the hard glint of anger in his eyes and knew he was not fooled. "Your list of conquests is quite substantial. Surely I know one or two."

"*My* list of conquests? You should look to your own list, my lord. It is quite lengthy in its own right, and if I am not mistaken, you will soon add to it." She nodded to the opera singer.

"Jealous, Countess?"

"Hardly."

The duke cleared his throat, and Lily realized she'd completely forgotten that he was still standing there.

"What are you doing here, Darlington?" the duke said, slurring his son's courtesy title. "I thought you didn't approve."

"I admit, Your Grace, my curiosity got the better of me. And I can scarce resist the allure of the Countess of Charm. In fact, we had an interlude earlier—"

"I've already discussed it with His Grace," Lily interrupted. "The topic is stale."

"Perhaps I can revive it." Darlington held out his arm. "Take a turn about the room with me, won't you, Lily?"

She was not deceived by his smile or his mild tone. She knew he was angry, and if she went with him, he would do something to make the situation worse.

"I do not think so," the duke said, taking Lily's arm. "I was about to give the countess a tour of the house. You shall have to excuse us." His fingers dug painfully into her arm, and she bit her lip to keep from crying out.

She could not stay, and she did not want to go. Cursing the untenable situation, Lily had no choice but to stumble along as Ravenscroft dragged her from the drawing room. No one but Darlington even noticed. She truly was alone here—and at the duke's mercy. Thankfully, the duke stumbled and leaned heavily on her, but had he drank enough to pass out, or would she have to fight him off?

Her last sight as she departed the drawing room was Kwirley's sneer and Darlington's scowl.

Six

ANDREW WATCHED HER GO. HIS FATHER LEANED heavily on her, his mouth beside her ear as he whispered God knew what. Lily laughed, but Andrew knew her well enough to know it wasn't an honest laugh. She might be fooling others into believing she was attracted to his father, but she was not fooling him. So then why was she going to the duke's bed? Did she want the title that much? The money?

Whatever her reasoning, he found himself inexplicably furious. Quite suddenly, he wanted to lift the Ming vase from the mantel and throw it across the room. Maybe he'd hit one of the lechers in the process. Half of London would thank him. But it wouldn't assuage his anger. Lily would still be in his father's bed. The old duke would still be undressing her, slobbering on her, rutting with her. The old fool wouldn't know what he had. He wouldn't appreciate the sprinkle of freckles across her face or the sardonic arch of her brow. Lily deserved better—not that he wanted her. She was like a sister to him, though he had to admit he had never kissed his sisters like he'd kissed Lily in the storage closet.

He ran a hand through his hair, discomfited by
the memory. He couldn't quite explain what had
happened earlier. He had not wanted to kiss Lily. It
had been yet another scheme to alienate her from his
father's affections. But once he touched her, once he
had her in his arms, all reason left him, and he could
think only of how sweet she tasted and how arousing
all the little mewling sounds she made were when he
kissed her deeply.

But kissing her had done nothing to stop her from
going to his father's bed. He was experienced enough
to know this did not mean his father would be asking
her for her hand in marriage, and Andrew could find
other methods to make certain this did not occur. But
he did not like to think of her under his father. Or
over his father... Andrew clenched his hands again.
He needed a woman to take his mind off what was
happening upstairs. He turned from the mantel and
surveyed the room. His father had certainly amassed
some of the most willing women in the entire country. He should have no problem persuading one or
more to join him in bed.

Andrew leaned on the mantel and tapped his fingers
on the ledge. Mrs. Arbuckle was eyeing him. She was
young and pretty with plump arms and cheeks and a
mass of blond ringlets. She spilled out of her gown in
an impressive display of flesh. She was quite delectable,
if one liked that sort of thing.

He turned his attention to the widows, Mrs.
Compton and Lady Euglin. Both were currently flirt-
ing mercilessly with his father's guests, but Andrew
thought he could lure one of them away. And then, of

course, there was Angelique. She was the opera singer, and he'd long admired her. She raised her brows suggestively when he caught her eye, and he started across the room. Yes, Angelique would take his mind off Lily. He'd already forgotten the courtesan.

"My lord," Angelique said, wafting her fan slowly, seductively. "I have been waiting for you to notice me for hours, it seems."

He bowed and kissed her hand. "You were never beneath my notice, fair Angelique. I've been thinking how to approach you again all evening."

"Have you? And I've been thinking of all the delicious hours we might spend together, if I could only see you alone. Would you like to give me a tour of the house?"

"I'd like nothing better." And yet he did not move to do so. Instead, he poured himself a brandy and sipped it, allowing Angelique to tease him with words and straying fingers. He should take her to his room. She was obviously more than willing. But he could not make himself do so. He did not want her. She lacked... something. Freckles across the bridge of her nose? A wild sweep of auburn hair? Laughing green eyes?

Devil take him if he was not completely besotted by that damned courtesan. And devil take him if he was going to stand idly by while his father defiled her. He started away. From far away, he heard Angelique calling after him. He gave her a distracted wave and headed for the stairs. Halfway to his father's room he realized the ridiculousness of his actions. He would not stop his father from defiling her. Could a courtesan even be defiled? And she had gone willingly. If he interrupted, he'd only be an annoyance to both of them.

He arrowed for his bedchamber instead. Once there, he dismissed his valet and loosened his cravat so it spilled down his white linen shirt. He still held the glass of brandy, and he replenished it and stared out his window, sipping it. He knew what the problem was. He'd become so focused on stopping this liaison between Lily and his father, he'd become obsessed with her. And she, being a courtesan, had exploited that weakness and bewitched him. What he needed was sleep. He would be able to look at everything with new eyes in the morning. Without bothering to undress, he flopped on his bed and threw his hand over his eyes. He fluffed his pillows then turned on his side. He turned on the other side and covered his face with a pillow. He tried lying on his stomach. Nothing worked. He was not going to be able to rest. Not until he stopped whatever was happening in his father's bedchambers.

He was a fool. He knew it. He knew he should leave well enough alone, but that didn't stop him from finding himself in the corridor outside the duke's bedchamber. A servant passed, and Andrew tried to look overly interested in one of the paintings on the wall. When the man was gone, he spun to stare at his father's closed door. He didn't hear any sounds. Were they sleeping? Was he too late?

Andrew approached the door, lifted his hand, then lowered it again. What was he doing? This was madness. He should...

Suddenly the door opened. Lily jumped and covered her mouth to stifle a small squeak. "Darlington," she breathed. "What are you doing here?"

It was the question he'd been asking himself for the past quarter hour. But instead of answering, he devoured her with his eyes. She was still dressed in the gown she'd been wearing earlier—a sober black gown that did not quite fit with her role here. It glittered with silver, making her porcelain skin look almost ethereal in the dim light. Her hair was a bit mussed, one long curl falling over the creamy flesh of her partly exposed shoulder. She did not look like a woman just emerging from a bed of sin.

And then he heard it—a loud snore. He pushed past her and peered into the room. His father was sprawled, fully dressed, on the bed. He lay face down, his enormous buttocks like a small hill on the large tester bed.

Andrew looked at Lily, and she looked back, her brows raised. "Not quite the scene you expected, is it?"

"I don't understand."

"Why should you be any different?"

He frowned at her.

"Is there something you need, Darlington?" she whispered.

"I'll walk you back to your room."

She shook her head. "I do not need an escort." She pushed him out the door. "Good night."

Andrew watched the door close. She was staying? For what purpose? He stuck a foot in the doorway, holding it open. "What are you doing?"

"I'm not ready to leave yet."

"Why not?"

"Go back to your room or to whatever you were doing, and leave me in peace."

She shoved him out the door and closed it in his face.

❦

Lily leaned back against the door, praying her conversation with Darlington hadn't disturbed the duke. She'd had to duck and twist and scamper to avoid the duke's nimble fingers. And when she'd finally persuaded him to lie down, she'd had to promise him all manner of wickedness before he finally fell into a drunken slumber. She'd barely begun to search the room when she'd heard footsteps outside and feared the valet was coming to attend to his master.

Instead, she found Darlington. Would the man not leave her alone? He was the most determined person she had ever met—and the most interfering. She needed twenty minutes to search the duke's chambers. Twenty minutes. Leave it to Darlington to rob her of even that much.

There was silence on the other side of the door, and she took a breath and scanned the room. She would begin with the desk. She could search the papers there quickly and then go through the drawers of his tall boy. She opened the first of the desk's drawers and rifled through the contents, not caring if she spilled half of them on the floor. She could claim their passion had overcome them and resulted in the room's disarray. Unfortunately, her quick perusal revealed nothing of rubies, nothing of Artemis, nothing...

Thump, thump, thump.

Lily jumped and spun to face the door. Now what? She glared at the door and willed Darlington to go away. She opened another drawer and spilled its contents on the floor, shuffling through papers, quills, and ink pots. She scanned the parchments, hoping to catch a reference to her fellow agents. Payments or promises of payments for services might also prove valuable. Did the man not keep a ledger?

Thump! Thump! Thump!

Lily stifled a scream of frustration.

The duke snuffled and stirred. Lily held her breath until he settled again and his snoring resumed. She was going to kill Darlington. She'd never killed anyone before, never wanted to. She had a very even temper. But Darlington was testing the limits of her patience as no one ever had.

The ledger was probably in the duke's library. That would be the next place she searched, as soon as she could access it. In the meantime, there was still—*THUMP!*

Lily jumped up, lifted her skirts, and raced to the door, pulling it open before Darlington's hand could come down again. "What are you doing?" she hissed. "Go away!"

"What are *you* doing?" He glanced past her, and though she tried to block his view by shifting her body, she knew he saw the mess she had made. "Are you trying to rob my father?"

Lily rolled her eyes. "Go away," she whispered. "You are not wanted here."

"Perhaps I should call for a magistrate. Then we'll see who is not wanted." He meant it, too. Lily could see in Darlington's eyes that he was eager to accuse her of something. It would be just her luck if he did call the magistrate and she was thrown out before she could complete the mission. None of the men working for the Foreign Office were in a position to come close to the duke or see the inner workings of his household. The Foreign Office was counting on her to find the traitor.

It was better to retreat tonight than to risk the entire operation.

"Very well," Lily said with a sigh. "I'll return to my room. I need to fetch my wrap." She closed the door again, gave the papers on the floor a last look, found her wrap, and opened the door.

Darlington was waiting for her. Why should she be surprised? The man was tenacious. She had to give him that much credit.

"I'll escort you to your room." He indicated she should precede him.

"That's not necessary." She stuck her nose in the air and walked away from him, but it was not long before he was beside her.

"You're up to something."

"You don't know what you're talking about," she said, not looking at him.

"Did you drug my father?" When she didn't respond, he grabbed her elbow and pulled her back. "Is that why he was unconscious?"

He was staring down at her and had her flattened against the wall, the edge of a portrait frame digging into her shoulder. "Did you happen to smell your father? He reeked of spirits. My guess is that he has been drinking since noon or thereabouts. He fell asleep without any aid from me. Even my charms failed to keep him awake."

A look of disgust covered the earl's face. "I suppose you become used to it after a while, sleeping with old men and lechers, allowing them to paw you, slobber over you."

Lily felt the heat rise in her cheeks, and she had to clench her hands into fists to keep from slapping him. She didn't know why his comments should anger her so. She'd heard them time and again, but she had always imagined Darlington was different. She had put him on a pedestal; she saw that now. He was just like everyone else—he saw only what he wanted to see.

She began to issue a scathing retort, and then changed her mind. "Don't forget that your love, Juliette, was quite recently a courtesan as well."

Darlington's eyebrows came together, and his face went dark. She would never understand why he was so loyal to Juliette. What did he see in her that made it so easy to look past her station as a courtesan, when he could not look past it in Lily's case? But Juliette could do no wrong. His unswerving affection made Lily suddenly angry. "She was pawed and slobbered on as much as any of us," Lily went on, though she noted the dangerous look on Darlington's face. "And don't forget that she chose all of those other men over you. Again and again and again."

His fist hit the wall beside her head, and Lily had to contain a jump. She had thought he would hit her. He'd had that look in his eyes, and she'd seen his fist coming. She turned to look at his hand now.

It was close, quite close. He pulled it away, and she saw the blood on his knuckles. "I don't want to talk about Juliette."

"I do. You know we were both under the protection of the Earl of Sinclair. He liked us to join him in bed together."

"Stop." His voice was low and murderous, but Lily could not stop herself. He'd had her kidnapped, insulted her at every turn, and now interrupted her vital work. She wanted him to be angry. She wanted him to be as annoyed and frustrated and furious as she was.

"You should have seen Juliette pleasure the Earl of Sin. He liked it when she would—" Lily saw his hand go up, and she flinched, but it was his mouth that came down hard on hers, silencing her. This time she was ready for it. This time she met him on the battlefield. She kissed him back, bruising his lips, tearing at his hair with her hands. He made an incredulous sound, and then his arms were around her. But she wouldn't be contained. She shoved him back, continuing her assault until it was he who was pinned to the wall and not her.

"How do you like it?" she asked, breaking the kiss. "How do you like being the one taken?"

He glared at her. She could see he hated her—no, he hated his desire for her. He wanted her, and he hated himself for that. Lily's heart swelled in her chest. *Darlington wanted her.* She shouldn't care. She should hate him, but she had wanted him for so long that to see the desire in his eyes, to feel his arousal pressed hard against her belly, was the ultimate fulfillment.

He might love Juliette—or think he loved the idea of her—but he wanted her—Lily. And, judging from the lengths he'd gone to in order to evict her from his father's bedchamber—he wanted her badly.

She had the sudden realization she could take him to bed. She could take his hand and lead him to her room. He would go with her. He was barely fighting his need for her now. It might take a bit of coaxing, more kissing, but she could have him. She had loved him for so long…

And if she bedded him, then what? Then his desire for her would be slaked, and he would go back to pining for Juliette and attempting to thwart her mission here. She would feel worse than she did right now. And she would be a prostitute in truth, because he would only be using her. Lily stepped back, letting her hands drop from Darlington's neck. This was not what she wanted. Not like this. She wanted him to care for her. She wanted him to pine for her, as he pined for Juliette.

That, she knew, would never happen, but she did not have to accept what he was offering now—a frantic coupling in the dark followed by his scorn in the morning.

She'd already taken that road. She'd been young, only sixteen, but she had learned from her mistake. She would not make it again.

"I'm returning to my room," she said. "Alone."

He stared at her, his eyes dark with longing that made her belly flutter and her legs weak. "Do not follow me." She forced her legs backward, forced herself to retreat, to leave him, though he was staring at her with undisguised need. She could almost feel his desire for her, and as soon as she was out of his sight, she began to run. Her slippers shushed loudly on the rug until she was certain he did not follow. Then she pressed herself against the wall, put a hand to her heart, and tried to catch her breath.

She was lost now. She had no idea if this was the way to her room, but she would worry about that in a moment. Running away from Darlington had been harder than she could have anticipated. She felt an ache now that she was away from him. She wanted him so badly, and yet she hated him as much as he hated her. She didn't understand it. She didn't want to. She had a mission to complete. Men's lives were at stake. She could not let them down. Something had to be done about Darlington's interference.

Perhaps if she found a way to keep him busy. The duke certainly had outings and entertainments planned. Perhaps she could make certain Darlington was involved in those. But even as she thought it, she shook her head. Darlington would never be occupied for long with picnics and archery. He had grown up on those pursuits. They would not keep his attention when he was so intent on keeping her away from his father.

A woman, then. That was the only way. Perhaps she could interest him in the opera singer. Everyone knew that, aside from Juliette, opera singers were his weakness. Lily did not relish seeing him with another woman, but she needed him out of the way. And she needed him out of the way immediately. With a sigh, she started back for the drawing room. It was early, and she had no doubt Ravenscroft's guests were still drinking and debauching.

When she reached the drawing room, it was unusually quiet. Perhaps she had misjudged the time. Could everyone already be abed? She knew country hours were earlier than those she kept in Town. Cautiously, Lily reached for the door's handle and pushed it open. Lord Kwirley sat in a chair by the fire, sipping what looked like port. He glanced up at her and raised a brow. "Back so soon?" he said with a sneer. "Did you find so little to entertain you?" He placed his thumb and forefinger close together. "So *very* little?"

"Where are the others, Lord Kwirley?" Lily asked. Why did *he* have to be the one left behind? Her luck of late was atrocious. Fallon had once warned her to stay out of Kwirley's path, and a warning like that from Fallon was not to be taken lightly.

He rose. "Outside." He walked to the serving tray, lifted a clean glass, and filled it with sherry. "Here you are."

"No, thank you. Why have they gone outside?"

"Not even thirsty after your exertions?" Kwirley shook his head. "You are wasted on a buffoon like Ravenscroft."

Lily frowned and peered over her shoulder. She did not want to go outside and look for the others, but it appeared she had little other choice. Obviously Kwirley was not going to help her by offering information. She'd have to see for herself.

"You are the determined one, aren't you?" He'd sidled closer while she'd been looking away. "They've gone swimming."

Lily blinked as much from surprise as the sharp scent of alcohol on Kwirley's breath. "Swimming?"

"Yes." He offered her the sherry again, and this time she took it. "The duke mentioned a pond at dinner, and they all seemed keen to try it out. Sans clothing, of course." He leaned close, so close she could see the stubble on his cheeks. He was a handsome man. He knew it, too, and thought his appearance gave him leave to act the perfect scoundrel. She was not impressed. "Will you join them?" he asked.

Lily wanted to curse. Even if she found the opera singer—what *was* her name?—she would undoubtedly be involved in some sort of groping and rolling about. This was hardly the time to persuade the singer to seduce Darlington. Lily's errand would have to wait until breakfast. "I do not think so," she told Kwirley.

"Too bad." He lifted a finger and stroked her cheek. "For you, I would have ventured out myself."

"Good night, my lord."

He grabbed her arm before she could take the first step. "Why in such a hurry? Is the duke awaiting your return?"

"Yes." She looked down at his hand. "Release me."

"What a little liar," Kwirley said, pulling her closer. "I am certain the duke is snoring loudly enough to wake the dead by now. That means you and I have plenty of time to become better acquainted."

"I do not wish to become better acquainted, my lord. I wish to retire." She pulled her arm, but he didn't release it. Instead, he set his empty glass on a table and took her by both arms.

"What did that little harlot tell you? That little

bitch!" He shook Lily, causing her to spill the sherry over her gown and onto the rug.

"Stop!" she said out of annoyance.

He shook her again, and she dropped the glass. It made a muted *thud* on the carpet. "Tell me what she said."

"Fallon told me to stay out of your path."

"Is that all?"

"Yes. Now unhand me before I scream and wake the house." She was not afraid, but she would have rather ended this expediently and quietly. The other methods she could employ would only anger Kwirley, and she did not need an enemy in the house.

"You didn't heed her advice very well, did you?" he said, rubbing his hands up and down her arms. "You are most definitely in my path, sweet Lily. What shall I do with you?" He walked his fingers over her shoulder and up to her chin, tapping her lips.

"My lord, do not make me scream."

"You won't scream," he said, caressing her exposed neck. "You do not want the whole staff alerted to your activities. They might tell your lover."

He was no fool. She did not want to have to explain what she had been doing in the drawing room with Kwirley rather than in Ravenscroft's bed in the morning. She wanted him to think she had been in his bed for most of the night. If Kwirley would not cooperate, she had only one more option. "My lord, do not make me hurt you."

"Oh, fair Lily. It is I who am going to hurt you." He smiled. "I like it that way." And then he crushed his mouth over hers in a painful kiss. His teeth sank into her lip, and she cried out in pain and tried to push him away.

He didn't move. He was almost twice her weight and easily a full head taller than she. He would not be moved unless it was his choice.

She would have to persuade him to make that choice.

He stuck his tongue down her throat, all but gagging her, but she clenched her hands resolutely and bit him. Hard.

"What the devil!" Kwirley yelled, jumping back.

"I told you not to make me hurt you." Lily tried to turn and run, but he came for her. As she knew he would. He made a grab, catching her arm. She pivoted and brought her elbow up and into his abdomen. She didn't connect as directly or forcefully as she would have liked, but it was enough to surprise him. Kwirley released her, and Lily ran. She had to skirt around a set of chairs someone had moved close together, and that cost her precious time. Kwirley caught her by the back of her gown, and she went down, landing hard on her face. Thankfully the rug was soft. She supposed that was one advantage to being attacked in a duke's residence.

Kwirley rolled her over. She knew how to fight him from this position. She'd been trained, though she hadn't used this training in a very long time— ever, actually. She would have kneed him, but she couldn't seem to catch her breath. The fall had been harder than she thought. She tried to breathe, even as Kwirley covered her mouth with his hand and sputtered something vile and awful at her. She couldn't hear him for the rushing sound in her ears, but she could imagine what he was saying.

His intentions were clear. He grabbed her wrists with one hand and began to ruche up her skirts with the other. He was smiling, his eyes glittering with desire. The man liked to cause fear and pain. Lily would give him neither. She struggled again for breath and shifted into position.

And then, suddenly, Kwirley was yanked back, and she was free.

Bloody hell, Lily cursed. *Darlington.*

Seven

DARLINGTON DID NOT BELIEVE WHAT HE SAW. KWIRLEY was attacking Lily. That much he could believe. The man was the worst sort of rake. The fact that such a bouncer had been invited into his home illustrated, beyond a shadow of a doubt, the lows to which his father had sunk.

Andrew absolutely could believe Kwirley was after Lily. What he could not believe was the manner in which she fought back. Her defense appeared coordinated. In fact, it even seemed somewhat effective. He had started into the drawing room as soon as he realized what was happening, and he kept thinking how fortunate for Lily that he had followed her down here. He had wondered why she did not return directly to her room. She was up to something, and he wanted to know what it was. He saw her conversing with Kwirley and speculated the two of them might be plotting something together.

And then Kwirley had gone for her, and she had fought back. He'd actually felt his jaw drop when she pivoted and elbowed the viscount. Where the hell had she learned that? And then he recovered himself and rushed in to save her. And not a moment too soon. She was on the floor, and Kwirley was going to rape her. With a roar, Andrew had run into the room, grabbing Kwirley by the shoulders and hauling him off Lily.

Kwirley had not surrendered easily or willingly, and that was fine with Andrew. He was sporting for a fight. He had wanted to hit someone or something since he'd first seen Lily walk into Ravenscroft Castle. Kwirley was a convenient target. The two men spun around, and Andrew landed the first blow. His fist hit Kwirley in the chin, knocking his head sideways. Kwirley bent over, but he came up with fists raised and in a fighting crouch.

Andrew recognized Gentleman Jackson's instruction when he saw it. But he'd spent his own fair share of time in the ring with the boxing master. He waited for Kwirley to strike. When it came, it was good—an uppercut to his jaw. It was so good, Andrew hadn't been able to sidestep it, but he was able to rebound. He pummeled Kwirley's belly until the other man was hunched over and vulnerable. And then Andrew gave the viscount a taste of his own medicine, striking him across the cheek and glancing his fist across the other man's nose.

Blood spurted everywhere, but Kwirley didn't give in easily. Andrew was grudgingly impressed. In fact, he'd been impressed enough that he missed the warning signs, and Kwirley's fist hit his jaw, sending him reeling backward. Andrew fell against a low table, causing the wood to smash under his weight.

Kwirley jumped on him, and Andrew rolled. Table legs and pieces of splintered wood cut through his wool coat and into his back and arms, but he was on top of Kwirley. He wrapped his hands around the man's neck, banged the back of the man's head against the floor, and then began to squeeze. Kwirley's face turned red then purple, and still Andrew squeezed. He could feel the blood thrumming in his veins, his heart racing, his anger fueling his strength as he squeezed and squeezed…

"That purple color is generally a bad sign," he heard a voice behind him say in a dry tone.

Andrew looked and saw Lily, standing with one hand on the back of a settee. She looked completely composed and unruffled. Her hair was still perfect, her gloves in place, her expression one of ennui—as though she witnessed one man strangling another every day.

She nodded to Andrew's hands, and he looked down at Kwirley's face.

"You can let go now," she said. "Unless, that is, you want to spend time in a gaol or in exile."

He was killing Kwirley. The man was no longer moving. Andrew released him and jumped back, horror dawning. Lily was instantly beside him. "Move aside." She bent, put a finger to Kwirley's neck, and knelt, still and silent.

"What are you doing?" Andrew asked. He'd killed the vile viscount, and she was kneeling beside the man as though a prayer would save him.

"Shh."

Andrew peered closer. Was the man still breathing?

For a moment, he wondered if fleeing to France or Italy would be better.

"He's still alive," she said finally, rising with an easy gracefulness.

"How do you know?"

"His heart is still beating. He's only lost consciousness." She smiled. "You won't have to flee to Italy after all."

"Italy? Not France?"

She gave him a look as though her reasoning should be self-explanatory. "He is unconscious, but there's no way to tell how long it will last. I suggest we not be present when he wakes."

"Very well. Follow me." There were any number of places he could take her, but for some reason he thought of the tapestry room. It was just to the right of the nearby staircase, and no one was likely to stumble into it. The library was closer, but the butler kept it locked. Books were valuable, after all.

She indicated he should precede her, and she followed him, closing the drawing-room door behind her. She didn't ask where he was taking her, which was to her credit. For all she knew, he could be taking her to his bedroom. Obviously, she trusted him. She was probably going to bow at his feet and express her undying gratitude for his efforts at saving her.

Perhaps the bowing was a bit much, but the gratitude was a given.

He ushered her into the tapestry room, leaving the door open a sliver. He watched as she peered around the room, and saw her eyes rove over the various tapestries. "These are exquisite," she said. "That uni-corn one, in particular."

It was the oldest and most valuable, and she had picked it out immediately.

"You have good taste."

She turned to him, raising a brow. "So I've been told." The window curtains behind her were still open. Some maid had forgotten to close them or had come by when he and Emma were talking and had not wanted to interrupt. The moon was full tonight, and the light spilled inside, casting a soft glow about her. Her hair, always so fiery in the sunlight, looked like banked coals in the velvet darkness. Hints of fire weaved their way through the upswept tresses, but they were quick and teasing, disappearing when his gaze caught one.

"Would you like to tell me exactly what you were doing in the drawing room?" she asked suddenly. His gaze returned to her face, and he realized she was angry.

"What *I* was doing?"

"Yes." There went her hands to her hips. "Did you follow me?"

Andrew frowned. What was this about? This was not how the conversation was supposed to go. Why wasn't she overcome with gratitude? "You should be thankful I did."

"Oh, yes, I am ever so thankful to be treated as some sort of prey for your stalking pleasure. How many times must I tell you to leave me alone?"

He stared at her. Did she not understand he was her hero? He had *saved* her! Again! "If I'd left you alone,

Kwirley would have... defiled you." There. Now she could not fail to see her debt to him.

"I had everything well in hand," she said. "You interfered."

Andrew shook his head. The woman was mad. "You were about to be raped," he said bluntly. "It did not look as though you had everything under control." But the image of her pivoting smoothly and elbowing Kwirley in the abdomen flashed in his mind. Perhaps that hadn't been simple luck?

"I know what the viscount's intentions were, and I know how to deal with them. I was momentarily out of breath. I would have incapacitated him, given a few more seconds."

"Oh, really?"

"Would you like me to show you?"

"Yes." The more he thought about it, the better it sounded. "Yes. Show me exactly how you were going to evade Kwirley when he had you trapped beneath him."

"Very well." She pointed to a couch in the center of a rug. "Move that aside."

He didn't take orders well, but he moved the item for the sake of efficiency. And then he watched in amazement as she knelt on the carpet, smoothed her skirts, and lay on her back. "I think I was in this position."

Andrew stared at her, and he wasn't thinking about proving anything to her any longer. He was imagining what she'd look like in his bed, with her hair unbound and swirling like molten fire about her face.

"My lord?" she said, shaking him out of his

fantasies, which were beginning to stray back to her kneeling beside him...

"Ah... your hands were above you." He crouched beside her. Did she really want him to straddle her? How was he going to accomplish that without illustrating just how much he liked seeing her in this position?

She raised her hands. "Like this?"

The movement caused her back to arch, thrusting her breasts out. Andrew took a deep breath. "Yes, like that."

She frowned at him. "Are you afraid I'll best you? Is that why you're hesitating?"

He laughed. "Hardly." If she wanted him to play the part of Kwirley, then he'd do it. He straddled her, grasped her wrists in one hand, and reached back with the other, resting that hand on her thigh. "I believe this was the position."

Her eyes were locked on his face now, soft green and impossibly large. She'd been fighting Kwirley, but she was not fighting him. He had her under him now. He hadn't even known he wanted her in this position, but leaning over her, his face close to hers, his hands holding hers, felt right. He could so easily kiss her.

He saw her swallow. "Proceed," she whispered.

He slid the hand on her thigh down and down, feeling the curves of her legs through the silk, until he reached the hem of her gown. And then his hand caressed the thinnest, sleekest silk of her stocking. He could feel her warm flesh underneath as he cupped her calf and moved upward.

Lily let out a breath and a low moan. He wanted to groan himself when his fingers brushed bare flesh.

Her skin was so soft. Once he'd been forced to hold his three-month-old nephew for several minutes, and Andrew had been amazed at the boy's downy hair and the tender skin on his cheeks. That was how Lily's legs felt—that soft, plump, untouched baby skin. And she was warm beneath him. She was looking up at him with those green eyes that always bewitched him. Why had he ever thought he wanted Juliette? He touched the skin of her thigh, pressed his hands between her legs and moved slowly higher. He already knew she would be hot and wet for him. He inched closer, watching her eyes darken further as he extended one finger…

And then she acted. He never saw it coming. Her eyes betrayed nothing. But her legs came up, and with a flexibility that shocked him, she connected a foot with the back of his head. He reared up, and she bent her leg, her knee just missing his most vital organ.

"Bloody hell, woman!" he yelled, releasing her. He jumped off her, and she sat gracefully. "You almost maimed me."

She smiled. "I told you I didn't need your help." She rose.

"Where did you learn to do that?" Andrew kept his distance from her, putting a chair between them.

"Oh, here and there."

It looked a hell of a lot more practiced than that.

"My point is that I can handle Kwirley."

"Good. You may need to."

"Yes, thanks to you, he will now want revenge." A section of her hair had come loose from her coiffure, and he was surprised at how curly it was and how long. It reached almost to her waist.

"Kwirley shouldn't even be here," Andrew said. "What kind of man leaves his wife at home for a week to attend a house party populated with courtesans"—he nodded at her—"and opera singers?"

"So you have noticed the opera singer."

"Pardon?"

"Nothing." She seated herself on the couch, smoothing her skirts. "I had no idea you were such a great believer in marital fidelity, Lord Darlington."

His nerves were settling now, and he pried his fingers loose from the chair back, still keeping it between them. He would be more vigilant in her presence from now on. "Aren't you?"

"I'm afraid I see very little marital fidelity in my circle," she answered. "But I don't believe it's an impossibility. My own parents were quite faithful, at least from my perspective."

Andrew raised his brows. "Your parents?"

She gave him an annoyed look. "I do have them, even if they no longer acknowledge me."

He had never thought of Lily—any of The Three Diamonds—as having parents. But the women hadn't materialized out of thin air. Even courtesans must hail from somewhere. It did not surprise him that her parents had disowned her. If they were respectable people, they would have no other choice.

"My father was a hero to me," she said. He looked up and saw she was watching him closely. "I thought he was the strongest, bravest man who ever lived. My mother was loving and kind. I was the youngest of five, and I'm sure I was very spoiled."

Andrew sat on the chair opposite her, intrigued enough to forgo the protection of his chair barrier for a moment. "Where did you grow up?"

She smiled. "The truth? London."

"What do you tell everyone?"

"York. I've often had people tell me I have a northern accent." She shook her head. "But I was born in London. My father had a position in the government. We were not rich, but we had a cozy house. My room was in the attic, probably because for a long time I was the shortest and the only one who didn't hit my head on the sloped ceiling."

"Do your brothers and sisters have your coloring?"

Her green eyes seemed to see right through him. "My red hair, you mean? It's natural. Was that what you were wondering?"

He was too smart to answer.

"Would you like me to prove it?"

Andrew reached for his drink and realized he didn't have one. He needed one badly. "I only meant that it is unusual."

"Yes, we must have an Irish ancestor somewhere. My sister Charlotte also has auburn hair, but she has brown eyes. My brother Robert has green eyes like mine, though. But we were discussing marital fidelity. Why are you such a firm believer?"

He considered. "Perhaps I'm not. Six months ago I would have said my parents had a perfect marriage, but now I have my doubts."

"If the duke kept mistresses in London, I never heard about it," she said. "That should restore some of your faith."

"Yes, but he has certainly made up for any lack since my mother's death. And there were the war years."

She made a slight movement, leaning closer, and he almost decided against speaking any further. But what could it hurt? She was not going to be as easy to dissuade as he had first thought. "He traveled extensively during the war, dragged my poor mother with him. They were gone for months at a time."

"Was he involved in the army?"

"I don't think so. He's no war hero. Come to think of it, I don't think I ever asked what he was up to. I suppose it wasn't my place to question him."

"Did he ever say anything about the French or any of our allies or enemies?"

"He commented on the situation, as any of us would. Why?" He leaned forward. "Why are you suddenly so interested?"

She smiled and flipped her hair, a gesture that looked too frivolous. "I am interested in His Grace's loyalties. I'm sure you can understand why."

"No, I don't." He rose. "What is it you want from my father? You have yet to answer."

She rose too. "I believe we've already had this conversation, and it is still not your concern." She turned and started for the door. "I will thank you not to follow me this time. I assure you I am going straight to my room and to bed. Alone."

He watched her leave, left with more questions than answers.

❧

Lily returned to her room, surprised she had not taken a wrong turn en route. She had not even been at Ravenscroft Castle for twelve hours. It seemed like weeks. She had Anna help her undress for bed and then dismissed her. When she was alone, Lily took a sheet of paper and a quill from her satchel and began to pen a note to Fitzhugh. She was brutally honest in her remarks, admitting she had been too heavy-handed when asking about Ravenscroft's activities during the war. She sat back, read over what she'd written.

The problem, as usual, was Darlington. She should have been able to question him with all of her usual finesse, but she found herself edgy and impatient in his presence.

She lifted her quill again, dipped it in ink, and wrote of Fallon: *Our mutual friend was correct in surmising that Lord D— will be a problem. He thwarts me at every turn. I will deal with him, but I may be forced to take less than appealing measures.*

Lily shuddered. It had been bad enough to endure Ravenscroft's touch for a few minutes before he'd fallen into a stupor. How was she going to tolerate him for any lengthy period of time? She knew if she was to be successful in this mission she might have to go to bed with the duke. Fitzhugh and his superiors had never said as much. It was not expected, but it was also part of the reason she'd been chosen for this mission. If she was a courtesan in truth, this aspect of her mission would not have caused her to blink, but for the life of her, Lily did not understand how courtesans tolerated bedding men they found repulsive. Desperation born out of necessity, she supposed. She was not quite that desperate yet. She had another idea, but she thought Darlington would like it even less than he liked the idea of her bedding his father.

And what did it matter what Darlington thought anyway? He was an impediment, nothing more. Except he was so much an impediment because she still wanted him. She had thought after his aborted kidnapping attempt she would hate him forever. She didn't. If he would stop kissing her, that would have helped. She could hate him quite easily until he kissed her or touched her—and then something happened. She took leave of her senses, and her body responded.

She had imagined thousands of times what it would be like to be touched by him, kissed by him, desired by him, but the reality exceeded her every fantasy. Perhaps her experience was too limited to indulge in truly sinful fantasies.

And that thought brought her to the other issue in the back of her mind.

She signed the letter and readied it to be posted. She needed to find a way to escape for a few hours tomorrow. A servant could easily post the letter, so that would not suffice as an excuse. Perhaps she could claim she had forgotten some necessary undergarment and beg to be excused from the afternoon entertainments to go into the little town nearby.

But then all the other women would want to go into town as well. The suggestion of an afternoon of shopping would be too tempting. That meant she would have to sneak away. It was an unnecessary risk—precisely what the countess had warned her against. But she had to see him again. It had been at least two years, and the last time it had broken her heart. She had vowed not to return. He was well. He did not need her. She had made the right decision.

But she had to see for herself. She had to see him one last time, if only to say good-bye in her heart.

The early morning might be the best time to slip away. The ladies would be abed, and the men would rise early to hunt. She glanced at her clock and sighed. That left her approximately two hours in which to sleep. Reluctantly, she summoned Anna again, and told her to wake her when the household servants rose to tend to the gentlemen. And then Lily fell into a light sleep.

The dew on the grass near the stables soaked her boots before she had even departed Ravenscroft Castle. Lily stood shivering in the misty morning, listening to the distant sound of hounds baying as the hunt began. Most of the grooms were engaged with the hunt, but she had found one still behind and asked him to saddle a good-natured horse for her. He'd offered to go with her, but Lily had refused. This was something she needed to do on her own. She'd lifted her riding crop and said she could handle any trouble, but now she patted her pocket and felt the reassuring weight of her small pistol. She did not think she would have to fire it. It would be enough to show it if she was accosted.

The groom brought the mare, an older horse who was gentle and slow, and helped her mount. She straightened her dark red riding habit then asked for general directions and started on her way, keeping well away from the men and their hunt. The sun had burned off most of the mist by the time she reached her destination. The air had warmed, and she was no longer cold. One look at the blue-streaked sky told her it would be a lovely summer day—the kind with puffy clouds and light breezes, carrying the scent of summer flowers.

It had been a summer day like this long ago when she'd met him. She'd been at a fair just outside London and had begged her parents to allow her to roam about with her friends. They had conceded, and she'd skipped off with two girls whose names she could barely remember now. They'd had a marvelous time. Between them, they'd probably had all of sixpence, but much could be had at a fair for very little in those days. And watching people come and go was free.

Lily would never know why he'd chosen her. He could have had his pick of any of the foolish young girls at the fair that day, but when she'd looked up from studying the heifers on display, she'd seen him watching her. He was handsome, devilishly handsome. And, of course, he was older. Her breath had caught in her throat when he'd smiled at her and approached. She remembered feeling her cheeks heat and knowing she was as red as the ribbons she and her friends had admired at one of the booths.

"I've been looking for you," he said, and held out his hand. It was such a romantic thing to say. Not that she would have found it romantic now. At five and twenty, she would have rolled her eyes at such foolishness and made a witty, but cutting, remark. At barely sixteen years of age, she was charmed. Impossibly charmed. And he knew how to charm young girls, or so she realized later—when it was too late. He made a great show of introducing himself and bowing politely to her friends, but he wanted her alone. And, despite her parents' warnings to stay with her friends, she went with him.

He bought her sweets and paid her admission to the menagerie and the boxing matches. And before he left her, he bought her the red ribbons she'd been eyeing. Her mother would scold her for purchasing those later—red was one of the colors that clashed horribly with her hair and complexion. He also arranged to see her again. He'd told her his name was Giles Westerly, and he'd bowed and said, "Lily Dawson, it has been a pleasure."

She'd been Lily Dawson then, not the Countess of Charm. If not for Giles Westerly, she might never have become the Countess of Charm, but she couldn't put all the blame on him. She had always loved adventure and excitement too much. The forbidden was all the more appealing to the girl in her who was tired of needlepoint and peeling potatoes and all of the other domestic chores that dominated her day and, seemingly, her life.

She'd lived for those clandestine meetings and the stolen kisses and delicious caresses that became bolder and more forbidden as the summer went on. Oh, she'd protested his roving hands and his nimble fingers, but she hadn't meant it. She'd been in love—or what passed for love at that age. She'd thought he loved her too.

But, of course, he hadn't. When he'd taken what he wanted, he disappeared, and by the time the leaves had turned, the romance was over and her virtue lost.

She shook her head ruefully at the memory as the mare topped a low rise. She was close. She remembered this rise—or so she thought. And when she reached the summit, she reined in the horse and looked down at the small cottage with its well-tended flowers and verdant fields. A puff of smoke came from the chimney, which gave her hope the family was home. She should have wished they were away for the day. Seeing him would give her no peace, as much as she tried to tell herself it would. That was a lie, and if the Countess of Sinclair had been here, she would have seen right through it.

But not even that formidable lady could have kept Lily away. She'd tried in the past, but Lily supposed she still had some of the foolishness that contributed to her fall all those years ago. A decade ago. Another lifetime.

And then the door opened, and her heart all but stopped. It was him. She would have known that face and that hair anywhere. She saw it every day in the mirror. He didn't see her, and that was for the best, because she was certain her face showed her every feeling. She had been prepared for the yearning—the longing to hold him, know him, this part of herself who had been so abruptly severed from her life. She'd not been prepared for the pain—the absolute anguish and despair that crashed over her when she saw him.

He was no longer a baby. He was growing up without her. He was his own person, and she, who at one time had known his every breath or cry, knew nothing of him now. Her arms ached to hold him again, tickle his tiny, plump toes, kiss his sweet brow, feel his chubby hand curl possessively about her finger.

The pain of her loss washed over her, and she would have crumpled had she not been seated atop the horse. Clutching her hand to her heart, she watched as the boy carried a bucket, appearing wholly absorbed in his own thoughts. She wondered what they might be. What did a boy of nine think about, imagine, dream of? Did he ever think of her? Did he even know she existed?

She hoped not. She could be nothing but an embarrassment and a disgrace to this boy. In London, when she was engaged in a steady diet of balls and routs, she never thought of what she was. She danced and laughed and flirted and spent others' money as though it were her own. Occasionally, she would catch a glimpse of herself in a mirror and wonder who the girl looking back at her was. But she could barely remember what it had been like to be Lillian Beatrice Dawson.

It was only when she was on the street in the cold light of day—when she had shopping or an errand or some ordinary task—that she was reminded of her place. She was a fallen woman, and respectable men and women crossed the street to avoid her. It was as though her vice was catching and could infect one by mere proximity. Her own parents would not see her. She had tried not once, but twice, to visit them. She should have learned after the first time, but she had never given up easily, even when the results were painful. And she could hardly blame her parents for disowning her. She had given them little choice. However, she did blame them for abandoning her when she had needed them most. The abandonment had not only stabbed her in the heart but left her at the mercy of the figurative wolves.

Her father had ordered her out without even a second look. Her mother had found her and gave her some money and food, but to her father, she was dead.

Even now Lily was angry at the man she'd once revered. He'd turned her out—scared and with child. Alone and defenseless. He knew London, knew what awaited her on its streets, and he'd abandoned her to that fate. If it hadn't been for the Earl and the Countess of Sinclair, she would be dead by now. Lily did not doubt that.

The boy looked up at her, his gaze curious. She knew what he saw—a well-dressed woman on horse-back out for a morning ride. He might wonder why she had ventured so far from the castle, as she was likely one of the duke's guests. And then she saw him turn toward her. Sweet boy. He had no idea how tempted she was to go to him. She wanted nothing more than to dismount. She would run to him, embrace him, wrap her arms around him as she had when he was a baby. All she wanted was to hold him one more time, to kiss his face, to tell him she loved him, she thought of him every day, she had not wanted to give him up. She wanted to see him laugh, hear his voice, hold his small hand in hers.

She never wanted to let him go again. Even now, the pain of losing him cut through her and left her breathless. Would it ever dull? Would she ever feel whole and complete once again? When would she wake without that vague feeling of wrongness? When would she open her eyes and not feel the crushing pain of remembering that a chunk of her heart was missing?

At times she wished her memory would fail her, so she would not have to bear the hurt.

He was nearing, and she knew her illusions about a reunion were just that—illusions. She would have to leave him. Again. He waved at her, his smile lighting up the hillside, and her heart clenched. Sweet boy. Handsome boy. She bit her lip to stanch the tears. He probably thought she was lost.

But she was not lost, and as she turned her horse, she knew it was time she returned to what she knew.

Eight

ANDREW STEPPED BACK INTO A SMALL COPSE AND watched as Lily spurred her horse back in the direction of Ravenscroft Castle. His own horse nickered quietly at the scent of the mare he probably recognized from the stable, and Andrew put his hand on the horse's nose and soothed the beast.

When she was away, he mounted the animal and urged him up the hill where she'd stood, looking down. He saw nothing unusual, nothing to warrant her attention. If memory served, this was the Musgrove home. The man was a gentleman farmer, and while the family was not wealthy, they were self-sufficient. Did they have only the one boy? Andrew couldn't remember, but he was intrigued. Everything about Lily seemed to intrigue him.

And now he would return home and see what other intrigues this day held.

He'd spent the rest of the late morning avoiding his father's guests. It had not been difficult because, with the exception of Lily and the men who had gone hunting, no one had been up and about. He'd found his sister in the music room, practicing her pianoforte as well as the harp. He'd listened briefly and then stepped outside to search for his father's steward. His father had been too occupied with his vices of late to take much notice of the estate, and Andrew had taken to meeting with the steward to discuss what needed to be done. But he'd barely left the house when he was accosted by someone else altogether.

"My lord," the opera singer purred, waving her fan in front of her face. It was a breezy day, and she did not need the fan, but he supposed it was for effect. And it was a lovely effect. Angelique was an attractive woman. He was rather surprised she had sought him out after the way he'd neglected her the previous night.

"Mrs. Howell. Good morning."

"Angelique, please," she said. "Care to accompany me on a walk?"

"Actually, I had business to attend to with the steward."

"Oh, is that all?" She fluttered her fan again. "Do you mind if I accompany you? I'm certain I shall find it fascinating."

Andrew sincerely doubted that. He did not find it interesting. But neither did he want the opera singer running to his father with a complaint. Andrew would be damned if he was going to be accused of not entertaining his father's guests. He offered an arm. "He is typically near the stables at this time of day. I thought to seek him there."

"Oh, good," she purred, but he saw her look down at her dainty slippers. They would be ruined if she stepped in manure or muck. "This is a beautiful estate, my lord," she said. "Did you enjoy growing up here?"

"How could I not?" He'd spent more time at Eton than he had here, but his sisters had told him it was a lovely place to grow up. But this was not a woman to whom he relished giving confidences. She was making idle chatter, not hoping for his life story. He supposed it was his turn to ask her a question, but he could not think of one. He really didn't care where she had grown up or what opera she was performing next or what she thought of the weather. Angelique did not interest him, and he did not feel like feigning interest today.

They walked in silence and had not made it halfway to the stables when the woman cried out and halted. Annoyed, Andrew glanced back at her. "Oh, dear. I do not think my slippers will survive a trek through that." She pointed to a muddy puddle. He had intended to step over it. Surely she could step over it as well. "Could you lift me over it, my lord?" There was the waving fan again and a flutter of her lashes.

Andrew smiled tightly, put his hands on her waist, lifted and arced her over the puddle. He set her down and started for the stables again. And then there was a pile of manure and then another puddle. Angelique had to be carried over each. Andrew was no fool. He could see her ploy. She had not come with him because she thought it interesting. She hoped to seduce him. He did not know why this annoyed him. She was an attractive woman, and he had been without a woman in his bed for some time. But he had wanted only to speak to the steward, and he was tired and did not want to carry her halfway across the yard. He did not want to flirt or tease or whatever else she had in mind. He wanted to finish his business.

And if only Pelham could hear him now. His friend the Duke of Pelham was always saying Darlington was too frivolous to be a duke. Darlington wasn't even a duke yet, and already he had become as sober and dull as Pelham. He wasn't even interested in opera singers anymore. That was not normal. Flynn would have suggested Andrew have a doctor examine him for signs of fever.

Finally, Andrew arrived at the stables and found the steward discussing a matter with the stable master. Andrew joined in their discussion of which conveyances needed repair and which it was more worthwhile to simply replace. He had not even touched on the topic of the fall harvest when Angelique gave a loud yawn and said she would have a look about.

Andrew gave the steward an apologetic look and attempted to return to the discussion. The steward was explaining the need for several more workers when they heard a loud clatter. Several grooms came running, and Andrew followed them to the saddle room. Two or three overturned buckets rolled on the ground, the grain that had been inside scattered about, and a stack of horseshoes had fallen from their hooks and lay on the ground. "I'm so sorry!" Angelique said. "I do not know what happened."

Andrew did not need to think very hard to figure it out for himself. Angelique wanted attention. She did not like to be ignored. He'd known enough opera singers to recognize the breed's need for constant petting. Normally, he was happy to oblige. Today he thought it best if he returned her to the house and spoke with the steward later. He gave the grooms orders to clean up the fallen items and offered his arm to Angelique. He walked back briskly, all but dragging her with him and not stopping to lift her over imaginary obstacles.

"What is the matter, Darlington?" she finally protested when they had nearly arrived. "You have all but torn my arm off."

He rounded on her. "I told you I had business. If you were only going to thwart me, why come along?"

Her hands flew to her hips, and she gave him an ugly sneer. "I'm so sorry, your lordship. I was given to believe my presence might be appreciated." She began to walk away, but he caught her arm.

"What does that mean? Did someone imply I wanted your company?"

"Your charming friend cornered me earlier, going on and on about how taken you were with me. Clearly, that is not the case."

"Who?" Andrew stepped back. "Lily? Lily told you to seduce me?"

"She did not put it quite that way. In fact, I rather thought *you* would be seducing *me*."

Andrew could feel his blood begin to boil. "And you thought when I said I had business with the steward, that was a ploy to lure you away from the house."

She shrugged. "I did hope."

"I'm going to kill her."

The woman stepped back. "Excuse me."

"Yes, please," Andrew said and pushed past

her. He stormed into the house and spotted his father exiting the dining room. "Where is she?" Darlington demanded.

"Who? What is it?"

Andrew peered beyond his father at the dining room. She was not there. "I beg your pardon. My apologies for disturbing you, Your Grace," he said and took the stairs two at a time. He found a maid and asked after Lily. The servants always knew everything, and this one pointed him to the duke's library.

Which meant Andrew had to turn back and head downstairs again. His father and the guests were gathered in the drawing room, and he evaded them and went to the library. It was usually locked. He had been inside it only half a dozen times. He pushed the door open and peered inside, spotting her immediately.

She, however, did not spot him. She was sitting in his father's chair, her attention focused intently on the duke's desk. She was studying one of the drawers and held a file and another object—perhaps a hairpin?

"What are you doing?" he demanded.

She jumped, and for an instant he saw fear in her eyes. And then her mask hastily returned. He had to admire how quickly she covered her surprise and fright. It made him wonder what else she was hiding.

"Are you attempting to pick the lock on my father's desk?"

"I beg your pardon!" She rose, hands behind her back so he could no longer see the file and the hairpin. "The duke himself gave me access to this room."

"So you could snoop about in his desk?" Andrew stepped inside and closed the door behind him. It was a heavy wood-paneled door. The entire room was done in dark paneling that reminded him of the Tudor era. The draperies were thick brocade things that blocked out all the light, and Lily or one of the servants had actually lit a lamp in order to see.

"So I might find a book to read." She lifted one off the desk and showed it to him. He crossed the carpet, took the book, and studied it. One of Fanny Burney's.

"You're quite clever. You did not grab the first book you saw—Fordyce's *Sermons* or some such rot. Now, where are they?"

She raised a brow.

"The file and the hairpin. Where are they?"

"I have no idea—"

He grabbed her other hand and pried it open. Nothing. It was empty. He rounded the desk and looked beneath it. Perhaps she had dropped them behind her.

"What are you doing?" she asked calmly.

"Where are they? Where have you hidden them?" He eyed her closely. "Do you have pockets in that gown?" It was a deep green color that matched her eyes. The skirts looked full enough to conceal a small object. He took a step toward her, intent upon finding those pockets, and she stepped back.

"Do not dare lay hands on me. You are obviously mistaken in what you saw or think you saw."

"Really? Then why did you send Angelique after me?"

A shadow flittered across her face.

"A-ha!" He pointed to her. "You weren't fast enough to conceal it that time. Yes, I know you sent

Angelique, and your plan to detain me did not succeed. Is this what you did not wish for me to see?"

"Excuse me," she said and attempted to move
past him.

"What are you really doing here?" he asked. "You
are not here for the house party. I thought it was to
catch my father in the parson's mousetrap, but that
wouldn't explain your little jaunt this morning."

She spun around, her face white with shock.
Finally! He had hit the mark, and quite accurately,
from all appearances.

"You *followed* me! You bastard!" She came at him,
and he expected her nails to rake over his face. He did
not expect a punch in the nose. He stumbled back,
more from surprise than pain, and bumbled into the
desk. When he recovered and sat forward, there was
a dagger at his throat. He glanced down at her hand.

"So you do have pockets," he drawled, careful not
to move his jaw overly much.

"Why did you follow me?" She dug the tip of the
weapon into his flesh, and he felt the sting of the prick.

"What were you doing that you wanted to hide?
And why are you holding a knife at my neck? Am I
supposed to worry you'll slit my throat?"

"Give me one reason not to."

Andrew looked into her eyes and felt a cold chill
skitter down his back. Suddenly that knife point felt
rather cold and deadly, much like her eyes at the
moment. He was beginning to believe she just might
be willing to use the weapon. "What the devil is
going on?" He was careful not to jostle her arm, lest
she dig the knife in deeper. "You're sneaking about,

holding a knife to my throat, trying to pick the lock on my father's desk. I'm beginning to think you are hiding more than your motivations for seducing my father."

She inhaled sharply, and he considered that perhaps it was not wise to have mentioned all of these matters when she still held the knife to his throat. And then, unexpectedly, she withdrew the blade and stepped back. "I carry a knife because there are times even a courtesan must defend herself against unwanted advances. I was in the library to fetch a book, and I was merely taking a ride this morning. There. That should suffice as explanation." The knife disappeared deftly into her skirts. "I believe a picnic is planned for the afternoon," she said, stepping back. "I should find your father before he misses me."

"There is one additional matter," Andrew said. She paused in her exit and looked back. "It's the matter I came to discuss with you, as a matter of fact."

"Can it wait?"

"The explanation should be simple enough. Why did you ask Angelique to seduce me?"

❧

Did the devil of a man know everything? Lily fumed, and then clenched her hands to control her anger. Anger would only prove he was correct. It had been a mistake to pull the knife on him. She should have acted as though her outing were nothing. Instead, she'd raised more questions. Some spy she was turning out to be. She was usually so calm and collected, but

Darlington had a way of angering her until she forgot what she really should have been doing.

But she would not forget now. She was through making mistakes, with allowing Darlington to rattle her.

"I have no idea what you are talking about," she said coolly. "I never asked anyone to seduce you. I am not even certain who *Angelique* is." But of course, that must have been the opera singer's given name.

"Don't you?" He gave her a long look, and she stared right back at him. He was not going to discompose her. She was no green girl.

He broke first. She saw the annoyance on his face before he spoke. "Angelique—Mrs. Howell—was kind enough to inform me that you told her I was quite taken with her."

"It's a natural assumption," she said with a shrug. Damn that Mrs. Howell! Opera singers could never keep secrets. They had to tell the world every trifling thought that entered their minds. "You do have a penchant for opera singers."

"I have friends who are opera singers."

She laughed. "Oh, I think they are more than friends."

"But that does not explain why you sent Angelique after me."

"I hardly *sent* her—"

"You wanted me out of the way." He took a step toward her. Lily put her hand on her knife again but resisted pulling it out. She had to remain composed. "You wanted to make certain you would not have to deal with me while you searched the library."

She laughed, though it sounded a bit too tinny. "Really, Darlington, are you even listening to yourself? Why on earth would I want to search your father's library?"

Now he frowned. Good. He hadn't figured that part out yet. And he wouldn't. He was cleverer than she had first thought, but he would never suppose she was a spy. No, he thought he knew her. To him, she would always be the friend of the woman he loved.

"You are looking for money." He had stopped advancing on her, and that was a good sign. Now, if she could just step out…

"Do gentlemen generally keep their blunt in the library?"

"I know what I saw!" He was exasperated, and that was good. Better him than her. "Damn it! I know there is something you are trying to hide. I know—"

"What is going on in here?" a voice boomed, and Lily jumped. Thank God she and Darlington were separated by several feet. The duke threw open the door and stormed inside. He was rather pathetic when he was in his cups, but when he was sober, he was a formidable man. She could well believe, when he was sober, that he could order the deaths of four men. He was cold and decisive, as powerful men often had to be. But, unlike his son, he had a weakness for women and wine. She would use that to her advantage.

"Your Grace!" Lily rushed to the duke's side. "Forgive me for taking so long to return. I found the book I sought, but the earl detained me. He seemed to think I was here without permission."

Ravenscroft looked at her, his eyes hard and cold. She stepped back slightly, a frisson of fear making its way along her spine. She did not like the expression in his eyes. Slowly, he turned his gaze to his son. "I heard you yelling at Miss Dawson. Is that how you treat my guests?"

"Father..." Darlington seemed to reconsider. "Your Grace, I know it is your custom to lock the library door. When I saw it was open, I chanced to look inside. I saw"—his gaze flicked to hers as though he was loath to refer to her so formally and politely—"Miss Dawson attempting to pick the lock on your desk."

The duke's expression darkened, and his hands clenched and unclenched. She could well imagine he wanted to snap her neck between his thumbs. Dear God, had she misjudged him? Was Fitzhugh right to warn her that the duke could be Artemis? If that was true, Darlington's accusations would lead to her death. She spoke hastily. "And, as I told *you*, my lord, you were mistaken. I was merely glancing through the book. There it is on the desk." She directed Ravenscroft's attention to it. But he was still looking at her, and his eyes were narrowed with suspicion. She held her breath. *No, no, no. Do not suspect. Damn Darlington! Do not suspect...*

"Is there something else I should know?" the duke asked. "I know my son is something of a gallant about Town. Have you and he ever——?"

"No!" she said quickly and with real horror in her tone. She didn't think the relief she felt was audible. He thought Darlington her lover. He did not suspect her of spying. "Lord Darlington and I have known each other for years, but he was always too in love with my friend Juliette to ever think of me." Lily did not look at Darlington. The last thing she wanted was to give him an opening to say something of what had occurred between them recently. She leaned close to the duke, making sure to rub her bosom against his arm. "I think he is upset that we are so taken with each other," she whispered in the duke's ear, making her voice husky and low. "The poor boy is still mourning his mother. Perhaps it is too soon for me to be here with you." She stroked his arm with slow caresses. "Shall I return to London and wait for you there?"

"No." The duke's answer was definite and affirmative. "I want you here." He pointed a finger at Darlington. "You are not yet master of this house. And while I am still alive, I will entertain whomever I wish without interference from you. Is that understood?"

"Yes, Your Grace." Darlington glared at her as he spoke.

"I have tolerated your presence here, Darlington, because this is your home, and your mother wanted all of her children welcome here." At that, Lily could see Darlington's jaw clench. She could tell he wanted to make some remark or other, and she could imagine what it would be. The duke's recent behavior did not exactly honor his late wife. But the earl was no fool. He kept his mouth tightly shut. The duke seemed to wait for his son to speak, and when he did not, he concluded, "But I will not hesitate to ask you to leave if it comes to that."

"I understand perfectly, Your Grace."

"You are dismissed."

Without another look or word, Darlington departed. Lily wanted to go after him. She had not wanted to witness his dressing down by his father. She had not wanted to be the catalyst for such a thing, but he had left her little other choice. And she was at the end of her options with the duke as well. It was time to choose her path and live with its consequences.

"Your Grace," she began. The duke turned and reached for her. She deftly sidestepped him, but this was no public ball or evening at the theater. She had nowhere to go, and he caught her hand and pulled her roughly to him. She crashed against his chest, and he wrapped a hand around the back of her neck, holding her still. She took shallow breaths as she stared into his dark eyes. One move and he could snap her neck. He could kill her.

"I am sorry you had to suffer his presence." Ravenscroft put a finger under her chin and raised it. "I will make certain he does not bother either of us again." He leaned down and kissed her. His other kisses had been drunken or laced with excited passion. This kiss was different. His mouth punished hers, his teeth grinding against her lips painfully, his tongue delving inside her mouth until she almost gagged. He held her neck in the painful vise and forced her to tolerate him. Lily closed her eyes, but it was all she could do not to scream for help and push him away. Not that anyone would come to her aid.

Finally, the duke bent and nuzzled her neck, his breath like the fetid exhalations of the three-headed dog Cerberus who guarded Hades. "I missed you. I find myself thinking of you all the time. Last night I disappointed you. I will not disappoint tonight." He looked into her eyes. "You will not disappoint me." His hand reached for her breast and squeezed painfully.

"That is what I wished to discuss with you, Your Grace." Lily swallowed. The proposal she was about to reiterate would very likely spur the duke to ask her to leave. Her departure now would jeopardize both lives and this mission. At this point, she would rather be asked to leave. It was all she could do not to tremble and show her fear. That was what he wanted. Fear aroused him, or so she surmised.

"Call me Hugh." He kissed her ear and dipped his wet tongue in it.

"I care for you a great deal, Your—Hugh. As I told you before, I am tired of protectors. I am tired of the life of a courtesan." As she spoke, she ran her shaking fingers down his chest. "And yet, I think—no, I *know* you and I would suit very nicely."

"Why do we not adjourn to my chambers and find out?" He released her neck and took her hand. Now she resisted. With an annoyed glance over his shoulder, he released her. "What is the matter?"

"As I said, I made it clear in London, I do not want a protector."

Now was the crucial moment. Would he throw her out? And would that not be a better option than securing his agreement? An engagement to the duke might spare her his attentions in the bedchamber now, but it would ruin her later. She had no intention of actually marrying the man, which meant one of them would have to call it off. No matter who called it off or the reason, she would end up the one damaged. Either she would be associated with a known traitor, or she would be the woman discarded by the powerful Duke of Ravenscroft. Either way, the gallants of the *ton*, those men who sought her attentions and ensured her livelihood, would consider her damaged goods. Speculation as to what the duke had found lacking would run rampant.

She would be done for.

She had no one in Town waiting to save her. Although the unions between the *ton* and the demimonde were generally perceived as mésalliances, they served only to elevate the courtesans involved. A broken engagement would send her to the bottom of the social ladder. Lily knew the Sinclairs would never allow her to return to the streets, but the fear haunted her nonetheless. What would it be like to have such a storybook ending? To know she was loved. To know she would be taken care of? To know she was safe?

Lily could not fathom it. And if she tried, she only began to hate her friends for having the one thing she never would.

Ravenscroft studied her for a long moment in which Lily felt as though her life hung in the balance. Finally, he nodded. "I will need time to consider such a momentous step."

"Of course."

He could not be completely surprised by her request. She'd hinted at it enough. He might have been expecting her to reiterate the demand. And he might have decided once he had her under his roof, he would tell her no and then do what he wanted with her anyway. She pushed the fear aside and ran a finger along his rough cheek. "But do not think *too* long. I'm not a patient woman." She could feel his gaze burn her back as she strode out of the room.

Nine

ANDREW HEADED BACK TO HIS ROOM, INTENT UPON packing his bags and quitting Ravenscroft Castle until the god-awful house party was ended and Lily Dawson returned to London, where she belonged. On the way, he passed the music room, and the sound of the pianoforte drew him in. Emma looked up from the instrument and smiled at him. In the corner he spotted her governess—what was her name again?—sitting in a chair and doing needlework of some sort or other. It seemed to him that women were always doing needlework.

"Pray, do not stop on my account," he told his sister. She nodded and began again. He had no idea what piece she played, but it was lovely, even if her fingers stumbled on occasion. "I have not seen you about lately."

"That is because you banished me," she said, her eyes on the sheet music before her.

"I?"

"You told Miss Peevy to keep me away from the amusements. I have been languishing in the nursery."

Andrew covered a smile. Emma could always make him smile. "Perhaps you should try acting rather than music. You seem to have a flair for the dramatic."

"Really?" She turned a page then glanced back at her governess, who was pretending, quite convincingly, not to be listening. "Do you hear that, Miss Peevy? The theater is not the work of the devil."

"Yes, miss," the governess said noncommittally. Andrew assumed they'd had this particular conversation previously.

"As you see, I am quite well protected," Emma said, fumbling the piece and squinting at her sheet music. "Oh, I see. I forgot about the E-flat," she muttered to herself.

"I am glad to hear it. His Grace's choice of company leaves much to be desired." He leaned on the instrument and watched her fingers.

"Well," she began again, correcting her mistake, "you would know, as I noticed you did not see the need to quarantine yourself from our guests' poisoning effect."

Drama was indeed her talent. "I sense discontent."

"Is it that obvious then?"

"Would a walk about the grounds alleviate your suffering?"

Her fingers paused, and she beamed at him. "It might." She glanced at her governess again. "But will Miss Peevy be capable of protecting me?"

"Doubtful. I will have to accompany you to ensure your safety. I trust you have no objection."

"None." She rose. "I shall fetch my shawl."

Andrew blinked. "You wish to go now? This moment?"

"Of course. I would not risk you changing your mind."

Miss Peevy stood, her face disapproving. "You will have to resume your practicing when you return."

Emma sighed. Clearly she had hoped to escape music for the day. "Yes, Miss Peevy." She pointed at Andrew. "Do not move. I shall return in a moment."

"Fetch your parasol as well!" her governess called, going after her.

A quarter of an hour later, he and Emma were walking the grounds of Ravenscroft. She pointed out all the places she remembered him causing mischief or injuring himself. Clearly she had idolized him when she was growing up. He did not know why he never saw it until now. She asked a tiresome number of questions about London, but he supposed that was natural in a girl her age. She would be coming out soon, and she probably had little else but her first Season to daydream of during tedious history lessons.

He answered her questions and attempted not to give her too much brotherly advice, and for the first time since his mother's death, he felt a sense of confidence. Perhaps he could do his sister some good, and that would mean he was not utterly worthless. He was not completely incapable of acting in a ducal manner.

From as far back as he could remember, the importance of his future role and title had been impressed upon him. And as far back as he could remember, his father had declared him a hopeless failure. Andrew was not a good student or a model son. He was far better at breaking rules than following them, better at making friends than making certain an estate ran efficiently.

And the House of Lords—he could not even stay awake for the interesting courses at Oxford. How was he going to manage when some old codger went on and on about the tax on wigs or some equally tedious topic? He should never have been born heir to the title. Why could Katherine not inherit it? She'd be a formidable duke.

Only the Duchess of Ravenscroft had ever believed in him. Only she had remained steadfast in her faith in him—even when he was gallivanting about Town, drinking himself into a stupor, and chasing every woman who so much as smiled at him.

His father had declared him a disgrace—ironic considering the duke's recent behavior—but his mother had never doubted him. Now he had no one who believed in him. No one to stand with him when the heavy ducal mantle dropped on his shoulders. Everyone thought him witty and charming and amiable. And he played his role well because the alternative was to show his true character. And no one wanted to drink with a man who was nothing more than an insecure lackwit whose only hope was to stumble through his tenure as Duke of Ravenscroft without ruining the family.

But here with Emma, Andrew felt a glimmer of hope for his future and that of his family. They were almost to the house when the steward found them. Andrew could see immediately something was amiss, and he sent Emma inside so the steward might speak to him privately.

"What is it, Helms?"

"There's been a theft from the kitchen, my lord."

Andrew frowned. "Go on."

"The cook discovered cheese, bread, and several jugs of her cooking wine missing."

"The cooking wine is not kept under lock by the butler."

"Correct, my lord."

Andrew motioned for the man to walk, and the two began in the direction of the kitchens.

"I asked Mrs. Fowler if she might not have miscounted or misplaced the items, and she assured me, quite vehemently, my lord, that she had not."

In other words, she'd taken offense.

"She is quite frugal and thorough, my lord. I have no reason to suspect she is mistaken."

"I will speak to her, Helms. It was probably one of our guests—perhaps it was filched for a picnic or a clandestine meeting."

The steward cleared his throat, and Andrew wondered how much he knew about the guests currently in residence. "In any case, keep your eyes open. Let's watch for anything else unusual."

"Yes, your lordship."

Darlington spoke with the cook and then a problem with one of the grooms demanded his attention and then the housekeeper wanted to speak with him about Lord Kwirley. Apparently, the viscount had made unwanted advances toward the parlor maid attempting to clean his room. He dealt with each issue as best he could, all the while wondering when everyone would begin laughing at the hoax. Darlington acting like a duke! How ridiculous.

By the time Andrew had finished addressing the

household matters, it was the dinner hour, and devil take him if he would be forced to sit at a table with his father and the Countess of Charm. Even though it was more trouble for the already overworked staff, he asked for a tray to be brought to his room and ate it there with a book in hand. He had begun it several weeks ago and had not progressed very far—he was not a great reader—but he had persisted because he thought it important to understand something of farming if he would one day inherit an estate that depended so heavily on that occupation.

If only his friends could see him now. He'd be laughed out of White's. The Darling of the *Ton* dining alone in his room, reading a book on farm practices. Good God, but he was as pathetic as Pelham.

A quiet knock sounded on his door, and he said absently, "Come." He glanced at his clock. It was a bit early for his valet.

"Am I interrupting?"

Andrew jumped to his feet and stared at the woman standing in his doorway. She wore a sapphire-blue gown and matching jewels at her throat and ears. The material pooled around her, shimmering in the lamp light. Her hair shimmered as well, and he realized she must have pinned small, sparkly ornaments in it to achieve the effect. Finally, he blinked, and the horror of the situation descended on him. "What the devil are you doing?" He crossed to her, pulled her inside his room, and slammed the door. It occurred to him, belatedly, he would have done better to have pushed her out, but even he did not have that much willpower. "You should not be here. If you are seen—"

"Will I cause a scandal? Oh, dear." She put a hand to her heart, feigning shock. "I fear my reputation would not survive."

"Hang your reputation. I care about Ravenscroft Castle. I don't know why my father insists on trying to run it into the ground." It was supposed to be his legacy. His throat burned, and he glanced toward a silver tray on a small corner table. "Care for a drink?"

"I thought you'd never ask."

Andrew smiled in spite of himself. Lily always managed to amuse him. Perhaps that was why he'd never thought of her romantically. She was approachable, and she made him laugh. She wasn't dubbed the Countess of Charm without reason.

He lifted a decanter in each hand. "Brandy or sherry?"

She gave him a disbelieving look. "Need you ask? Next you will offer me ratafia."

"The brandy then." He warmed the glass then filled it half-full and handed it to her before pouring his own. The caramel liquid slid cleanly and sweetly down his throat.

"This is very good," she said, and he noted she was looking around curiously now. He wondered what she thought of his room. He'd always been something of a hedonist, and he'd indulged in expensive rugs, heavy draperies, and a large bed replete with piles of pillows and plush bedclothes. He had two hanging presses to hold all of his clothing. Andrew was the first to admit he'd been a bit of a dandy. But that was before.

"What do you think?" he asked when she continued her appraisal.

Her gaze fixed on him once again. To be under the

scrutiny of those emerald eyes was rather provoking. He sipped the brandy again.

"It's comfortable, but then I'd expect nothing less. You're not exactly austere in your lifestyle."

It was true, and for whatever reason—the remnants of his earlier confidence—he took offense. "And what do you know of my lifestyle?" he said. "What do you know of what I've been through—what my family has been through—these past months?"

"You're right," she said, surprising him with her easy capitulation. "Your mother's death has changed you. I see that. I judged on appearance alone." She gestured to his room and then stepped closer to him, almost seeming to confide in him. "That is why I came to speak to you. I wanted to apologize for this afternoon."

"I'm the one who should apologize. I accused you unjustly."

She seemed to consider before she spoke again. "Appearances, as we just discussed, can be deceiving, Lord Darlington. There's more to me than you see."

"I'd be interested in seeing more of you then." The words were out before he could stop them, before he even really knew what he was saying.

She gave him a weak smile. "I don't think that's a good idea. But my real apology was about your father. I did not mean for the two of you to quarrel."

He laughed. "Quarrel? You mean, you did not want to witness my dressing down."

She sipped her brandy and gave him a considering look. "Why is it so difficult for you to trust me and so easy for you to think the worst of me?"

"I'd like to trust you, Lily." He set his empty

brandy glass on the table. "But I find it difficult when I catch you attempting to steal from my father."

She shook her head. "I thought you knew me better than that."

"Exactly." He pointed at her.

"Thank you for the drink." She handed him the brandy glass, but when he took it, she did not release it. "One last caveat. Everything is not always as it seems."

"If I cannot believe my eyes," he murmured, his fingers closing over her warm hand, "what can I believe?"

"What you feel," she whispered. "What you know"—she lifted a hand and put it on his chest—"in your heart to be true."

They stood frozen for three beats of his heart. He counted them, the flesh of her hand infusing warmth into him. And then, as one, they came together. He did believe in what he felt, and what he felt was desire. Arousal. Need. It was pure and visceral and only waiting for the right opportunity to be let loose. No one would interrupt them now. Nothing would save her from him now.

Or perhaps it was he who needed to be saved?

⁊ↄ

She was in his arms, and no matter how many times her mind screamed that this was a mistake, she could not seem to step away. His mouth covered hers hungrily, and she devoured him just as eagerly. When she touched him, everything inside her came alive. Every sensation was heightened—she felt the fine weave of his linen shirt, the hard muscles of his chest, the stubble on his jaw as his mouth met hers. The lamps flickered weakly; his face had been in shadow from the moment she entered his room. She touched it now with one hand, learning its planes and ridges, its slopes and edges. Her fingers raked through his thick, dark hair. It was soft and naturally curly.

She moved to kiss his neck and nip at his ear, catching his scent—a mixture of brandy and leather. She flicked out her tongue, teasing him just below the ear, and he inhaled sharply. Lily couldn't have said why she did such a thing. She had wanted to taste him, to lick his skin and see if it tasted as delicious as he looked.

He pulled back, his dark eyes even darker from arousal. "What the devil have you done to me?"

"Should we stop?" she asked, surprised her own voice should sound so breathless.

"Yes."

They stood for a moment, looking at each other, and then he kissed her again. This time he was the one exploring. His hands roved her back until they cupped her bottom, and slid to shape her hips then to measure her waist. Her breasts felt heavy and sensitive as his fingers edged closer. She'd spent years attempting to stop men from groping her. Now, she wanted his touch more than she could have ever imagined.

One warm palm settled over her breast. His hand was strong and pleasantly weighted. He held her then caressed her, causing her nipple to peak and harden almost painfully. "Yes," he murmured, leaving her mouth to torment her neck and shoulder. "Now you know how painful that hard, unfulfilled arousal can be."

She supposed she should make some witty comment

in return, but she could not think of one. She could think of nothing but his hand moving in slow circles around her nipple, the sensation making her body tingle all over and making her lower belly begin to throb and ache. She hadn't expected this reaction. Of course, she hadn't expected this to happen. She was not in the habit of bedding men, despite her role as a courtesan. But even if she was the most experienced Cyprian in London, she thought Darlington's touch would have undone her. There was something about him that pulled at her. It always had, and she'd always known, even in the midst of her fantasies, that if he ever were to bed her, he'd realize she was no courtesan.

"I have to taste you, Lily," he was saying now as he pushed her backward in a slow sort of dance. "I have to see you."

"We should stop," she whispered as her legs bumped against the bed.

"Yes," he said. "You should leave. Walk away."

Instead she allowed him to lift her onto the bed and to kneel above her. His dark curls spilled over his forehead and cheeks, and she lifted her hands to push them back. He was so handsome with that boyish face and those dark, liquid eyes. And the way he was looking at her made her insides turn to porridge. She'd dreamed he would one day look at her like this. His hand on her back loosened the fastenings of her new gown, and when he brought his fingers around, she could feel them on the skin beneath her gaping bodice.

"You're not walking away."

"I can't. I want you too much."

"Lily." He stared at her, his expression one of surprise and desire. She felt him, hard and heavy at the juncture of her thighs.

"You will have to act the gentleman and end this."

"Oh, Lily." He shook his head. "Didn't you know? I'm no gentleman." He bent his head and kissed the swell of one breast, his warm tongue laving over her skin until it pebbled with pleasure. His nimble fingers made swift work of her bodice, and then he had to struggle with her stays. "Why..." He grimaced. "Do women..." He bit his lip in concentration. "Wear so many..." With a last flick, she felt the stays give, and he pushed them down. For a long moment, he just looked at her.

"So awful I've left you speechless?" she finally joked. She was beginning to feel nervous, and she always turned to flippancy when she felt nervous.

His gaze flicked to her eyes and remained there. "I am speechless, but I would not describe you as awful. Quite the opposite, I assure you." His voice was low and husky now. "May I touch you?"

"It would be cruel of me to allow things to go this far and then deny you that much."

He gave her a small smile. "It would. I have dreamed of touching you like this."

"You needn't flatter me. I'm already half-undressed and lying beneath you." She took his face in her hands. "Just kiss me. It will be enough." She interrupted whatever he was about to say by pressing her lips to his. She felt his hand on her breast again, and this time the contact was skin on skin. His skin was deliciously warm and not at all as soft as she would have expected of an earl. She felt calluses on his fingers and liked the rough feel of them on her tender nipples.

And then he pulled away, and it was his hot, moist mouth on her. His tongue teased and his mouth sucked until she was panting with need. "You are so beautiful," he said, and she opened her eyes and saw he was looking down at her with wonder.

"Quiet," she said, putting a finger to his lips. "Just kiss me."

"Ah, but where?" His grin was devilish now, and when she laughed he waggled his eyebrows suggestively. "I was quite serious," he said when she didn't respond after a moment. "Where would you like me to touch you?"

Was she supposed to tell him? Wasn't he supposed to do what he liked and wonder later if she'd enjoyed any of it? Besides, a man with the experience and reputation of the Earl of Darlington should know what to do. Of course, he probably thought she had as much, if not more, experience than he. After all, she was the last of The Three Diamonds. The three of them were known for their seduction skills. Not that any of the men who lauded them knew of these skills from personal experience. But everyone knew someone or other who had heard from someone else who had been one of their lovers.

Lily realized she was going to have to play the part of the courtesan now too, if she did not want to make Darlington suspicious. And suddenly, she felt quite cold. This was the reason, even when she found a man she was attracted to, she did not take him to her bed. She did not want to play a part during such an intimate moment.

That and the fact that she'd always been in love with Darlington.

"Don't tell me you're going to play shy."

"No," she said slowly, thinking carefully before she spoke. Her mind was fuzzy with arousal and desire. "But I do not want to play the courtesan with you, Darlington. I had hoped we were more than that."

"Yes," he said, his look serious. "Then you'd better call me Andrew." He bent to kiss her breast again, and she felt the heat simmer inside her. "I'd like to hear my name when you scream from pleasure."

"Ha!" She laughed at his arrogance, but then one hand slid under her skirts, and she felt his deft touch on her silk-clad calf.

"Not laughing now, are you?" he asked, stroking up and up until he reached her garter. "I wonder…" His fingers continued their slow journey, higher and higher.

"You wonder?" she said breathlessly. Her body clenched in anticipation of his touch where she most craved it.

"If you are one of those forward women."

"I think that fact has been well established," she panted as his fingers made circles on her inner thigh. "And verified, as I am in your room now, doing this."

"Oh, that doesn't make you forward."

She laughed again. "Really? Pray tell? What constitutes a forward woman?"

"One who wears drawers under her gowns." His hand slid higher, cupping her bare sex. She moaned in response, and her whole body felt a jolt of painful yearning when his hand slid away again. "No. You're not forward at all. I hardly even think you deserve to be called a Cyprian."

She took a shaky breath before she replied. "You are ridiculous. You do know that?"

"I know your skin is flushed." He stroked one breast, cupping it. "I know your breathing is rapid." He placed his hand over her chest, which was rising and falling as she tried to catch her breath. "I know you are wet for me." His hand slid under her gown again, and this time he did not merely cup her. He slid one finger inside her then pulled it out slowly, stroking her as he did so. Lily gripped the bedclothes. She could feel the pressure building. She needed him to touch her again and to continue touching her. She'd felt this sensation before, this need, but the end had not been at all satisfactory. She was not unaware that her body craved a release. She had heard other courtesans discussing it. But she had thought perhaps she was not capable of such a feeling. Now, as he slid two fingers inside her, she groaned and began to hope.

"I've always been curious," Andrew said, as though what they were doing at the moment was a common occurrence.

"Have you?" she said between moans. She was writhing against his hand. She tried not to, but her body had its own priorities, and decorum was not one of them.

"Is that your true hair color?" One finger pulled out and circled a particularly sensitive nub, and Lily gasped and moaned.

"Yes!"

He frowned. "Yes that is your true hair color, or yes you like this?"

"I don't know." Her hips were pushing off the bed, rubbing her body against his hand. "Yes to both. I…" And then, quite suddenly, her world exploded with color. She gripped the bedclothes tighter and pulled her whole body inward as pleasure imploded within her. It was over far too soon, but it left her breathless and shaken.

Reluctantly, she opened her eyes and looked into his face. He was not smiling now. His eyes were dark with intensity. "I must see that again."

She blinked at him, puzzled and too overcome to speak. She tried to slow her breathing, to calm her racing heart so she could say… what? Something. Was *thank you* appropriate?

"Do you mind if I look?"

"What?" She pushed up on her elbows, and his eyes widened. "I like that position. Don't move." He gathered her sapphire skirts in his hands and tossed them to her waist.

"What are you doing?" she asked as he moved between her legs.

"I want to see if you are truly a redhead."

She shook her head as he lifted her chemise and tossed that up too. "You are."

"I told you." She tried to push her skirts down, but he stayed her hand.

"Not so quickly. I told you, I want to see you climax again."

Lily shook her head. "I can't. I mean, what you did… was… sufficient." How did courtesans talk about these things? She sounded like she was sixteen, which would have been the last time she'd been with a man.

"Sufficient?" His brow darted up. "Is that supposed to be praise?"

It was very strange to be arguing with him when she was in this position. "Andrew..."

"That's right. You will be screaming that in a moment." He lowered his head, and she felt his hands caress her thighs again.

"This isn't necessary," she began, but she had to admit it did feel rather nice. And then one finger brushed over that sensitive place again, and she yelped. She was still tender. Too tender. "No, I—"

He lowered his mouth.

"What are you doing?" she all but screamed. Not that she made any effort to stop him. She might be shocked, but she was not a fool.

He grinned up at her, looking like the debauched rake he was, positioned neatly between her thighs. "I think you know." He flicked his tongue out, touching her, and she jumped. "Hold still." His eyes still on her, he did it again. She jumped again.

"That won't do." He placed his hands on her thighs and spread her legs, opening her to him. Lily had never felt so exposed in her life—or so aroused. "You are so beautiful," he said, looking into her eyes.

Before she could answer—not that she knew what she would say—he dipped his head again and swirled his tongue around her. She inhaled sharply and clutched the bedclothes. She had heard other courtesans describe orgasm, and she had expected it to feel wonderful.

But this… this was beyond wonderful. What he was doing to her now was amazing. Her entire body thrummed with pleasure, and the intensity grew as his mouth continued its gentle torture. "Yes," she moaned, unable to stop herself. "Yes!" Her hips rose off the bed, and her hands clenched tightly as the pleasure crescendoed. "Andrew!"

As though he'd been waiting for her to say his name, he laved her one last time, and she came apart.

Lily opened her eyes groggily some time later and stared up at the canopy above the bed. It depicted a hunting scene between a lion and a deer. She could not help but feel she was the deer, and Darlington was the lion. She turned her head and found him lying beside her, propped on one elbow. He was smiling at her, looking quite smug. She supposed she would have to allow him his moment. He had earned it. She closed her eyes again, and he said, "I hope you aren't falling asleep."

Ah, here was where she had to pay for her pleasure. He would definitely expect her to reciprocate. She opened her eyes. "Not at all." She put an arm about him and pulled him close for a kiss.

"More?" he said, tone incredulous. "You are insatiable, but unfortunately there is not time."

Lily blinked when he pushed back from her. He was accusing her of being insatiable? She was only trying to give him what he wanted. But then why had he pushed her away? Perhaps he didn't want her.

"My valet will be here shortly. I don't want him to find you here."

"Oh." She sat and pushed her hair out of her eyes.

"I'll dress." She tugged her gown up, and he assisted her. She was not surprised he knew how to dress a woman. He was almost as proficient as her maid.

"I could send him away," Darlington said, trailing a finger along her shoulder before pulling her sleeve up. "But then he'd be intrigued and insist on finding out why. The man is more curious than a cat."

"I understand." And she did. She did not want to be found here. She didn't even know how this had happened. She'd come here to apologize and ended up in Darlington's bed. And did that really surprise her? Did she really not think something like this would happen if they were alone together? Was that not why she had worn the new blue gown? In the back of her mind, she had hoped this would happen. And she had let it, because in the morning, Darlington would know, and then everything would change.

Ten

"MY LORD," HIS FATHER SAID AFTER ANDREW HAD broken his fast. "I'd like a moment of your time. Your sister is already waiting."

Andrew raised his brows, but he nodded when his father indicated the library. He passed one or two of his father's guests entering the dining room, but most were not yet out of bed. Emma was indeed seated inside, her hands clasped in her lap. Her tense posture made her look nervous, but she loosed her twined fingers when Andrew entered. He grinned at her, trying to put her at ease. No doubt this was something about the house party. The duke intended a ball or some other nonsense.

"Be seated," Ravenscroft said. "I will be only a moment." He stepped outside, and Andrew took a seat in the chair beside Emma. There was a small sitting area across from the desk with a couch and two chairs. Emma had claimed one, and he took the other. He closed his eyes, still weary from the all but sleepless night before. After Lily had left, he had not been able to stop thinking about her. He wasn't even certain how he'd had the willpower to let her go. When she was near, he could think of little besides touching her, holding her, kissing her. And then when he did have her in his arms, he could not seem to take his fill. He wanted more, drawn to her like a gambler to the faro tables.

But he'd resisted her.

Yes, he'd been concerned about his valet. Phibbs was nosy, but Andrew could trust him. He would not have revealed anything to the other servants or to the duke. It had been something he'd seen in Lily's eyes. She'd seemed resigned, as though she thought she was obligated to pleasure him.

That wasn't what he wanted. He didn't want to be another man who expected something from her. If she gave herself to him, he wanted it to be willingly.

But self-deprivation had not led to a peaceful night. He couldn't seem to stop thinking about all the times he and Lily had been together at a ball or a dinner party or the theater. He'd done nothing but look at Juliette, when the woman he should have been paying attention to had been right beside him. Had he really been so blind? Had he really never noticed how beautiful Lily was—how her eyes glittered emerald when she laughed and turned to mossy green when she was aroused, how delicate her pale skin was and how it flushed slightly when she was uncertain?

There was so much he'd missed. The small hollow at the base of her throat. The hints of gold in her hair. The way her eyelashes swept across her cheeks when she closed her eyes, and the pale pink of her lips.

Should he remedy his inattentiveness now? He wanted her too much to let her go. Granted, wooing her might take time. He did not think she had quite forgiven him for having her kidnapped. He would have to make that up to her. What had he been thinking? He'd no excuse other than he'd still been in the throes of grief over his mother's death and his father's abhorrent behavior immediately following it. Lily had every right to be angry with him. She'd been doing only as she always did—courting a wealthy, powerful man. And yet she'd admitted to having been in love with him.

How had he never seen it? How had he resisted kissing her for so long?

The door opened, and his father entered again. Andrew stood, taking a step back when his father moved aside to admit someone else.

Lily.

"What is she doing here?" he said, his voice more gruff than he'd intended.

She didn't answer, but her eyes met his, and he couldn't quite read the expression in them. Regret? Apology? She looked beautiful in a pale green morning dress with a white gauzy overlay. Dark green ribbons tied in bows dangled at her elbows, just above the exposed skin of her forearms, and another ribbon graced the modest neckline. But Andrew could well imagine the swells of her breasts beneath that ribbon. She'd had her hair styled simply, pulled back by another dark green ribbon, the auburn curls trailing smoothly down her back.

"Darlington, I must insist on civility toward Miss Dawson," the duke said. Andrew shut his mouth, but he clenched his fists. He did not like where this was headed.

"You know my son," the duke said, all but dismissing him. "But have you met my daughter? Emma, this is Miss Dawson. Miss Dawson, my daughter." Lily curtsied, and Andrew expected her to admit she'd met Emma before, but she remained silent.

Andrew's unease grew.

"You may be seated," the duke said. Emma and Andrew resumed their seats, and the duke sat beside Lily on the couch. Did he know? Andrew wondered. Had someone seen her entering or leaving his room? If that was the case, why was Emma here? And why were his father and Lily sitting together as though a united front? Andrew glanced at Emma, but she was already looking at him. She seemed to know what this was about.

"It's a pleasure to meet you again, Miss Dawson," Emma said. She looked at their father. "We met only informally when Miss Dawson first arrived."

"I see." The duke, never one to sit for long, rose and moved to stand before the fireplace.

"Thank you, Lady Emma. We haven't seen much of you these past few days."

"And you won't, either," Andrew muttered.

"Lady Emma is busy with her studies," the duke said. He cleared his throat. "We could exchange pleasantries all morning, but as to the reason I called all of us together. Emma. Andrew." He nodded at each in turn. "I want you to meet your new mother."

The room blurred, and Andrew felt as though he was stuck on a runaway carousel. From far away he heard Emma say, "Congratulations. When is the happy day?"

"We have not set a date yet," the duke answered. His father sounded as if he was in a tunnel. Andrew shook his head to clear it, but even as it cleared, he shook it again. He did not—would not—believe what he was hearing.

"Darlington?" his father said, voice stern and full of warning. But Andrew stared at Lily. She didn't look back. She was looking at the duke, and she was smiling as any prospective bride would.

"I do not believe this," Andrew said. Lily still didn't glance at him. She seemed quite absorbed by the rug. "You cannot possibly think to marry her."

"That is exactly what I have in mind," the duke said. "I see no reason why I should not."

"She's a bloody courtesan! She is paid to pleasure men!" Andrew yelled then turned hastily to his sister. "My apologies."

"Don't mind me." Emma's eyes were wide.

"I mind." The duke glared at his son. "Emma, leave." Emma made no move to rise.

"How can you do this to my mother?" Andrew demanded.

"How can I do this to your mother? As though she was a saint who deserves my sacrifice! As though she never—" He broke off. "You did not know her as well as I, Darlington, and so I will forgive you. But she is dead, and I deserve happiness. Lily makes me happy." The duke put his hand on Lily's shoulder, and Andrew flinched. Seeing his father touch her made him furious. He could not allow himself to think of the duke touching her anywhere else—touching her for the rest of the old man's life. For much of the rest of Andrew's life. His father was correct on one account. The duke was not doing anything to his late wife. The duke was taking Lily away from Andrew.

At some point, Lily had become his. Perhaps he'd always considered her his.

Andrew looked at Lily, who was carefully avoiding his gaze. "Lily, do you have nothing to say?" he asked.

She looked up at him, her expression calm. How could she be so calm? How could she have come to him last night when she knew she belonged to another? To his own father!

"I think His Grace said all there is to say." Her gaze remained on him. She did not look worried in the least. In fact, her eyes seemed to challenge him to reveal their secret. What would she do then? Did she want him to say something? Did she want a way out?

He was not going to give it to her. If this was what she wanted, then she could rot in the pit of her own making. He was going to pack his things, return to London, and wait for his father's death. That would be the moment he'd have his revenge. He would return to Ravenscroft Castle when it was his and summarily evict her.

Andrew rose, aware he was being rude. "Then I wish you every happiness. Good-bye." He strode for the door, threw it open, and walked into the saloon, heading for the staircase to his room.

"My lord!" He recognized Lily's voice and continued walking. She caught his elbow at the staircase, and he gritted his teeth and turned his head to glare at her hand.

"Remove your hand from my coat." His tone

perfectly expressed his feelings at the moment—her hand was offal, and he did not want it to touch him.

"I wanted to tell you," she said, her expression pleading. It was such a different expression from the one she'd worn in the library, he was momentarily taken aback. "I tried."

"When?" he said between clenched teeth. "When I was firmly ensconced between your legs?"

She had the gall to blush. A courtesan who blushed! Was this another of her deceits?

"I want us to be friends."

"We cannot be *friends*," he said, his tone mocking. "Not when you presume to take my mother's place. Bloody hell! I feel like Oedipus."

"No one will consider me your mother. I ask you, am I really so unworthy to become the Duchess of Ravenscroft? I am good enough for your bed but not for your dining room, is that it?"

That wasn't how he felt at all. But at the moment, he didn't know what he felt, only that he did not want her to marry his father. He wanted her for himself. Did he want to marry her? Hell if he knew. He rarely thought of marriage. He would marry one day. It was expected. But marry a courtesan? Despite the Duke of Pelham's recent example, it was not done. His father had an heir, and he was an old man. He could do what he liked. Andrew had always done what he liked as well. But now it seemed the roles between father and son had reversed, and Andrew must be the responsible, sensible one.

"Enjoy your residence in every room, Miss Dawson. I'm returning to London." He started up the stairs again.

"My lord!" This time the voice was not Lily's. He turned to find the steward hurrying through the entrance hall.

"Whatever it is, Helms, you shall have to take it up with my father. I am for London."

"I see," the steward said, looking dubiously toward the library. "It relates to the matter we discussed the other day, my lord."

Andrew frowned. "The theft from the kitchens?"

Lily moved aside as he descended the stairs.

"Yes, my lord. A groom has been injured. He was exercising one of the hunters and was assaulted. The horse has been stolen."

"What?" Darlington's mind was reeling. "There must be some mistake." This sort of thing was blatant indeed. A horse was not a jug of wine or a crust of bread. A hunter of the sort his father kept in his stables was worth a small fortune.

"There is no mistake, my lord, as much as it pains me to say so. When he was discovered, the groom was brought back to the stables and laid on a pallet. He is awake now, if you'd like to interview him."

"Have you interviewed him?" Lily asked.

Andrew frowned. "This really does not concern you, Miss Dawson."

"All the same, I'd like to accompany you, Lord Darlington."

"No." He turned his back on her and motioned to the steward to lead the way to the stables. A moment later, Lily was at his side. "Miss Dawson, you are not welcome."

"I gathered as much, my lord, but I think I might

be of assistance. I asked if the groom had been interviewed because an earlier interview may have wearied him, in which case it might be better to wait to speak with the man."

"That is a good point, madam," the steward said. "I spoke with the groom briefly and gained the information I have from the gentleman who found him, a neighbor on a nearby farm."

"Good. Then you can judge the groom's earlier statements against those he makes now. You will want an accurate account, Lord Darlington."

"I will, and I still maintain this incident has nothing to do with you." If the steward had not been present, he would have said something to the effect that she was not the duchess yet. But there was no need to start the servants gossiping before his father announced the engagement. Perhaps the duke would yet come to his senses.

"I promise not to interfere," Lily said. "I will be as quiet as a mouse."

Andrew scowled. The woman was persistent. How he longed to tell her, in no uncertain terms, to go back to her diversions. But Andrew had been raised as a gentleman, and everything in him rebelled against such behavior in front of the servants. Because it was not only the steward listening now. He saw one of the parlor maids dusting nearby, and a footman was standing at the ready to move a couch back to its proper place for her.

Andrew gave a nod and started for the stables again. He walked quickly. Usually, if he was accompanied by a woman, he walked at a slower pace to accommodate her shorter legs, heavy skirts, and delicate slippers. Not today. If she could not keep up, she could return to the house. But she did keep up and without protest. She was at his elbow, moving just as quickly as he and with surprising grace. When they reached the stables, she was not winded at all, though her face was pleasantly flushed from the warm air and sunny sky.

Andrew looked away, well aware he no longer had the right to look at her with the desire that always seemed to bubble under the surface when she was near.

"Mr. Helms," she said as they neared the building. "Did I hear there was a theft in the kitchens?"

The steward looked at Darlington. Andrew sighed and waved a hand in resignation. She was obviously determined to interfere.

"Yes, madam. There was a theft a day or so ago."

The trio paused in the doorway. "And what was taken?" she asked.

"The cook reported cheese, bread, and several jugs of her cooking wine missing."

She nodded, and Darlington interjected, "Might we go inside now, Miss Dawson?"

"One more question, my lord, if you will permit me." She turned back to the steward. "Would you say the amount of food taken was enough to feed one man or more than one?"

"I..." The steward seemed surprised by the question. Andrew was surprised as well. It was an astute question, and one he wished he had thought to ask. It might be helpful to know whether they were dealing with a lone culprit or a group of men, especially if the steward thought the two incidents connected.

"I will have to ask the cook to be certain, but my impression was that it was enough food to feed a man for a day or so."

"And now that man is also in possession of a horse." Lily looked thoughtful.

"If it is the same person, yes." The steward gestured to the stables. "Shall we go inside?"

"By all means," Andrew said. "Give us one moment alone, please." He waited until the steward disappeared from sight and turned toward Lily. "What do you know about this?"

"Nothing yet," she said. "But it interests me."

"Obviously. Are you some sort of Bow Street Runner?" He was joking, but she looked as though she was actually considering the question.

"Something to that effect. Your groom is waiting."

She was impatient to see the man, which Andrew found strange. Why would she take such an interest in a groom? "After you, Miss Dawson." He followed her inside and found Mr. Helms waiting outside the grooms' quarters.

"We have him in here, my lord."

Andrew entered and saw a young man lying on a pallet. Another groom sat beside him, but he excused himself with a deferential nod when Andrew entered. He couldn't quite keep from gaping at Lily as he passed her, though. Unlike most beautiful women, she didn't seem to notice the attention.

The injured groom tried to rise, but the steward told him to remain still. Andrew didn't recognize the lad, who was really little more than a boy, and he understood this might have been the first time the groom had been in the presence of one of the family. "Be at ease, lad," Andrew said.

"M'lord," the boy rasped, grasping his side. "I apologize for losing Annabel. I'll leave soon as I'm able."

"Leave?" Andrew looked at his steward.

Mr. Helms took over. "Lord Darlington is not here to dismiss you, Abraham. He only wants to know what happened."

"Has a doctor been to see this man?" Lily asked. Abraham turned his head, and his eyes widened considerably.

"I will summon the doctor at the earl's request, madam," Helms said.

Andrew nodded. "Do so, Helms."

The steward nodded and hurried to carry out his orders, and Lily moved in, sitting on a low chair beside the groom's pallet. "Is Annabel the hunter?"

"Yes, m'lady."

She smiled. "I'm not a lady. You can call me Lily."

The groom stared, slack-jawed. "Oh, no, miss. I couldn't do that!"

"You're very sweet, Abraham. Tell me about the man who took Annabel. Was it an ambush, or were you able to see him?"

"I think I should ask the questions," Andrew interjected. This was his servant and his house, after all. It seemed he should do something other than stand about and watch her take over.

"By all means," Lily said. "I have overstepped."

That was better. "Abraham," Andrew began, but he could not think of any questions. "Ah… were you able to see the man who stole Annabel?"

If Lily thought it amusing that he repeated her question, she hid it well.

"I did, m'lord. I were exercising her in the north fields—"

"Why not in the paddock?" Lily asked.

"The duke likes for the hunters to be ridden three times a week," Andrew answered. "He thinks it keeps their hunting instincts sharp."

"Yes, m'lord. We was taking a leisurely ride, and I spotted the man lying near a tree. Looked near dead to me. But when I got down to see if he was still breathing, like, he threw me over, kicked me"—he indicated his ribs—"and mounted Annabel. She protested, but he swore at her and kicked her hard, my lord. She were a good horse. She didn't want to go with that blackguard."

"What did he look like?" Lily asked. Andrew frowned, but she seemed to have forgotten about him. Again.

"He were dressed as black as the night, miss. He had longish black hair and black eyes. Reminded me of the Grim Reaper, he did."

"Had you ever seen him before?" Andrew asked.

"No, m'lord. Never."

"One more question, Abraham," Lily said. "I know everything happened quickly, but did you happen to notice if the man had a white streak in his hair?"

The groom's eyes widened. "You know him, miss? He had a patch o'hair was white as snow."

"Thank you, Abraham. I hope you recover quickly." She looked at Andrew. "I'll wait outside."

Andrew stared at her. Where the hell had that

question come from? What did she know that she wasn't telling anyone? He made some remark to Abraham and went after her. She hadn't waited—not that he expected she would—and he caught up with her next to the paddock. She heard him coming and paused beside one of the whitewashed railings.

"Where the——?"

She held up a hand. "I already know what you're going to ask, and I cannot answer your question."

Andrew glared at her. She had bloody well better answer his questions. "Are you involved in this?" he demanded.

"Not in the way you think. I can tell you this. The man your groom described is almost certainly Lucifer."

"Who?"

"A criminal of the worst sort. He was the owner of a gambling hell called Lucifer's Lair. He is a thief and a murderer."

"And he is here? You believe this man is the one who has stolen from us? Why? I fail to see how this Lucifer is connected to Ravenscroft Castle or to my family."

Lily looked down, seeming to consider. Finally, she looked up again, and her eyes were hard emeralds. "If your father has what Lucifer wants, Lucifer will kill him to possess it again."

Eleven

OF COURSE, SHE WASN'T CERTAIN RAVENSCROFT HAD what Lucifer wanted or exactly what it was Lucifer sought. She assumed it was the names of the Diamonds in the Rough—five elite spies responsible for supplying the information that led to Bonaparte's ousting. She wanted that list too—as proof of Ravenscroft's complicity. But Lucifer must have known the spies' identities. There had to be more he wanted. There had to be something else Ravenscroft possessed. Something Lucifer wanted, and she already knew he was willing to steal and kill for what he desired.

She certainly cared nothing about protecting the duke from Lucifer. Ravenscroft had made his own bed. The very real certainty that Lucifer was prowling about told her Lucifer, at least, believed Ravenscroft had information he wanted. But that wasn't enough to arrest the duke. The man was a peer of the realm—a wealthy, powerful peer. She needed proof he was a traitor, proof he possessed the rubies promised as payment to the assassins hired to kill the King's men.

And if she discovered Ravenscroft was the infamous

Artemis in the process, all the better. Unless, of course, he killed her first. She was walking a thin tightrope on this mission, juggling too many balls—Ravenscroft, Darlington, Lucifer. Something or someone was going to fall.

Darlington made some motion and caught her attention. He looked striking in his morning coat and perfectly tied cravat. He wore trousers, though, and they were snug but not nearly as tight as usual. When her gaze rose to his face, she forgot her worries for the moment and smiled at his expression. He stared at her in that perplexed way she adored. He so often seemed perplexed by those around him. He'd had the same look, though it had been mixed with anger, when Ravenscroft had announced their engagement. She sighed at the thought of that ordeal. How could Darlington believe she would marry Ravenscroft after what they'd shared together? She supposed he thought she did such things all the time. She was a courtesan, after all. And it was for the best he believed it. He was on the verge of returning to London. That would remove one of her juggling balls. And Darlington would be safe in Town. Much safer than he was here. Perhaps she could persuade him to take his sister as well.

"It probably is best that you return to Town. I'm sorry it's under unpleasant circumstances, but you will be much safer. I'd really prefer you took your sister with you, if your father will allow it."

"*I* will be safer?" Darlington asked incredulously. "What about you?"

She hoped he would not employ any misplaced

chivalry. He'd not shown much propensity toward it before now. "I can take care of myself, I assure you."

"Then you really expect me to believe that my father, the third Duke of Ravenscroft, is in league with a man named Lucifer, who is a thief or worse?" The sun was behind him, and the wind blew gently, ruffling the gold-limned curls in his dark hair. She wanted to reach out and stroke that hair, run her hands through its softness. "And not only am I to believe that rubbish, I am to then run away, leaving an old man and two women here with such a blackguard?"

"I said—"

"Yes." He grabbed the arm she'd been gesturing with and held her wrist. "You say you can take care of yourself. I can well believe it, but what I wonder is how you came upon any of this information, and what it has to do with you."

"I am not at liberty to divulge that information."

"Not at liberty? Why? Does it violate some sort of Cyprian code?" His hand on her wrist clenched. "Is the Crown using Impures as spies now?" He laughed, and then his eyes grew serious. "Good God. Does Fitzhugh have something to do with this? I will kill the man if he's involved you in one of his so-called missions."

Her instinct was to defend Fitzhugh. The man was a decorated war hero. But she refrained, knowing it would only lend credence to Darlington's suppositions. "I will not discuss it, my lord." She pulled her arm out of his grasp. "Now, I suggest you and your sister remove yourselves before Lucifer grows bolder and enacts whatever plan he has fermenting in his wicked mind." She had learned that sometimes disengagement was the only way to avoid revealing too much. She did not want to lie to Darlington. She had done quite enough of that. And she could not tell him the truth, not without putting him in danger. She wanted to tell him the truth. She wanted to share her fears with him, but that was her own selfishness—selfishness and the misplaced need to find someone she could trust and confide in. Darlington was not that person. And so she would tell him nothing. Instead, she started back toward the house. Her thoughts were jumbled with all she'd learned, and she bypassed the drawing room, which sounded as though it was occupied by numerous guests now, and started for her room.

The maid was changing the bedclothes, but she dismissed the girl and sat down at the small, feminine escritoire to compose a letter to Fitzhugh. She began it listing all she had seen so far and her current circumstances. She was describing her false engagement and Darlington's suspicion when her maid, Anna, knocked on the door. "I'm sorry to bother you, madam, but this letter came for you. It's from the Countess of Sinclair."

"Thank you. You did right to bring it immediately."

The countess had not had time to receive her letter, so Lily assumed this missive must have been written when Lily left Town, or perhaps even before. She set aside her report and broke the seal on the countess's letter. It was brief and to the point, as was all of the countess's correspondence. It stated Lily should be careful not to compromise her identity in any way. Lily knew the countess was warning her against going to see her son. Included was a brief report from an investigator the countess had hired a year or so ago. Lily read it incredulously. The countess had sent a man to travel to Nottinghamshire to ascertain that Lily's son was being treated well by his adopted family. The investigator reported the boy had no idea he was even adopted and was treated as well, if not better, than any natural child would have been.

Lily felt tears well in her eyes for her son's good fortune. No one could know how many hours she had spent worried and anguished over her baby, wondering if she had made the right decision, if he was well, happy, loved. Why had the countess never shared this information with her? Lily almost laughed, because she knew why. The countess did not want Lily blubbering all over her with gratitude. Lily's own mother might have disowned her, but the countess was a more than adequate substitute.

Another knock sounded on the door, and with a sigh, Lily shoved the letters inside the desk drawer. Anna entered and informed her everyone was dressing for a light afternoon repast. Lily closed her eyes and consented to the tedious dressing ritual. Would madam prefer the gold or the brown gown?

The meal was, of course, a ridiculous waste of time. She had managed to avoid Kwirley the past few days, but she could not escape him this afternoon. He was sullen and almost abusive. That would all stop when Ravenscroft announced their engagement. She had persuaded him to wait until they both returned to London, so they might make the announcement at a ball Ravenscroft held in Lily's honor, but she could not trust that he would wait. It was in her best interest to ensure news of the engagement was never made public, but she was also well aware she might have to sacrifice her own interests.

Her tension about what Ravenscroft would say or do, coupled with Kwirley's insistence that every third sentence contained cutting remarks aimed at her, made the meal all but unbearable. And if worries about Ravenscroft and Kwirley were not enough to make her stomach hurt, Darlington did not join them. He had made his distaste for the guests clear, but now she wondered if he had learned some new information about Lucifer that kept him away. How she wished she had the freedom of a man. Right now she would have liked to walk the grounds and snoop a bit to see if she could find any evidence of Lucifer's presence. She was not an expert at surveillance, but she knew what to look for. But if she mentioned going for a walk, half the men in the room would offer to accompany her. With her luck of late, she would end up on the arm of Lord Kwirley.

Afternoon turned to evening, and Lily was forced to change yet again. This time she donned a gold silk gown with a shimmery overlay. The V-neck bodice was low enough to display her favorite sapphire necklace, nestled in her cleavage. She had no time to complete her letters, but she was able to excuse herself after the fourth dinner course, claiming a headache. Once again, Darlington had not made an appearance, and she considered changing into a dark cloak and sneaking past the drawing room later, when the guests were quite foxed, to take a look about outside on her own. She would have to take her pistol, of course. Lucifer could very well be lurking.

Anna was helping with dinner and would then dine with the servants, so Lily knew she had plenty of time to herself. She opened her door, closed and locked it, and went immediately to her desk. She pulled open the drawer and inhaled sharply. Her letter to Fitzhugh, as well as the countess's letter, were missing.

"Looking for these?"

She turned and watched as Darlington moved out of the shadows on the far side of the room. In his hand, he waved several sheets of parchment.

"Those are personal."

"Yes, I've noted that. They are *quite* personal." He stepped forward. "Are they true?"

She didn't answer. She had been foolish to leave them in an unlocked drawer, but she did not think they revealed anything at a casual glance. She was still not certain what Darlington thought he knew. It was better to keep silent, rather than give anything away. "May I have them back?" She rose and held out a hand.

"No. I want to know what you're doing here. Did Fitzhugh send you?"

She met his gaze in stubborn silence. She did not blame him for trying to discover her secrets. He was desperate to protect those he loved. But she would help him more by staying silent.

"Is he your superior? Is that why you are reporting to him?"

She knew every effective interrogation technique as well as she knew the lines on her palm. If he thought merely questioning her would succeed in gaining information, he was quite mistaken. He moved closer, and she tensed. He looked furious, and the hard glint in his dark eyes was dangerous.

"What exactly do you do for the Crown? Are you a spy?" He grasped her arm and hauled her against him. "Are you here to spy on me and my family?"

She merely stared at him. He knew more than she had anticipated, but he wasn't certain. If he was certain, he would not be here, questioning her.

"You will answer my questions," he said. "I deserve an answer."

"No, you don't. This has nothing to do with you."

He released her, all but shoving her away from him. It hurt to see the contempt in his eyes, but engendering his dislike was the least of her worries. It was her own fault for allowing him access to her heart. And for daring to hope he might fall in love with her and forget, for one moment, the lovely Juliette. Oh, but how she wished she could confide in him. She wished she could tell him everything. But that was folly. Dangerous folly.

"If you will not answer my questions freely, then you leave me no choice."

Lily felt a chill run down her back and into her legs. "What do you mean?" Her gaze flicked to the letters he held, and she caught her breath. He had read the one to Fitzhugh, but she had been careful in her wording. He could guess at what it meant, but he could not be certain. But she had forgotten the other letter she received—the one from the countess. The one that contained that detailed report. "No choice but...?"

"I read the letter from the Countess of Sinclair. You have a son."

Lily shrank back, bumping against the desk and rattling the lamp on top. "I don't know what you're talking about," she whispered.

But Darlington was looking at the letter. He was reading it, and she had never felt so naked. She had never felt so exposed. "I followed you, remember? The Musgrove boy is yours. I cannot believe I never saw it before. He has your coloring."

Lily clenched the desk, her blunt fingernails digging into the soft wood.

"I didn't piece it together until now." He waved the letter. "Who knows besides Lady Sinclair?"

She swallowed and attempted to force her lips to move. "You." Her mind was whirling faster and faster, making the room swim. She had made a grave error—an amateur error. She should have burned the letter as soon as she received it. The countess should never have sent it, but she was not a spy. She was not expected to know the protocols. Lily was, and she did.

But she had not followed them, and now she would pay the price. The Diamonds in the Rough and the Crown would suffer for her own stupidity.

"This is privileged information then," Darlington said. He was not taunting her. He was not crowing. She could see he took no pleasure in besting her. But he would not shy from using what he had, either. She knew the set of his jaw and the determined line above his brow. He would do what he felt necessary to protect his family. "What do you think the *ton* would do if it knew your secret?"

"I don't care." This was true enough. "I do not think they would care beyond the fact that it would give them something new to gossip about." This was also true. There was hardly an Impure about who did not have at least one child. If the child was a by-blow of a peer, the gentleman usually provided for his offspring's rearing. The prince regent even gave titles to his illegitimate children. Having the child of the prince was a mark of prestige.

But Lily's child was not the son of a peer or even a gentleman. And she had not been a glamorous courtesan when she'd birthed him. She'd been a scared, lonely sixteen-year-old girl. All she had wanted was to survive.

She did not care if the *ton* knew her secret. But she did care, very much, that the identity of the boy should be revealed. What would the child's life be like if he found out he was adopted? If he found out he was the child of a courtesan? Would his friends turn their backs on him? Would he be the target of scorn and ridicule? She could not allow that, not any more than she could allow another of the Crown's men to die at the hands of a paid assassin.

"What do you think my father would say?"

Lily paused. "He would understand. I would explain the circumstances."

"And what are those circumstances?" He waved the letters again, and Lily wanted to snatch them. She knew such an effort would be useless, but the urge was there nonetheless. "That the child of his intended is living a few miles from here?"

"You cannot ever reveal that!" she sputtered and immediately regretted saying anything. She should have said nothing, but words had broken free before she could contain them.

"And if I do?"

She wanted to beg. She wanted to throw herself at his feet and plead. Would it make any difference? Did she have any choice? Bile rose in her throat at the very thought. She had only ever begged once before, when her parents had found out she was breeding. For her pains, they'd thrown her transgressions in her face and mocked her efforts to ask for forgiveness. "He's an innocent child," she said. "If you reveal that I am his mother, it will change the whole course of his life. If you read that"—she pointed to the letter—"you know he does not know he is adopted. He does not know who his mother is. If he learns, it could ruin him."

"Then tell me what I want to know. You hold the boy's future in your hands." His arms were crossed, his face stony. How could he be so harsh, so cruel? She had thought she knew him, but now she was not so certain.

"I cannot. No matter the consequences."

"Fine." He started away from her. "Then I go to my father."

Lily swallowed the bile in her throat. "No." She went after him, grasped his wrist. "Please. Andrew, please." She was out of options, so she fell to her knees. Her son was worth this humiliation. She would do it for him. She had done worse.

Darlington tried to pull his hand away, but she held it tightly. "My lord, please. I beg you not to expose my son. If you must expose me, so be it, but spare him."

"Stand up." He shook his hand free and grasped her shoulders. "I do not want you to beg."

"I have no other choice. What do you want from

me? I'll give you whatever you want. I'll do whatever you want." She reached for the fall of his trousers. Pleasuring him might not change his mind, but it would stall him. It would give her time to think.

He took her hands. "No. Do you think I would use you like that?"

She did not know what to think anymore. He pulled her to her feet. "You are blackmailing me," she pointed out.

He sighed. "I cannot even do that. You obviously love this child, your son. He does not know you are his mother, and you would sacrifice for him. Do you not see I, too, am trying to protect those I love?"

"Yes."

"And yet you won't tell me what I ask. I must resort to blackmail." He spat the word as though it left a bitter taste on his tongue.

"There are some sacrifices not mine to make."

He swore and crumpled the papers in his fist then turned away from her, resting a hand on the mantel. "How am I supposed to take a boy's mother from him? How, when I know how that feels?"

"Andrew." She put a hand on his shoulder. "I am sorry for your loss. Please understand I would never think of taking your mother's place."

"Then what are you doing here?"

She looked away.

"Is this something to do with the Lucifer you mentioned? Is that what Fitzhugh and the Foreign Office are interested in?" He stared at the fire, and she could see his mind working. But did he have enough information to puzzle it out? She did not think so, but she dared not underestimate him. "You said my father may have something Lucifer wants, and this Lucifer is the man causing the recent mischief. In that case, I should alert the authorities. We cannot have Lucifer attempting to break in and steal my family's property."

"You can try to do so," she said, "but if you tell your father, he will stop you." At least, if her suppositions about the duke were correct, he would stop his son. He would not want the authorities involved.

"You think he would risk the safety of his home and family?"

She gazed at him directly, allowing him to come to his own conclusions.

He shook his head. "You have no intention of marrying him, do you?"

"Does that relieve you? I will not defile your home or presume to take your sainted mother's place." She turned away, trying to hide the bitterness in her voice.

"I was wrong," he said, catching her elbow. "I was wrong to say that about you. I… it was my grief speaking." It was Darlington who turned away then, and though Lily knew this was the perfect opportunity to reclaim the letters—now when he was distracted—she could not do it.

"Andrew, why do you still grieve for your mother?"

He glanced over his shoulder, his expression one of contempt. "Because she was the only person who ever loved me."

Lily stared at him, at the naked pain etched on his face.

"I loved you," she whispered.

He gave a bitter laugh. "And look how I treated you. I never told her. I never thanked her."

"I'm certain she knew you loved her."

"I'll never know." He laid his forehead on his arm, and Lily's eyes widened in surprise. She had never seen him like this and did not know what to say or do to make it better.

"I never told her," he said, voice muted. "I never told her I loved her. I never told her how much I appreciated all she had done for me."

"She knew." Lily rubbed his back.

"When I was first at Eton," he said, his voice little more than a whisper, "I hated it. I was small and scrawny, and I made an easy target. I was lonely, too. My mother used to write me a letter every day. Those letters saved me time and again when I felt I could not go on. I knew if I made it one more day, I would have another letter from my mother." He looked up, his expression rueful. "You can see why the other lads beat up on me."

"Not at all. You were a little boy. Of course you missed your mother."

"She gave me the advice that helped me through it."

"What was that?"

"Make them laugh. If they were laughing at me, they couldn't hit me—at least, not as hard."

"Is that how you became so charming?"

"I was always charming."

Lily rolled her eyes.

"But that was when I learned to use it." He straightened. "This has nothing to do with you—"

"But it does. I know what it is like to send a son away, although my circumstances are somewhat different." Perhaps if she told him. Perhaps if she revealed something of her past, he would keep her secrets—at least long enough for her to complete her mission.

"Is that why you became a courtesan?" he asked.

"I was a fallen woman. I had no other options open to me."

"You could have kept the child."

She shook her head. "I was sixteen when he was born. My parents had disowned me, and I was living on the street in the worst part of London."

"What about the father?"

"I don't think he ever knew I was with child. We spent barely a summer together, and I was little more than a child myself. I hardly knew what I was doing."

"Bastard."

"Oh, he's not completely to blame," she said, putting a hand on his arm. "I knew it was wrong. I knew that much. But I was so dazzled by him. He was handsome, and he dressed like one of the dandies I sometimes saw on the streets. I fancied myself in love. No one ever looked at me, you see, and he made me feel beautiful and special."

Darlington huffed. "I can hardly believe that. You must have had admirers."

"No. I was an incredibly shy child. I had to learn to overcome that to ma—to become a successful courtesan." She had almost said *masquerade*. She could not allow herself to drop her guard around Darlington. She had to remember he was very much her enemy.

"But even if you were reticent, there is still the obvious." He gestured to her as though his point should be clear.

"The obvious?"

"You are beautiful."

She gaped at him. She almost argued. She had never been called beautiful—that was a term reserved for women like Juliette and Fallon. She was always *charming*, as if her personality somehow made up for what she lacked in appearance. But Darlington was absolutely serious. He was not attempting to flatter her. He called her *beautiful* as though it were fact. "You say things like that," she said, her voice breaking, "and it makes it incredibly difficult to hate you."

His brow rose. "And?"

"And I *need* to hate you, Darlington."

"What if you didn't?"

"Then… this." She grabbed him about the shoulders and kissed him. She expected him to go rigid with surprise, but he wrapped his arms around her and pulled her tightly against him. She was lost. She knew that now. She was completely in his power.

Twelve

ANDREW DID NOT WANT TO THINK ABOUT WHAT HE was doing. His was alone in the bedchamber of his father's intended. He was kissing her, his thoughts and intentions far from brotherly toward the woman who might one day be his stepmother.

Except all of that was a lie. She was hiding something, hiding a lot, from him and from his father. Andrew was not certain of the details yet, but it was coming together in his mind. He would figure it out. And when he did... what? He could not reveal her secret to Society. It had been an empty threat. Not simply because she was right about the damage it would do to the boy, but because he couldn't hurt her. Could she not see he wanted to protect her? Why would she not trust him? Did she think he could not see there was more to her than she allowed others to glimpse? The mystery surrounding her, the secrets, intrigued him.

No, he could not use her son against her, but he could use the boy to gain information about her. He could demand she include him in her... in whatever it was she was doing in Nottinghamshire. He pulled back, aware this might all be an attempt to seduce him, a form of bribery so he would not reveal her secrets. He wanted her, but not with that between them.

"I won't reveal your secret," he said. "I want your help."

She looked up at him and blinked, seeming almost dazed. "I know."

"What I mean is, you do not have to do this to persuade me to keep quiet."

"I never would." She moved to kiss him again, and with herculean willpower, he held her at bay.

"But I do want something, and I want you to agree before this goes any further."

She frowned at him, and he understood her confusion. He was confused as well. At some point he had developed… not scruples, exactly, but something suspiciously resembling them. "What do you want?"

"I want to be part of whatever it is you are doing at Ravenscroft Castle."

"No." Her response was quick and definitive. She attempted to step away, but he had no intention of allowing her warm, supple body out of his arms. And he would secure her help. It was the only way he could save both of them.

"Yes," he demanded. "You will include me."

"You already said you would not reveal my secret."

"But that does not mean I will make things here easy for you. I can reveal other things to my father, which may make him question his engagement to you." He glanced at the mantel, where he had left her letters. He saw her look at them, knew she was thinking of her letter to Fitzhugh.

"I'll consider it."

"Good."

"And what makes you think this"—she gestured to his arms wrapped around her—"will go any further?"

"This makes me think so." He bent and took her mouth with his. The moment their lips met, he felt the frisson between them. Something akin to the flash of fire when it is first ignited. She fought the spark. He could feel her trying to pull away, trying to resist. He had given up resisting. He could no longer keep his desire for her at bay.

"We cannot do this," she said, turning her head to deny him access to her mouth.

"Lily." He touched her cheek and tilted her face to his again. "We were meant to do this. Do you think this—what we feel when we touch—is common? You must know it's not."

"You should go." But she didn't mean it. He could see in her eyes she wanted him to stay.

"Don't make me beg," he said.

"I thought I was the one who was begging."

He gave her his most wicked grin. "Give me a few moments more."

She hesitated when she should have fled, and he took advantage, kissing her again. His hand slid up her back to trace the bare skin of her neck and cup the back of her head. Her flaming hair was heavy in his hand, and his nimble fingers plucked pin after pin from it, allowing them to fall useless on the rug. Finally, her hair tumbled down, sweeping over his arm. It was longer than he'd imagined, and wavy but soft. He threaded his hands through it, kissing his way to her neck. He wrapped his hand in her hair and brought it to his nose, inhaling deeply. It smelled of apples and fresh cream, of all things, wholesome and sweet. He kissed the tender flesh of her neck again. His lips brushed that soft skin, pressing so lightly that he could feel her shiver.

"Cold?" he murmured.

"No. Warm. So very warm."

He traced the lace at the bodice of the gold shimmery gown she wore, marveling at the accuracy of her statement. Her flesh was warm to his touch, flushed and slightly pink. Andrew had an encyclopedic knowledge of women's clothing, and he quickly loosened the fastenings holding the bodice in place. The silk material fell aside, leaving her in skirts and stays over a thin, filmy chemise. He had tasted her before, kissed her here, taken her flesh in his mouth, but he found himself eager to do so again. Almost too eager. His hand shook as he pulled at the stay's lacings. When he looked at her face, she was gazing up at him, her eyes large and liquid.

He wondered what she saw in his face. Desire? Certainly. Need? Definitely. Fear? God, he hoped not. He wanted this to be right. He had never wanted anything so much in his life. And he reminded himself he was a fool to worry. She was no virgin, and yet he felt as though there was something new for both of them in this coming together. He had always bedded women because his body craved the pleasure. But he had all but forgotten his own needs. It was her needs he thought of.

When her stays opened, he allowed the weight

of his hand to rest over the cloudlike thinness of her chemise. He could feel her heart pounding under her fevered skin, and at his touch, she gave a little moan. That sound pleased him inordinately. He hooked a finger in the small loop with which she'd tied the neck of her chemise and tugged. The loop opened, and the material rippled down her shoulders, pooling at her elbows and exposing her exquisite breasts and the sapphires nestled between them.

Now she would see his hands shake, and he could not seem to control the tremors. She was perfect. He watched as her nipples hardened and puckered under his gaze, then lowered his mouth to take one dark, ripe bud between his lips. His hands remained fastened on her shoulders until he was certain he could control their shaking. As soon as his cool lips touched her warm flesh, she arched back and dug her nails into his upper arms. Her surrender was all but complete, and it made him want her that much more. He was hard for her now, eager to explore all of her body as he explored the fullness of first one breast and then the other.

He caught a glimpse of her flame-washed body in the light of the fire and wanted her naked before him. Bending, he swept her into his arms.

She laughed, and he looked down at her as he crossed to the bed. "I've amused you?"

"I've never been carried to bed before."

"Good." He laid her down and stripped off his coat, then loosened his cravat. He wanted to touch her, skin to skin.

"I had no idea all that romantic talk of yours was not simply for show."

"I hope you don't expect me to start spouting poetry." He pulled his shirt over his head.

Her eyes widened appreciatively, and he had to admit he felt a certain sense of satisfaction in knowing she found him desirable. He had not spent all those hours in the boxing ring for naught. He reached for the fall of his trousers then thought better of it. Instead, he rolled her over. She laughed again, which pleased him for some reason.

"Now what are you doing?" she asked, looking at him from over her shoulder.

"Unhooking your skirt and then untying your petticoats." He spoke as he performed the actions.

"I could stand."

His hand stroked the curve of her bottom. "I like you like this."

And then the garments were gone and the chemise with it, and she was left in her stockings and garters, the skin of her pale bottom painted with colors from the flickering fire. How he wanted to raise her hips and take her then and there. But he held off, instead lowering his mouth to her back and skating his wet tongue over her warm flesh.

She giggled and then moaned, her hips rising on their own so her bottom cupped him where he ached. He continued his descent down her spine, licking the indenture of her lower back then kissing it softly. One hand delved under her, lifting her pelvis so the other hand could slide between her legs. He found her fold warm and wet for him as he stroked her. She moved against him, pushing into his hand, and when he slipped two fingers inside her slick opening, she groaned. He slid in and out of her, readying her, surprised when he felt her muscles tighten so quickly. "You are ready for me," he whispered into her cinnamon hair. "Let go. I want to feel you climax."

"Andrew." She was holding back, but her body would not be denied. She writhed against him, and it took but a small adjustment of his fingers until she went over the edge. She clenched around him and cried out, muffling the noise into the covers on the bed. Even in passion, she was no fool.

When she stilled beneath him, he began to kiss her back again, and she rolled over, looking up at him with eyes impossibly green. "Your turn," she said.

He knew what she meant, but he wanted to be inside her. He wanted to pleasure her even as she gave herself to him. "And your turn again," he said.

Gently, she pushed him back and loosed, awkwardly, the fall of his trousers. He sprang free, and she pushed the material off his hips and then took his hard length in her hand. He groaned at her gentle touch, knowing she must be teasing him. She stroked him then bent to touch him with her tongue. In one move, he rolled over, pinning her beneath him. "I want to be inside you."

"No."

He had been about to kiss her, and it took a moment before her refusal broke through the haze of his desire. "No?"

"I've made that mistake in the past, as you well know. I won't risk it again."

He thought to ask how she managed with other men, but he did not want to speak of other men at the moment. And then she was pushing him back again and lowering her mouth to him, and he could not really think at all. He would allow this. For the moment.

She kissed him, then licked, her pink tongue tentative and sweet. He had to clutch the bedclothes when she put her lips around him, but just when he was gritting his teeth in anticipation of exerting extreme self-control, she withdrew and... kissed him again.

What the devil was she doing? It was not unpleasant, but neither was it what he was expecting from a renowned courtesan. She took him again, so clumsily he all but gaped at her. He could have sworn he felt teeth. "Ouch!"

"Sorry," she said with a sheepish shrug. And then she went back to kissing him—quick little pecking kisses that were more suitable for a grandmother's cheek than for... Now what the devil was she doing? She had him in some kind of vise grip. He supposed there was a first time for everything, because at this point, he just wanted her to stop.

"You've never done this before," he said, the words out before he could prevent them.

She glanced up at him, guilt in her eyes before she hid it. "Yes, I have."

"With whom?"

She straightened indignantly. He wasn't chastised. He enjoyed the view. "How dare you ask me to reveal such a thing!"

"I only want to know if the man survived."

She looked rather disheartened at that statement. "Was it that awful?"

He contemplated his answer. He did not want her trying again, but he did not want her to order him out either.

"Your hesitation is all the answer I need," she said with a sigh. "I suppose you might as well know the truth. You won't believe it." She paused and considered. "Or perhaps you will."

Instinct told him this conversation led in the wrong direction. He made a point never to converse with women in bed. It led to emotional outbursts he wanted to avoid. But he could not imagine Lily making such an outburst. Of course, he would have said the particular French trick she had been performing—even when it was done badly—was still good. But the world was obviously off its axis. "The truth about what?"

She pulled the covers over her shoulders, wrapping them protectively around her body. "I'm not really a courtesan."

Whom did she think she was speaking to? He knew her. He had been to more social events with her than he could count. She was one of The Three Diamonds. She was *the* Fashionable Impure.

She was watching him, noting his response. "I knew you would not believe me."

"Are you telling me you are not one of The Three Diamonds?"

"No. I am telling you The Three Diamonds was a fabrication we created in order to survive in London. I had birthed a child out of wedlock. I was a fallen woman. The Countess of Sinclair suggested I embrace my status, rather than attempt to hide it."

"The Countess of Sinclair?" Now this was too much

altogether. Angry, he stood, yanked his trousers back up and rounded on her. "The wife of your protector, The Earl of Sin, told you to join the demimonde?"

"Yes. She told all of us."

The woman did not look mad, but she was sitting there making no sense and expecting him to believe it. "Was this before or after she found you and your fellow Diamonds in bed with her husband?"

"I've never been in bed with Lord Sinclair. I've never seen his bedchamber. He's like a benevolent uncle to me. Society began to whisper that we were engaging in all manner of lewd acts with the earl, and the countess realized that everyone would believe whatever they wanted, regardless of what the truth was. And so she let them believe it."

He shook his head. What she'd said, what Lily told him, was impossible to fathom. "She's the pity of every woman and half the men of the *ton*," he said. "Why would she allow that?"

"Because she's kind and selfless and loving."

Andrew had never met the Countess of Sinclair. He'd never wanted to. But he knew who she was. He had been to functions where she was present. He would have described her as a dragon—and that was being kind—but Lily seemed to think the woman a lap dog.

"All of Society thought we were under the protection of Sinclair. That elevated our status and gave us instant notoriety. We became desirable in every way. I never even had to take a man to my bed to maintain the illusion. It was enough that everyone thought I was bedding everyone else."

"But men—"

"Lie?" she offered. "No, no. I'm sure no man ever lied about one of his conquests."

Andrew paced back and forth. He could not believe this. It was difficult to fathom. The Three Diamonds had fooled everyone.

Or had they? Did Fitzhugh and Pelham know the truth? Was that why they had no reservations about marrying the so-called courtesans? And then another thought occurred to him. If Lily was not a Cyprian, neither was Juliette. She had never been a courtesan. No wonder she never wanted him in her bed. He looked up and found Lily watching him, her mouth pursed. "I already know what you are going to ask. No, Juliette was no more a courtesan than I was. Whether she ever invited a man to her bed, I do not know. Our position gave us independence." She gestured to the bed where they had been wrapped around each other a moment ago. "As you see."

He did not want to believe it, but he knew it must be true. And so Lily really had no experience pleasuring a man. She had been used, at a very young age, by a man who left her, and had limited experience. And he'd expected her to behave as a fallen woman. He'd treated her—

"I want you to leave." She tossed his shirt to him, hitting him in the face. "Go now."

"If I offended you earlier, I apologize. I did not know. I did not realize. Lily, I should have—" He gestured helplessly. There was so much he should have done differently. But he could make it up to her now. He could be tender with her. He could proceed slowly, reassure her, cherish her and the experience.

He wanted to. Suddenly, he wanted that more than anything else.

"Please go," she said, her face set in stone and her tone a perfect match.

"Lily." He started for her, and she scooted back, holding her hand up defensively.

"Out! Now!"

"What the devil? What have I done?" But he was already pulling his shirt over his head. He would not stay if he was not wanted.

"Do you really not know? Can you really blame me for wanting you to leave after your first thought when I reveal my secret is of *her*?"

"No. Lily, she wasn't my first thought."

"So you did not think of Juliette? You did not try and piece together why she had never asked you to her bed?"

The fire crackled.

"At least you are honest," she said with a sneer, but she looked close to tears. "I love Juliette," she said. "She is my dearest friend and will always be. But right now, I hate her and you both. Out!"

Andrew did as she ordered.

❧

Lily told herself it was for the best. An intimate relationship with Darlington would make what she had to do that much more difficult. She looked at her rumpled bed and at her clothing strewn about the floor in wanton disarray. How had it even come to this? She had walked in to find him in her chamber, reading her personal mail, and they had ended up—her mail!

She jumped to her feet and ran to the mantel. She snatched up the papers and pawed through them. There was the letter from Lady Sinclair and the accompanying report from the investigator she had hired. Thank God! She fed it to the fire and watched it burn. She turned over the last paper she held in her hand, expecting to see her letter to Fitzhugh. But the paper was blank. She stared at it, willing words to appear in her hand. And then she searched the mantel again, peered into the fire, turned over her clothing and her bedsheets.

But the letter to Fitzhugh was not in her room.

And that meant Darlington still had it.

Bastard!

Well, she could steal it back. Then it would be his word against hers. She need not feel any compunction about doing such a thing. After all, he had stolen it from her in the first place. And after he had stolen it, he had proceeded to seduce her—the scoundrel!

Oh, very well. She'd wanted to be seduced, so she could hardly fault him. She did not know why she should suffer such weakness when it came to him. Why could she not refuse him, when she had refused hundreds of other men who were equally handsome, wealthy, or charming?

Because you love him.

No, she did not love him. She did not want to love him. She had put those feelings to rest—several times—and she refused to succumb again. He loved Juliette. He would always love Juliette, and even if, by some miracle, he came to love her, she would always be second to the one and only Juliette.

Lily reminded herself she was at Ravenscroft Castle for a reason, and that was what she needed to focus on. As soon as she had the evidence she sought, she could leave and forget all about Lord Darlington.

As she pulled on a night rail and climbed under her covers—alone—she tried not to think too much about what her life would be when she left Ravenscroft Castle. A return to life in London as The One Diamond? More likely The One Piece of Coal. Once word of her engagement was public, she was ruined. And did she really want to return to London? London was where her friends were, but it wasn't any fun going to balls and routs without Juliette and Fallon. She knew she would always be welcome at Somerset, but it was in Hampshire. And lovely as the Earl and Countess of Sinclair were, it was rather uneventful there.

She could go abroad. The Foreign Office would love to send her to the Continent. That work would be exciting—and dangerous. But she questioned her skills as a spy in light of this most recent endeavor. Darlington seemed to have caught her at every turn. She had never claimed to be one of the Foreign Office's best. She had her talents, interrogation and—like her father—good instincts. But this venture had taught her nothing if not that when she strayed too far from missions that capitalized on her strengths, she floundered.

At times like this, she wished she could see her father. Perhaps she might have benefitted from his experience. But as far as she knew, he was still living in London, and he must have known who she had become. She had never hidden her identity, only concealed some of the facts about her past. She was not difficult to find, and yet neither he nor her mother had sought her out. At times, she had hoped one of her sisters or her brother might have contacted her. Did they know why she had been sent away? Did they ever miss their little sister on Easter Day or when a new baby was baptized or one of them married?

She missed them, and never so much as on days when the weather was perfect and she strolled in the park, catching glimpses of ordinary families taking the air. She would always pause and watch as the children—not sons and daughters of peers, but common children as she and her siblings had been—kicked a ball or raced after ducks or joined hands to make a ring and then fall down. That had once been her life.

But her family had made a clean break, and she was truly alone in the world now. Once or twice she had spied on her brothers and sisters, on their little families. But seeing them so happy, so normal, hurt too much. Did they ever wonder what had become of her? Did they ever wish they could sit and have a cup of tea together, reminisce about their childhood games and pranks?

No, they had all forgotten her. She was the Countess of Charm now. Lily Dawson was only a memory.

With a sigh, she flopped back on the pillows and settled in for a long night. She would not sleep; that much she already knew. She was feeling too melancholy and too self-pitying. But she would hang herself before she tossed and turned all night, thinking of Darlington. And so she locked her hands behind her head and began to plan.

The next morning she stayed abed long after she knew the rest of the house was awake. The day had dawned bright and clear, and this was to her advantage. Outdoor amusements would be planned, leaving the house relatively empty. When she was certain her absence had been noted, she sent Anna to give her regrets. She had an awful megrim and would stay in bed. Anna had merely blinked at this directive. Undoubtedly, she was thinking that Lily had never before stayed in bed from a headache, but she kept her thoughts to herself. And that was why the girl kept her position.

Anna departed, and Lily lay in bed, feeling restless and impatient until finally the house quieted. She sent for Anna to help her dress, asking enough questions about the activities planned for the day that she felt comfortable with the window of time she had available.

"Lord Darlington went with them," Anna said, as she pulled Lily's hair back into a simple tail.

"Oh?" Lily said, feigning disinterest.

"They needed another male to even out the numbers."

Lily frowned. "Who else stayed behind?"

"Lord Kwirley."

"Ah." That did not surprise Lily. The man had probably indulged too much the night before.

"He is still abed," Anna said, as though confirming Lily's suspicions.

"Thank you, Anna," Lily said, rising to inspect Anna's work in the cheval mirror. "It is a lovely day. Why do you not take a few hours to yourself? I imagine most of the other maids have gone with the party—a boating party, you said?"

"Thank you, madam." Lily bobbed and departed.

Lily was practically right on her heels. She wanted to go to Darlington's room, but if the party had recently set out, the maids would be in the family's chambers, making beds and straightening up. That meant now was the ideal time to search the library.

She was not very good at picking locks, but she managed to gain access to the library and the duke's desk. She had broken the lock on the desk out of her clumsiness, a matter which became all the more frustrating when she realized the locked drawer contained nothing useful for her purposes.

She left the library and stood in the grand entrance hall for a long, long moment. Was there nothing the duke was hiding, or had she missed some vital clue? She could search his room again. Her last search had been hasty and incomplete, but she could not be certain the maids were finished and had moved on to the guest chambers yet. That left the music room, dining room, saloon, various parlors...

The tapestry room? That room appeared the sole province of the family. Perhaps she should search there. She thought she remembered a small table or two inside. But would the duke really hide something tying him to Lucifer in a tapestry room? She had to search to be certain. She was rapidly running out of time and options. If she did not find something to implicate the duke soon, she would be called back to London. The duke might be smitten with her while she flirted and teased him here, but if they parted, she was under no illusion his interest would hold. She would lose the connection she had with him, and then the Foreign Office would have to start anew.

How many agents would die in the meantime? Even now one of Ravenscroft's assassins might be targeting the Diamonds in the Rough. Could she ever again face Fallon if Fitzhugh was one of the agents murdered?

Lily set off for the tapestry room. She took several wrong turns, which was to her benefit, as she looked lost and confused when she encountered servants. Finally, she found the right corridor and started for the room she sought. But once outside, she paused. She could hear voices inside. Maids? No. It was a man's voice and… there was something familiar about the woman's voice.

She almost turned and retreated to her room, but then she heard the man's words quite distinctly. "I can satisfy your appetite, little wench." Kwirley. She knew all of his uninspiring innuendos.

There was a gasp then a small screech, and Lily did not hesitate. She lifted the latch and stumbled inside.

Thirteen

Kwirley turned to look at her, his body shielding the female he held in his clutches. Lily was perfectly aware she might have mistaken the scene, but she was willing to take that risk.

"Unhand her."

"This does not concern you, Countess. Go charm someone else."

"Let her go, my lord, or I will scream and alert the household."

"Lady Lily." The girl's voice was breathless and her face pale as she peered around Kwirley's shoulder.

Lily inhaled sharply at the sight of Darlington's young sister. She mentally drove daggers into Kwirley's eyes. "How could you?" she hissed. "Let her go, or the duke will hear of this and have your head for assault."

Kwirley must have seen something in her eyes, because he released Lady Emma and took a step back. He dusted his hands together as though ridding himself of the lady's touch. "We were only having a spot of fun, wench. No need to swish your skirts at me."

"Out." She pointed to the door. "And if you are smart, you will hie back to London and your wife now."

He gave her a mocking bow and walked, unhurriedly, out of the room. Lady Emma's legs buckled, and Lily rushed forward and guided her into a comfortable chair. "Are you harmed?" she asked. "Did he hurt you?"

"I am fine. I do not know why I am shaking."

"It's perfectly natural after you've had a fright. Shall I ring for your governess or a maid to bring tea?"

"No!" The girl grabbed her elbow before Lily could start for the bellpull. "No. Please. I do not want anyone to know of this." She buried her face in her hands, and Lily could just make out the words, "I am to blame."

Lily took the girl by the shoulders and ducked her head so she might speak to the poor child directly. "You are not to blame. Lady Emma, listen to me. You did nothing wrong."

"You don't understand," the duke's daughter said. Her shoulders were shaking now, indicating she was beginning to sob. "I encouraged him. He gave me compliments, and I was flattered. I agreed to meet him here. I knew I shouldn't. I knew it was wrong, but he said I was pretty and—" Her words were lost in a heave of sobs.

Lily sighed. She well knew the power of an older man's charms on a young, inexperienced girl.

"Your choice was unwise," Lily admitted, "but that does not give him leave to insult you. Come. I'll escort you back to your chambers."

"You won't tell anyone, will you, Lady Lily?"

"I'm not a lady."

The girl blinked tear-stained eyes at her. "I thought you were a countess."

"The title is… honorary. Lady Emma, I would like to keep your secret. The—"

The tapestry-room door swung open, and Darlington stood in the opening. His face was a mask of anger, and his arms were crossed over his chest as though he were a human barricade. "What secret are you discussing?"

Lady Emma gasped. "Andrew! Were you eavesdropping?"

He ignored his sister and kept his gaze on Lily. "Tell me what is going on."

"No!" Emma cried.

"What the devil have you done to her?" Darlington demanded, stepping into the room.

Lily felt her anger rise. "I've done what you wouldn't. I've protected her."

"What rubbish is this?" He looked from Lily to his sister. "I would protect her with my life."

Lily looked at Lady Emma. "He needs to know what occurred. You are not safe here. You should have been sent away before your father's companions arrived."

"No," Lady Emma whispered. "Please do not tell him."

"I will not. You will tell him. I shall wait outside." Lily stepped outside the door and closed it, giving the brother and sister privacy. She did not try to listen, but she suspected even if she had, she would not have been able to hear anything. Emma was too distraught to speak loudly, and Darlington would have to strain to hear. Suddenly, the door opened, and Darlington emerged with his sister. He looked furious. Lady Emma did not even glance in her direction.

"Wait here," Darlington directed. "Do not leave this room until I return."

Lily did not particularly care for the way his finger jabbed in her face, but she made no comment and returned to the tapestry room. After what had almost happened to poor Lady Emma, she barely remembered why she had come to the tapestry room in the first place. When she did remember, she sighed, wishing, for once, she did not always have to play so many parts in life. But she had a mission, and now was the perfect opportunity to search the room.

She went to work quickly and efficiently, going from one decorative table to the other, looking for drawers or secret openings. She found none and decided to look behind the tapestries. What better place to hide a safe? She peered behind one, moving the heavy drape aside and grunting with the effort. It was almost too dark in the room for her to discern whether or not anything was behind the tapestry, but she ran a hand along the wall and felt no protrusions. When she emerged, Darlington was standing in the room, watching her.

Lily almost jumped. The man should have been a spy. He had an uncanny ability to move about without being detected.

"Is that why you came here? To search it?" he asked pointedly.

She saw no reason to lie. "Yes."

"And that is why you claimed to have a megrim."

"I wanted to be left behind."

He shook his head. "I do not know what you are looking for, but you are not going to find it."

Lily said nothing. She did not wish to invite further conversation on the topic.

"And yet," he continued, "I am glad of your persistence and your ridiculous search—whatever it is for. You saved my sister from Lord Kwirley."

"She told you what happened?"

"She tried, and I pieced most of it together."

Lily saw his hands clench and open.

"I'm going to kill that bastard. How *dare* he lay one finger on her?"

"That sort of thing will do nothing to harm Kwirley's reputation and everything to ruin your sister's."

Darlington stared at her, anger blazing in his dark eyes.

"You know the *ton* as well as I. No matter what the truth of the matter may be, Society will assume your sister behaved improperly. Even if you claim nothing untoward occurred between them, the old biddies with nothing better to do than sip scandal broth will whisper that Lady Emma is compromised."

"So I do nothing?"

"You do what you should have done in the first place. Send Lady Emma away."

She saw his jaw tighten with fury, and she knew she had overstepped. He was going to roar at her. To her surprise, he raked a hand through his hair, collapsed into a chair, and buried his face in his hands. He looked very much the twin of his younger sister in that moment. "I want to be angry at you, but I am to blame. I was consumed by my father's romantic liaisons. I didn't think of my responsibilities."

"It was your father's responsibility not to invite such men to the sanctuary of his home, but your father is concerned with his own pleasures at present. Is there somewhere you can send her until the house party has ended?"

"My sister Katherine will take her. She will probably appreciate a visit from her younger sister, and it will give Emma time with her niece and nephew."

"Have her pack tonight and send her first thing in the morning." She knelt beside him. "And do not blame yourself. There is enough blame to go around without you adding to it."

He looked at her for a long time, so long that Lily began to feel her cheeks heat. Finally, he took her hand. She tried to pull away, but he would not release her. "There is something I want to say. Something I need to say after last night."

"There's nothing you have to say on that subject I care to hear." She yanked her hand away and stood, starting for the door. She would have to return later and search the tapestry room then. Unfortunately, the other venue she needed to search, Darlington's room, was also an impossibility at the moment as the earl had returned to the residence.

"It's about Juliette," he said to her back.

Her steps faltered. She did not want them to, but her legs went weak and her feet stumbled. She swallowed and straightened her back. "You've made your feelings about her quite clear."

"Lily."

She walked away before he could say anything further. She had been hurt enough. She would not allow him to drive the stake any deeper into her heart. Perhaps, with time, her feelings for him would fade. Until she could escape him and his house, she must limit their contact and conversation.

Lily would have liked to burrow under her covers, but she could not afford to be absent. She did not have the evidence she needed against the duke, and he might do or say something crucial. She spent the evening dining and drinking with the duke and his friends, trying to act her usual charming self, despite all the turmoil in her mind and heart. At dinner, she'd been seated across from Kwirley, and the viscount made a point of sneering at her. He almost seemed to want her to expose him. She ignored him and fawned over the duke. Ravenscroft, in turn, drank far more than he ate and was deeply in his cups by the time the men joined the ladies in the drawing room.

The duke came up behind her and pulled her roughly into his lap, whispering lascivious comments in her ear. She tittered and giggled as was expected, while inwardly cringing. At least the faux engagement would buy her time and keep her from having to blockade him from her bedchamber. If the hard length she felt against her backside was any indication, he could hardly wait to take her there.

At one point, still perched on the duke's lap, she looked up and saw Darlington had entered. Her heart sank when she saw the disgusted look on his face. She deliberately looked away. The duke was her mission. She could not concern herself with Darlington's assumptions and judgments. By the time she was finally able to escape the duke and retreat to her bedchamber, Darlington was gone. Relieved, she closed her door, searched her room to be certain she was alone, then with Anna's help, readied herself for bed and climbed under the covers.

She fell into a deep sleep, where she dreamed a hammer pounded nails into her coffin. With a gasp, she bolted up and realized the pounding was not a hammer at all but someone at her door.

"Who is it?" she called out.

"Darlington."

Lily shook her head in amazement. Was the man really such a loggerhead? "I do not wish to see you. Go away."

"You will come to the library, or I will be back to drag you," he promised. She heard his footsteps leading away, and she frowned.

If this was a ploy to seduce her, why had he knocked on the door? And why had he spoken from without, so other guests might hear?

And what was happening in the library?

Because she was curious, and because she had no doubt Darlington would return to drag her forcibly, as he'd threatened, she rose, donned a robe and slippers and, taking a lamp to guide her way, padded to the library.

She heard voices even before she reached the doors, and her sense of unease increased. When she stepped inside, she gasped in a breath. Darlington was watching her. He stood beside his steward, and the state of the men's attire told her they had not yet been to bed. The butler, who looked as though he had been abed, and the housekeeper, who wore a robe and slippers like she, stood at the other end of the room, whispering quietly.

"Well," Darlington said. "You are either a very good actress, or you are as surprised at this as we are."

"What happened?" she asked, turning in a circle to survey the damage. Papers were strewn everywhere, books lay in teetering piles, the expensive chairs and couches were ripped open and the stuffing covered the floor, reminding her of a sheep shearing.

"We thought you might be able to tell us," Darlington said. Even in the midst of this chaos, he drew her gaze. He was so handsome, and she couldn't help but stare at the bronze skin of his throat where his cravat hung loose and his shirt was open. Glancing down a bit farther, she noted the tight trousers, made all the more scandalous because she knew what was under them now.

"I have been in bed. I assure you, I had nothing to do with this." She glared at him, willing him to keep silent about what he had read in her letters.

"But you know who did." Darlington's gaze on her did not falter. She was angry with him for dragging her into this, but she could not afford to show it.

"Where is His Grace?" she asked. "Has he not been informed?"

"We are not able to rouse him, madam," the steward said.

"I see." She should have realized that would be the problem. The duke had drunk like a sailor tonight. Darlington was still looking at her expectantly, so she shrugged. "I do not know why I was wakened. I have nothing to contribute."

Slowly, Darlington turned to the butler and house-keeper. Addressing them by name, he said, "Why don't you retire? We will deal with the cleaning up in the morning."

"Yes, my lord." They left eagerly, and Lily imagined they were thinking about the work they would have to face in just a few hours.

"Perhaps you could attempt to rouse my father again," Darlington said to the steward.

"Yes, my lord." He left, and Lily turned to the door as well.

"I shall also retire." She started for the exit.

"I do not think so," Darlington said. "Tell me what you know."

"Nothing, as I said." She reached for the door handle.

"What about Lucifer?" he asked.

Her hand on the handle stilled. She closed her eyes, knowing to answer would involve her further, and feeling as though Darlington had a right to know. His home had been violated. "This incident is further proof he is nearby." Ravenscroft had documents or papers, most likely pertaining to the Crown's spies, and Lucifer wanted them.

"You will help me capture him," Darlington said.

She turned to face him. "No. I want nothing to do with him." She did not say capturing Lucifer was not her mission. Ravenscroft might be a threat in that he ordered men's deaths, but Lucifer actually killed them. He was far more dangerous, and she was not equipped to deal with a murderer. Not out here by herself without any other agents to assist her. Darlington was capable of taking care of himself, but she was not certain how much of a match he was against a man like Lucifer. "I suggest you have footmen serve as perimeter guards for the time being."

"That will be done, but it will not solve the problem. We must locate this Lucifer." Darlington moved across the room, advancing on her. "He has been inside my home and dared to do this." He gestured to the ransacked library. "This is not to be tolerated."

"Nevertheless, I cannot assist you."

"You can, and you will."

"Or else?" She already knew the power he held, the secrets he knew.

He bent close and whispered in her ear. "Do not make me threaten you, Lily. It's not a gentlemanly thing to do."

She turned to face him so her nose brushed his. "You won't do it. If you were going to reveal my secrets, you would have done so already. I warn you not to persist in making threats you can't keep."

Instead of fuming, he touched her cheek. "Are you angry? I rather like you when you're angry." His finger trailed down her skin, and he bent close. Lily knew she should pull away, avoid the kiss, but she could not quite make herself do so.

"What the devil is going on in there?" a familiar voice boomed. Lily jumped away from Darlington and out of the path of the door just in time. It swung open and barely missed her. The Duke of Ravenscroft stood in the frame, scowling at his wreck of a library. His hair stood up, and his eyes were bloodshot. He looked all of his almost-sixty years tonight. "What happened?" he said, turning about, much as Lily had upon entering. His gaze fastened on her. "What are *you* doing here?"

She glanced at Darlington before answering. "I thought I heard a commotion, and when I came down, I saw the light on."

The duke looked from her to his son, his expression skeptical.

"There have been several thefts and incidents lately, Your Grace," Darlington said. "We think this might be related."

"Incidents?" The duke's eyebrows rose. "Why was I not notified?"

"Mr. Helms did not want to trouble you or your guests," Darlington said smoothly, though it was clear to Lily the steward had gone to the man he knew was really running the estate.

"Well, I am troubled now," Ravenscroft lamented, bending to sift through papers and allowing them to fall like sand through his hands. "Whoever did this will not go unpunished. Helms!"

The steward, who had been standing just outside the library, hurried inside. "Yes, Your Grace."

"Tomorrow you will find the man who did this."

"Yes, Your Grace."

"Get out."

"Yes, Your Grace." He left quickly, and with a muttered pardon, Darlington followed. Lily tried to escape as well, but the duke caught her arm. His grip hurt.

"What do you know that you are not telling me?"

the duke demanded. His breath was hot and foul against her cheek.

"I do not know what you mean, Your Grace."

"I may be old, but I am no fool," Ravenscroft said, digging his fingers into her tender flesh. "There have been too many coincidences involving you. You are up to something."

"Your Grace," she said calmly. "You are frightening me."

"I wish that were true. Then I might actually believe your stories." He released her. "But I don't frighten you, Lily. I should, you know. You should be afraid, because if you are involved in this, in any way, I will kill you." His dark eyes were fierce and ominous. This was no idle threat. He stalked out, and Lily clutched her hands into fists.

If she had not been frightened before, she was now, though she would fight it. *This* was the Duke of Ravenscroft she had been searching for—the man willing to kill men for his own purposes. A traitor and enemy of the Crown.

But why? Why did he want the Diamonds in the Rough dead, and where were the rubies he was promising the assassins? Was he working for another country's government? A country that wanted England's top spies dead? Was the duke the notorious Artemis? In which case, she was as good as dead. She closed her eyes, resolved to fight her fear, conquer it, because she knew she was close to the third act now. The trick was to stay alive for the finale. When her legs were once again steady beneath her, she returned to her room and lay awake with her hand on the knife beneath her pillow.

❦

Darlington sent a message through Lily's maid for her to meet him in the stables. He intended to search every inch of the estate for this Lucifer's hiding hole, and he wanted Lily with him. Perhaps she would see something he did not. Perhaps he would only keep her from causing some other mischief at the house. Or perhaps he just wanted to keep her close. Nevertheless, he was prepared to drag her from her bed when she stepped into the stable, her eyes blinking in the sudden darkness.

"I thought I would have to physically remove you from your bed," he said, moving into the light so she would see him easily.

"I'm certain you would have enjoyed that."

"I would far rather drag you into bed." Her eyes widened in surprise at the admission. Andrew gestured to the stalls. "Do you have a choice of mount?"

"No. I am not familiar enough with your horses. Where are we riding?"

"I thought you might direct me. I beg your leave for a moment." He moved farther into the stables and returned with two grooms, whom he directed to saddle two riding horses, his favorite gelding and a fast but gentle mare for Lily. The two of them waited outside while the horses were prepared. The day was cloudy and gray, a change from the sunny, clear days of late. Rain showers threatened, but he noted she had brought a shawl. That would protect her from a light rain, at least.

She glanced at him, and he looked away quickly.

Not for the first time, he had been caught admiring her. It was difficult not to admire her. She was a beautiful woman with her auburn hair piled on top of her head in a mass of curls and coils. Her riding habit was snug, the dark emerald color making her look regal. If she had chosen another path in life, she might have become a lady. She certainly behaved as such. She might have made some duke a powerful duchess.

The horses were finally ready, and he and Lily set off by tacit agreement toward the woods at the rear of the house. When they were out of the grooms' earshot, Andrew slowed his horse and fell into step with Lily's. "I think the woods the most likely hiding spot."

She nodded her agreement.

"He could be hiding in the village," Andrew added a moment later.

"I think such a man would have been noted and mentioned. He has a striking appearance, quite handsome from what I understand."

"You have not seen him?"

"From a distance. He does not have the sort of looks I admire."

"And what sort is that, Lily?"

She cut her gaze to him. "You will not receive any compliments from me, my lord."

"You wound me."

"Hardly." She spurred her mount forward, and he allowed her to lead briefly then charged ahead. When they reached the outskirts of the woods, they slowed, and Lily motioned to him to approach. "I suggest we ride into the woods and tie the horses to a tree when the foliage becomes thicker."

Andrew frowned. "What will stop him from stealing our horses?"

"He has a mount. He no longer needs one. If we are lucky, he will never see our horses. But if we ride them and come upon him, he will hear us long before we ever spot him."

As a lad, Andrew had done his share of tracking animals for sport. He knew what she suggested made sense and only wished he had thought of it himself. With a nod, he motioned her to follow him into the woods. The path was not wide enough for two horses, and he led until they reached a small stream where the brush seemed to thicken. "We leave the animals here," he said, pointing to the stream. "If we ford here, it might serve to obscure our trail."

Lily blinked at him. He could see what she was thinking. She was not eager to cross the water, but she did not argue, only tied her mare to a tree then removed her boots and stockings.

Andrew tried not to watch her, but he might have caught a flash of ankle or calf as he removed his own riding boots. When she was ready—her footwear cupped in the skirts of her riding habit—he started across. The water was colder than he'd anticipated, and he stifled a small yelp. She made no sound whatsoever, crossing behind him with grace and speed. She faltered on the other side of the stream, where a steep incline forced them both to climb up loose dirt, but he grasped her elbow and pulled her to the top.

Once at the crest of the bank, he did not release her right away. He held her arm for a moment longer than necessary, looking into eyes that matched the vivid green of the forest around them. She stepped away, averting her gaze and moving to a log where she sat to don her stockings and boots. This time Andrew did not look at her. He was on slippery ground in more ways than one, he knew. This interest in her was more than the simple desire to bed her. There was that, but he had wanted women before that he could not have. He had wanted one in particular.

But those women had never consumed his thoughts as Lily seemed to. Even now, when he knew he would be rebuffed, he was drawn to her. He wanted to touch her, kiss her, hold her. In most cases, a woman's disinterest was enough to cool his ardor. He did not know why he could not seem to allow Lily to go her own way.

When she was ready, he gestured to the right and then to the left, allowing her to choose their path. She studied both then gestured to the left. He led the way, and they moved without speaking through the woods. After several hours, they paused by another branch of the stream where they had left the horses. Andrew cupped his hands to drink the cool water then produced a handkerchief with bread and cheese from the satchel he carried over his shoulder.

Lily took a share with a nod of thanks then looked away as she ate it, her eyes scanning the woods around them. Andrew supposed he should be thankful she didn't insist on chattering until he went mad, as some women did, but he did wish she would say *something*. Finally, he could stand it no longer. "How are you faring? Should we return?"

She raised a brow at him. "I hardly think now is the time to worry about my welfare."

She was correct, of course. If he wanted to concern himself with her well-being, he would not have demanded she accompany him. "Perhaps I regret my decision to invite you."

She smiled at his use of *invite*, as he had known she would. He understood her so well, even when she did not speak her feelings. "I do not regret my decision to accept your invitation." Her mouth curled in a rueful smile. "I am happy for the time out-of-doors, even if the weather is less than ideal."

A light rain had been falling for the past hour, but they were somewhat shielded under the canopy of trees. Still, Andrew could see the drops of rain disturbing the calm stream, and he looked up to gauge the condition of the skies. Pewter-gray clouds promised the dreary weather would continue.

When he looked back at Lily, she was staring at the ground beside the rotten tree stump where she perched. He thought he might move away, give her some time to herself and her own thoughts, but then she rose and moved to study a nearby bush. She bent, studied the ground again, and turned to him. "Have you trespassed on this ground?"

"No." He moved closer, feeling his heart begin to pound. "Have you found something?"

She gestured to the soft earth. "A footprint. A man's boot, I think."

Andrew studied the print and another she pointed out as well. He placed his own foot beside it, but his boot was slightly larger. "It might not be his," she murmured.

"It's the first sign of anyone we've seen all morning. You stay here, and I'll investigate." He started into the brush, following the logical path the man might have taken, even as fallen leaves obscured other prints. He should have realized she would never obey orders, but he was still surprised when he paused and she came up beside him. He frowned at her, but she ignored him and gestured ahead.

He saw the flash of color at the same moment she motioned. Moving silently now, he moved a leafy branch aside and looked into a small, man-made clearing where a red handkerchief fluttered against a tree.

Fourteen

ONE THING LILY HAD LEARNED WHEN WORKING FOR the Foreign Office was to trust her instincts. She had excellent instincts. She looked into the clearing and knew this was Lucifer's camp. He was hiding here, biding his time, waiting to strike. He'd searched the duke's library for the documents he wanted and had not found them. But he could not expect to be able to search the estate again with impunity. He had left too much evidence of his search to hope to continue acting with stealth.

And that was what concerned her. If he was no longer worried about being detected, what would the man do next? He had lost his gambling hell. If he regained the documents detailing information about the Diamonds in the Rough, he could sell that information to any number of foreign governments. He could live quite richly on the Continent at the expense of the lives of England's heroes.

Once again she reminded herself Lucifer was not her concern. He was already a wanted man for his evil deeds. The key was to prove Ravenscroft guilty of buying the names of the Diamonds and hiring men to have them killed. In that way, she was no different from Lucifer. They were searching for the same thing. The fact that Lucifer was here should damn the duke, but without a mountain of evidence, one did not accuse a powerful peer of being a traitor. At this point it was a matter of whether she or Lucifer found the evidence first. And that rivalry gave her reason to interest herself in the camp.

"We should search it," she said, moving through the opening Darlington had cleared in the trees. It was raining harder now, and as she stepped into the clearing, water plastered her hair to her forehead and ran in rivulets down her face.

"We should return to the estate and contact the proper authorities." Darlington stood rooted in place. "This is Ravenscroft land, and Lucifer, or whoever is camping here, is trespassing."

"It's Lucifer," she said. "I can feel it."

"All the more reason to return immediately."

She glanced at him. "Are you frightened?"

"No." His steady gaze told her he spoke the truth, and if she was not a spy for the Crown, she too would have gone to the local constables. But she needed information.

"I want to see if there are any clues to what he plans next."

"It won't matter," Darlington argued. "He will be sent to gaol."

She turned over a log with the toe of her boot. The ground beneath it was still fresh, indicating it had been recently moved and situated beside the fire pit. The rain had long since extinguished the fire and cooled the tinder, so she could not ascertain how recently someone had been here. "You have a great deal of faith in the Nottinghamshire patrols. The Bow Street Runners have been searching for Lucifer for months, and he's eluded even their very best."

A large swath of canvas had been stretched over a low-hanging branch to form a tent of sorts. A greatcoat and a saddle blanket, most likely from Ravenscroft's own stable, had been added to supplement the structure. Lily moved the material aside and peered inside. As she waited for her eyes to adjust to the gloom, she felt Darlington move beside her. "That wine is from the kitchens," he said, gesturing to a jug. He had good eyes. Her own were just now making out the forms and shapes.

"And I am willing to wager that flour sack has foodstuffs inside." She glanced at Darlington. "This is your thief."

"Yes, but where is he?"

"If the horse were here, we could assume he was nearby. As it stands, he could be anywhere."

"I don't like it. If this man is who you say, he is dangerous. I want you back at the house, where you will be safe."

She almost laughed. Safe? From whom? From Lucifer? He was probably stalking about the estate now. From Ravenscroft? He'd already threatened to kill her. From Darlington? One of these times he kissed her, she would not have the strength to stop him from doing more. She was as safe in this camp as she would have been anywhere else, which was to say, not safe in the least.

"I do not need a protector," she told Darlington, moving into the tent. "You brought me here, and now I want to look in this sack. Perhaps it contains more than food." She lifted the sack and prepared to dump the contents on the ground.

"I didn't bring you here for this," Darlington hissed. "If he returns now and we have to leave quickly, he will know we've been here."

He was correct. She was cold and wet and losing focus. She pawed through the pouch, pushing aside a hunk of cheese and a crust of bread, pulling a leather pouch out and opening it. "Why did you bring me here?"

"Because I didn't think you'd be safe at the estate without me."

Despite her eagerness to peer at the contents of the pouch, she couldn't stop from staring at Darlington. "Who would endanger me?"

"Lucifer. My father—"

"Your father?" she said sharply. Perhaps Darlington knew something after all.

"Might we discuss this at a more opportune time?"

"Yes. I'll be only a moment." There was something inside this pouch. Something Lucifer wanted to protect from the elements. She would look inside and then she would make Darlington tell her what he knew about his father. She could not allow his statement to pass without explanation. If he knew something that might implicate the duke, she would find it out.

She untied the pouch and lifted the flap. Inside, neatly stacked, was several hundred pounds. She rifled through the money, ignoring it, until she found a letter of transit. No, make that three letters of transit. The name on each document differed. She supposed one of these was his true name, but she did not know which. Finally, she found a crude drawing of what appeared to be Ravenscroft Castle. Lucifer was making a blueprint of the estate. It was unfinished, but a quick perusal told her he had been inside more than she had supposed.

"I hear—"

"It's a horse," she said. She'd heard it too. "We had better go now." She tucked the pouch into her blouse.

"What the devil are you doing?"

"He was foolish enough to leave it here," she whispered, pushing him out of the lean-to. "I'm not leaving him with money and a means of escape."

"Are you mad?"

"Possibly. He's close now. Hurry!" She led him to a thick grouping of trees as the hoofbeats closed in. He was walking the horse, probably leading it by the halter. There were too many low-hanging branches here to allow a man to ride. She pulled Darlington behind one of the thicker tree trunks and ducked into a crouch. Once Lucifer was busy starting the fire or tending the horse, they could sneak away.

She heard leaves moving and the sound of the horse's breathing. Around them, the rain continued to fall, making a soft and steady *whoosh* sound as it splashed against the leaves. The wind blew the higher branches and chilled her, and she huddled close to Darlington as she tried to hear where Lucifer might be.

She remembered how she had always wanted to be invisible when she was a child. Her father had once told her his job was to be invisible. She understood what he meant now. He would always be remembered as a hero. He had been one of the men to thwart the attempted invasion of England by *La Légion Noire* at Carregwastad Head near Fishguard. Cecil Dawson had indeed been a resourceful man and an asset to the Crown. She could only hope not to dishonor his reputation. And right now, her success depended on her invisibility.

But she would not rely on it, and so she withdrew a slim blade from her boot. Darlington gaped at her, but she did not look away. It was better he knew she was serious about her work, better he knew she understood danger and could counter it. Perhaps it would soften the blow when she had his father arrested. To lose two parents in one year would be hard for any man. To lose a father because the man was a traitor to his country would be devastating.

She heard a man swear, and the striking of a rock, and she nodded to Darlington. Thankfully Lucifer's first task was to start a fire. That was not an easy feat in this sort of weather, and she heard his frustration. When he gave it up, he would return to his tent and find his leather pouch missing. She did not want to be near when that happened. She replaced the dagger, and with Darlington, trekked back the way they had come, through increasingly heavier rain. Lily was soaked to the bone and knew she would be thankful for a warm fire and dry clothes.

They forded the first stream with ease. The water had risen since they'd crossed, but it was a narrow, burbling thing. When they reached the next stream, opposite where the horses were still tethered, she knew immediately they had a problem. She did not care about wading in up to her waist. She was soaked through anyway, and now the rain was pouring down in sheets, but she feared if she did wade in, she would be carried away. The stream's current was rapid, sweeping branches and large logs and even a small creature, hanging onto a fallen tree limb, downstream.

"We can't cross here," Darlington said, raising his voice so it might be heard above the sound of the storm. "It's too dangerous."

"Agreed. What should we do?"

"Find shelter."

"Most of our supplies are with the horses." She pointed across the impassable water.

"We'll find something." He motioned for her to follow him, and she tried, but her skirts were heavy with water and clung to her legs. Finally, Darlington took her arm and all but carried her away from the open space beside the stream. The rain was not as heavy under the canopy of the trees, but she was so wet, it made little difference. She shivered with cold and tried not to think about warm fires and hot tea.

And scones. She would give anything for a scone at the moment. She was famished.

She knew she should be helping Darlington, but she was weary and ready to collapse. He had dragged her into this. Perhaps it was only justice that he should have to find the way out.

"Here!" Darlington yelled, pointing to two large trees that had fallen into each other at some point years before. Their trunks formed an inverted V, which Lily could see would provide some protection from the elements. She would have preferred her bedchamber, a hot brick at her feet, and steaming chocolate in her hands, but she would take this for the present. Besides, agents for the Crown did not whine and complain.

And sometimes she was quite weary of being an agent for the Crown.

She allowed Darlington to drag her under the inadequate shelter, pulled her shawl over her head, and crouched down. She expected him to do the same, but he scurried about, appearing to gather fallen branches and handfuls of leaves. It did not take long for her to ascertain what he was doing. He spread some of the leaves at her feet, making a sort of soft place for her to rest, and arranged the branches over her head to fortify the shelter. Within a quarter of an hour, the structure was really quite tolerable. She made room for him when he finally joined her, and leaned back against one of the tree trunks, closing her eyes.

"You're shivering, and your lips are blue," he said.

"I've been told I look good in blue." She would not begin complaining and feeling sorry for herself now. If she started, she would not be able to stop. She was also perilously close to tears, and crying was absolutely out of the question.

"You must be the strongest woman I know," he said, awe in his voice. She opened her eyes. "You have not uttered one word of complaint or protest."

"I assure you, I have cursed you and the heavens in my thoughts without ceasing."

"As well you should. I was wrong to drag you with me."

She laughed. "You are quick to admit when you are wrong, my lord. I do admire that trait. I only wish you would come to these conclusions *before* you make the mistakes." She closed her eyes again and felt them burn with exhaustion.

"As do I. But I wouldn't have found Lucifer alone."

She suspected he would have, and probably much more quickly. After what she'd seen, she was reasonably certain the man causing trouble at Ravenscroft Castle was indeed Lucifer. And perhaps she had stalled his escape by taking his papers and his blunt. Perhaps the travel papers would provide the Bow Street Runners with evidence or a clue to assist them in his capture, should he elude the authorities in Nottinghamshire.

"I've asked this before, but I hope I have earned your trust since then. What is it Lucifer seeks?"

She opened her eyes. Looking at him, his hair shaggy and disordered from shaking off the excess water and running his hands through it, his eyes as weary as hers, and his skin pale with cold, she knew she could trust him. And she also knew it was time to tell him the truth.

"I am here on behalf of the Crown."

He nodded. "I had thought as much, but I didn't realize women worked in that service."

"That is why we are so effective. There are very few of us, and I was chosen because my father was a spy. I inherited many of his skills."

Darlington frowned. "So you're a spy? Like Fitzhugh?"

"I've never been abroad, but from time to time the Foreign Office asks me to collect information on a person of interest."

"That's rather brilliant of them." The rain finally slowed to a steady drizzle, and they were able to speak without shouting. "You do meet everyone and go everywhere. No one would suspect you had any motive other than pleasure if you flirt with a foreign ambassador or a French émigré." That was accurate, but Darlington was skirting her true mission here. "And that is why you have continued to masquerade as an Impure. I wondered why you would keep up the pretense, especially after your friends retired."

She nodded. "My lord, I wonder—"

"Andrew. With all we have been through, it's time you called me Andrew. I already call you Lily."

She had called him *Andrew* many times in private, silently in her mind, but now she did not know if speaking his name aloud, if agreeing to such familiarity was a good idea. Her emotions for him were already precariously close to the surface. More steps toward intimacy were to be avoided. "You may not want me to be so familiar when you understand my true reason for being here."

"Go on." He did not look concerned, but he had not fit all of the pieces together yet.

"I do not always collect information on foreign dignitaries and émigrés. Sometimes one of our own is accused of treason." She saw the moment he understood her point. She watched the hardness creep about his mouth and the corners of his eyes, almost as though he had gazed at Medusa and was slowly turning to stone.

"You think you have evidence my father has done something treasonous."

She nodded. "I was sent to collect undeniable proof. In London, and when I first arrived, I found it difficult to believe your father could be guilty, but Lucifer's presence here has changed my mind. Lucifer would not be here if your father did not have what he wanted."

"You have said as much before—that my father possessed something Lucifer wants. I imagine there are any number of items a duke possesses that a criminal like Lucifer would covet."

Of course Darlington—Andrew—would say as much. Would she love him if he was less loyal, less eager to defend his family? "Lucifer believes the items he seeks belong to him. They were stolen and sold. Lucifer killed the thief. He could kill again."

"What items were stolen?"

"I am here to discern that information. We know names and dossiers on the Diamonds in the Rough were taken, but there must be more."

"Who are the Diamonds in the Rough?"

"The Diamonds in the Rough were five elite agents for the Crown. They are largely credited with supplying the information that led to Bonaparte's eventual defeat and exile."

"And you think my father has information on these men—these spies?"

"All that and more, yes. This information would not have come cheaply."

The rain had finally stopped, and the skies were slowly clearing, but Darlington's face held the thunderclouds now. "I understand it would take a man with vast resources to pay the price most likely demanded. But my father is not the only man in the country with a large fortune. You cannot arbitrarily accuse him of this."

She fought for patience, fought not to feel insulted. "It is not arbitrary. One of the Diamonds caught a man trying to kill him—an assassin. When questioned about his employer, the man said it was a gentleman who promised him three rubies as big as his fist."

Darlington's eyes widened, and Lily knew she had the answer she wanted.

⁂

Andrew knew there had to be some mistake. Those rubies had been in his family for centuries. His father would never part with them, especially not to pay some thug to kill a group of spies who had nothing whatsoever to do with the duke or the family.

"I see you've heard of the rubies," Lily said. He glanced at her and winced. She resembled a drowned mouse. With her hair wet and clinging to her pale face, she looked young and vulnerable. She was shivering, and he moved closer to share body heat. Not that he was much warmer. He would have given her his coat, but it was as damp and cold as the rest of their clothing.

"They are part of the Ravenscroft legacy," he said. "They are not a secret, but I find it improbable that my father would have promised them to a thug on the street."

"What else would he have to offer?" Lily asked. "I beg your pardon, but I was obliged to research your family's finances. There is money held in trust for you and for Lady Emma, but the money that was not protected is gone."

Andrew felt his indignation rise. How dare she pry into something so personal? And how dare she misrepresent the family's situation! "You are mistaken. It is true the estate revenues have been down the past few years, but a few good crops and a bit of renovation on some of the cottages will bring in capital and an increase in rents."

She shook her head. "This loss is far more than one or two good crops can repair."

"Do you have experience in managing an estate?" he demanded. "You should stick to what you know."

"Andrew." She touched his shoulder, and he barely tolerated her hand. "I know you dislike the mention of finances."

"It is not done."

"And that is why you do not know the situation. I do not imagine you would ask your father about his management of the estate, but the Crown has documents that prove your father lost enormous sums on war speculation. He bet against his own country, and he lost."

"That cannot be correct." But her words triggered something in his mind. He remembered how angry his father had been when Bonaparte had been defeated. At the time Andrew had been preoccupied with his own concerns—mainly winning the lovely Duchess of Dalliance—but now his father's unpatriotic sentiments stood out.

"Are you certain?" she asked. "I saw copies of the

schemes he partook in, and I also paid a call on your father's banker in London."

"He wouldn't have spoken to you."

She smiled. "I am not charming you now, but I will remind you, I earned my sobriquet."

Andrew felt violated. He did not know why, as he had done nothing wrong. He had never been what some might call economical, but he generally lived within his means. In any case, he did not gamble away the money he owed for his rents or buy more waistcoats than he could afford simply to look fashionable. He had six thousand a year, and he managed his income well.

But he had been concerned to see Ravenscroft Castle fall into disrepair. He considered it a byproduct of his mother's death, but the damage was too great to have progressed so quickly. Perhaps the real problem was that his father did not have the funds to make the necessary repairs or hire the requisite number of servants.

He shook his head. No, whatever disdainful qualities his father possessed, he was not a traitor. "My father is a loyal Englishman," he said. "We fought with Henry V at Agincourt, and in the Wars of the Roses. The duke would not have invested in schemes that would harm England, and he would not finance the murder of English agents."

"Then why is Lucifer here?"

"You tell me!" Andrew stood. This conversation was ridiculous. He would have stomped home except he remembered the stream. He could have forded it. He was strong, but Lily could not make it, and no matter the accusations she made, he would not abandon her in the woods.

"I don't have the documents with me," she said, "but I would not lie to you."

He gaped at her. "You've lied about everything! You are an agent for the Crown, not a courtesan."

She glared back at him. "I told you before I was not a courtesan, and keeping my true reason for being here was a necessary omission. But when you have asked me questions directly, I told you the truth. I told you about my son."

He was not going anywhere, so he sat beside her again. He did not want to hear what she would say next, but by the same token, he knew he must listen.

"You know something," she said. "I see it in your face. I've said something that hits close to the mark."

He clenched his jaw and did not answer. He would confront his father. This was a matter to be dealt with in private, within the confines of his family.

"Lucifer will stop at nothing to reclaim the documents pertaining to the Diamonds in the Rough. He has resorted to murder before, and he will do it again. For that reason, I am thankful Lady Emma will be sent away. But no one is safe—not you, not your father, not the staff. I cannot help you if you will not help me."

"You have no intention of helping. You want to accuse my father of treason."

"Your father is *guilty* of treason. Once I find the evidence that proves as much, I will turn it over to my superiors. My job is to protect the agents of the Crown. Already your friend Fitzhugh has been the target of several attacks. He may not survive the next one."

"Even if what you say is true"—and he had a sinking feeling some of what she said had merit—"why would my father want to kill these men? Why would he promise them jewels that have been in our family for generations?"

She looked down. "I don't know."

"But you have a theory."

She glanced up, and her green eyes were filled with pain. "You don't want to hear this."

It was too late for that. Far too late. He needed to know all of it now. "Tell me."

"I suspect your father is the notorious assassin, Artemis. He killed valuable British agents during the war, but the Diamonds in the Rough always eluded him. I think he wants to prove he can kill them to bolster his pride and line his pockets."

"For profit?"

She hesitated, and he could see she did not want to say more. He grasped her wrist to keep her from moving away.

"Profit?" he asked again.

"The French have been defeated, but we have other enemies. The Diamonds in the Rough are the best we have. If they are killed, or worse, captured, Britain's intelligence community will be hobbled."

Darlington shook his head, but it was more out of horror than denial now.

"We know there are traitors in the Foreign Office. Fitzhugh tracked and captured the man who sold the identities of the Diamonds to Lucifer. There will be others. If so, your father may have been approached by these men. It is vital we question your father and have him order the cessation of the attacks on the Diamonds."

Her hand shook as she spoke, more out of passion now than cold. The rain had ceased, and patches of her hair had actually begun to dry. He had never seen this aspect of her before. He had never thought of her in any role other than that of seductress. But clearly she was clever and brave.

Andrew was not certain he had the courage to travel alone to the enemy's lair, to risk discovery and the accompanying perils. And for what? Loyalty to King and country? She could have no other motive. Quite suddenly, he felt ashamed. He had not fought in the war. He had not cared what happened to the men who did, not really. Casualty numbers meant little to him. He had always cared for his own pleasures, and as the heir to a dukedom, he had been safe from inconveniences like war. Had he ever done anything for his country? Had he been living with a traitor and not even known?

If these accusations were true, he could save his father. He could expose her and alert his father to cover his tracks. Lily knew this. He could see in the wary manner she watched him that she knew he had the upper hand. And she had risked telling him anyway.

"I'll help you," he said. "I'll help you find the evidence you need."

"No one is asking you to betray your own father," she said, turning his grip on her wrist so she cupped his hand in both of hers.

"And if he is a traitor, and if he orders the deaths of these men and profits from it, am I supposed to revel in one day being a beneficiary of that treachery?"

"The scandal on your family, if he is found guilty, will be all but insurmountable."

"In that case," he said, "my cooperation may be the only way to save the dukedom."

She nodded. "You do your family service."

"No. I have not. I have not served my country either, but that is going to change." He lifted his free hand and cupped her cold cheek. "I admire you, Lily, and now that I know your true purpose for being here, it is impossible for me to allow you to continue unprotected."

"I can take care of myself," she said, straightening her back and all but bristling at the idea that she couldn't.

"I know you can, but I can take care of you too." He leaned close to her, brushing his mouth against hers. "Let me."

Fifteen

She froze, not sure how to respond to Darlington's kiss. She wanted to kiss him back, but was this some sort of deception? She had just told him his father was a traitor. He should have hated her. Instead, he praised her and kissed her.

As he wrapped his warm arms around her cold body, she melted into the welcome heat of him. She was so cold, inside and out. When he touched her, she realized how much she missed this sort of simple human contact. She tended to avoid physical contact since the night Sinclair found her, broken and bleeding. It was different with Darlington. When he touched her, he set her on fire. Now she craved that heat.

She did not regret what had transpired between them. He'd shown her she could take pleasure in the physical aspects of a relationship, but how would she feel if he wanted more? They were not married, he had not proposed, and she did not want to bear another child out of wedlock. She could not allow him any further intimacy.

Slowly, gently, Darlington pulled away and cupped

her face in his hands. She was warm now—from his lips and the closeness of his body. His hands were flooding heat into her chilled cheeks. His dark eyes studied her face with an intensity she hadn't thought he was capable of. "I've never felt like this before," he said, his voice so low she almost thought she imagined his words. "I've never known a woman like you."

His tenderness overwhelmed her, punctured her defenses. "I've always been in love with you," she said. "You know that."

"Despite my frequent lapses into idiocy."

"Despite those." She laughed. "Perhaps because of them."

"I want you," he told her, his fingers tensing slightly on her tender flesh. "I know this is not the place." He gestured to the woods, where the leaves glistened around them from the recent rain and the glimmer of late afternoon sun peeking through the clouds. "I feel as though I've waited an eternity to have you, Lily. Let me come to you tonight."

She shook her head. "I cannot. I know that sounds ridiculous coming from a so-called courtesan, but I do not want another child. I made that mistake once, and I will not repeat it."

"I know precautions."

Lily had heard of these precautions. One did not associate with courtesans and ladies of ill-repute for long without learning something about the ways in which one prevented the birth of unwanted children. But whether or not he possessed French letters or knew of some other method, a child was only part of the issue.

He sat back, releasing her cheeks. "If your feelings have changed—"

"No." Her entire being mourned the loss of his touch. "My feelings haven't changed, and please do not think this is some scheme to force you to propose marriage. I know who you are and what your responsibilities entail." No man of noble birth would ever want her.

"Then what is it?"

She studied the damp ground beneath them, lifting a small stick and pushing it about to form various designs. Could she tell him? Could she confide in this man what she had confided to no one? Lord and Lady Sinclair had rescued her, but they had not asked questions. They undoubtedly knew she had sinned, but once she entered their house, it was as though a new life had begun. She was no longer that girl.

She glanced up at Andrew, sighed at the tender way in which he watched her. She should tell him if only to turn that tender look into one of disdain. He would not want her when she revealed the truth. And that would make it easier for her to give him up for good.

"You don't know me like you think you do," she said to begin. "You don't know the truth about me."

"I know you are smart, brave, and resilient. I know how I feel about you. How I feel when I am with you. What else need I know?"

"After the birth of my child, I had nowhere to go. My parents had disowned me."

"What about Lady Sinclair?"

She shook her head. She often perpetuated the misinformation that she had known the earl and countess for years, because she did not want to speak the truth. "I did not know the countess then, and my mother had turned her back on me. I don't blame her. I had disgraced my family. I had no one to blame but myself."

"And yet it seems kindness and loyalty should win over reputation."

"You say that because someone in your station can afford a little scandal. You can survive a scandal. My family's position was one step away from ruin. Creditors could call in debts. My father could have lost his position. The landlord might have turned us out."

"I see."

She doubted that, but she knew he tried, at least.

"I had the baby in a charity hospital, surrounded by the other women who had nowhere else to go. And then I had nowhere else to go. I had no money, no skills, no connections. A few days after the birth, I was told there was no more room for me."

She'd wandered the cold streets, still sore and bleeding, taking what charity she was offered, sleeping in doorways or church graveyards. The only thing she had cared about was her child. Somehow she had to care for him, provide for him, protect him. "I stole and I cheated and I—I did all manner of things I'm not proud of, but I cared for my baby. And then it began to rain. It rained for a week, and I had no protection. I huddled on stoops when I could, and I begged passersby to spare something so I could give my child shelter."

She'd begged, her dirty hand extended toward those more fortunate, those who passed her by and pretended not to see her. She'd known hunger and cold and desperation.

"One night an older woman passed us. She barely glanced at me—and then she came back." There was something caught in her throat, but she ignored the way it tightened, and soldiered on. "She took me inside a coffeehouse, bought me food and drink, and she told me about her daughter, a married woman who was barren. She talked and talked about her child and the girl's husband, and I didn't understand at first. I was so hungry. All I cared about was the food and keeping my little baby dry, but then she put twenty pounds on the table. I think I almost fell over. It was a fortune to me then. I would give her my child, and she would give me money. No questions." Save one. The woman had asked for her name. Her real name.

"Lily." Andrew's hand on her arm tightened, but she couldn't look at him.

"I took it. I was so weary. I knew I couldn't go on much longer. I sold my child." She looked into his eyes now. "What kind of person does that?"

She wanted to see condemnation, expected it, but his face showed only anguish.

"It must have been difficult to let him go."

She waved her hand, because if she spoke of that now, she would never be able to continue. She could not think of losing that small defenseless child to an uncertain future. She could not bear to remember having that part of herself, a part she had nurtured and grown with her own flesh and blood for months. The child who had been with her constantly, who had moved within her, his little flutters and kicks and hiccups her constant companion during the loneliest time in her life.

No, she would not think of that now.

"He was safe, or so I prayed, but I was lost." She'd considered just stepping off a bridge into the Thames, ending it all. Her child was gone. Another woman held him in her arms, smelled his sweet hair, rocked him to sleep. Her family had abandoned her. She was as good as dead to them. But as she'd stood on London Bridge and stared at the rushing water below, she could not make herself take the last step. She wanted to live. She wanted to believe the world had something more for her than this miserable, invisible existence.

And then she'd stepped back onto the bridge and laughed so hard she'd clutched her empty belly. She had always wanted to be invisible. One should be careful of wishes.

She'd been robbed not long after—that precious money gone—and she'd gone back to desperation. She'd resorted to selling her hair, though the price was not very good. Blond hair was prized above her unfashionable red. And then one night she'd been jarred awake by a man's stale breath and his heavy body. She'd been sleeping in the doorway of a church. Sometimes the vicars were kind and let her sleep inside. Not this one, and she was vulnerable and exposed.

She tried to fight the man, but she was weak from lack of food and groggy from sleep. The pain and the terror and the humiliation had been more than she could take, and she'd gone away in her head for a little while. Even now, years later and miles and miles away, she could not make herself go back there. Not completely.

But she remembered that when he'd finished, he'd tossed her a coin before doing up his breeches and walking away. She'd eaten the next day.

She felt the burn of tears behind her eyes and looked away. She could not look at Darlington as she told him what must come next. "I had fallen as low as I could. Used and left for dead. But I took that money. I had no other choice," she whispered. "I should have died, but I was stubborn. I wanted to live."

"Lily." His voice was anguished, and he pulled her into his arms. She tensed, certain he had not understood her. Why would he be holding her? Shame and mortification heated her cheeks all these years later when she thought of how she'd sold her child, how she'd been raped, but instead of fighting, she'd taken the money as though she were a common whore.

She pulled back and forced herself to look at Andrew's handsome face. It was the face she had dreamed of beside her, the face that, not so long ago, she had lain in her soft, cold bed and wished were there with her. The face she knew she could never have.

And perhaps that was why she'd chosen him. He did not want her, and she was safe. She could love him from afar and never have to fear she would shrink from his touch as she'd learned to shrink from men on the streets of London.

"You don't understand. I sold my child." There, she'd said it. Before today, she'd never said it aloud, and now she'd admitted it twice. She could feel her face flaming, but she went on. She had to tell him all of it now. "I could have fought for my child, fought that man off, but I didn't."

She watched him, waited for the disgust, but his
face showed only compassion, much as the Earl of
Sinclair's had the night he'd found her.

"Lily, Lily," he whispered, and took her in his arms,
enveloping her in his warmth. The way he said her
name... it was almost as though she were as precious
as the flower she'd been named after. But she was
soiled. Ruined.

She pulled back, out of Darlington's arms. "How
can you touch me? I told you what I did."

"You were a child. You did what you must in
order to survive. And, if you recall, I touched you
before, when I thought you were a courtesan."

She shook her head. "That's different."

"Why? Because the beds are softer and the protectors wear silk and brocade? Do you know one reason
I held onto my infatuation—" She began to protest,
but he cut her off. "Yes, it was an infatuation. I know
that now. But I clung to it because I wanted to save
her. I thought I could take her away from that life, the
life of an Impure."

"You couldn't have hoped to marry her," Lily
said, astonished. But if she was honest with herself,
and there often seemed so little reason to be honest,
she knew there was a flicker of hope in her words. A
flicker for herself.

"I don't know what I thought, what I hoped. And
I don't know what you went through, but thank God
you found a way out."

"I don't understand."

"We can both agree I am no saint," Darlington
admitted with a smile. His thumb stroked her cheek

reverently. "I'm no one to judge. How did you escape it? How did you become a 'diamond of the first water'?"

"The Earl of Sinclair."

"Your protector."

"My savior," she corrected. "Both the earl and the countess. He found me, broken and bleeding, brought me home, and she took me in. Juliette and Fallon were already there. I told them I was from York, because I didn't want them to search for my family in London. I don't know if the countess believed it, but she never asked me any questions. She must have suspected something."

There was no question Lily was, at the very least, a fallen woman. She remembered she'd stood in Lord and Lady Sinclair's vestibule, marveling at the soaring ceiling and the enormous curved staircase. The footmen had stood so straight, so regal. They pretended they didn't even see her. She hadn't wanted to be seen. She'd been dressed in rags. Her hair—the little she had left—had been dirty and matted, and she had blood on her face from a blow she'd been given by a man she had fought off.

That was when Sinclair had found her. She'd stumbled into a dark corner in an alley, not really looking where she was going. She was burning with fever by then and so weak she could not think. She'd known she was ill, that she needed proper food and sleep, but she could hardly afford the most meager provisions. She'd lain down on the cold pavement and closed her eyes. She would probably have died there if the earl's coachman hadn't seen her and tried to shoo her away.

The earl had returned as she struggled to her feet, the coachman urging her to move along.

But instead of turning away from her, the earl had lent an arm for support and given her his handkerchief to wipe away the blood on her lip.

She'd stared at him, not understanding. "What do you want?" she asked.

"Nothing a'tall, my dear," the tall, slim, white-haired man had said in his deep, gentle voice. "Allow me to show you this kindness. I assure you, you will owe me nothing in return."

"Ha!" She'd laughed in his face and pressed the handkerchief back into his hand. She would not soil the fine linen with her stink. "I am not that naïve." Not anymore.

"Madam, I assure you I speak the truth."

She narrowed her eyes. No one had ever called her *madam*.

"His lordship speaks the truth," the coachman volunteered. "You can trust him."

Lily had looked from the coachman to the gentle-man, took a deep breath, and nodded. She'd pressed the clean, fresh-smelling linen to her mouth and accepted the coachman's hand as she climbed into the carriage. When she saw the velvet squabs inside, she said, "I should ride outside with the coachman. I'll spoil your seats."

"I'll not hear of it," the man said. "You are cold, and you will come inside. I have a blanket and a warm brick for your feet. I could care less about a little dirt."

She was so unused to kindness of any sort at that point that all she could do was gape at him. Finally, she'd climbed inside and sank into the seats. She was asleep within moments, letting her guard down, which was not like her. The earl had shaken her gently awake when they'd arrived at his Mayfair residence, and she'd stumbled inside, stumbled to another life.

She looked at Darlington now. "The countess did not so much as blink at me."

"She must be a kind woman, despite all appearances to the contrary."

Lily laughed. "She does have a way of making sure her wishes are followed. God knows I never had a chance. She marshaled Fallon, Juliette, and me into ladies, though it must have been a trial. Fallon, in particular, had no idea how to behave. I at least knew the basics."

"You were born to be a lady," Darlington said, his hand touching her hair. "Even now, soaking wet and covered with dirt, you look every bit the part."

Lily rolled her eyes. "They do not call you 'the Darling of the *Ton*' for nothing."

"Actually, no one calls me that anymore. Not since I called all my former friends empty-headed fops and publicly accused my father of lechery. And, of course, I insulted the *ton*'s favorite Fashionable Impure."

"Juliette?"

He tapped her nose. "You."

She did not know what to think of this new interest in her. She had wanted his attention for so long that she could scarce believe she actually had it now. And what would she do with it? After what she'd been through, could she go to bed with a man and not remember that horrible violation years ago?

He stood and offered his hand. "We should return. The rain has slackened enough that the water in the stream should have returned to its previous levels."

She took his hand and stood, suddenly eager to return to Ravenscroft Castle. Now that she had Darlington's support, she would have more access to the duke's private rooms. That should make the search faster. All she needed was proof Ravenscroft was involved in the scheme against the Diamonds in the Rough, and the Crown could take action.

They started back toward the stream, she holding his hand in a comfortable intimacy. How strange that this contact should feel so natural when, in the past, she had lived for weeks on one smile directed at her or one brush against his arm. Darlington moved aside a low-hanging branch so they might pass without having to duck. Standing on the other side was a smiling Lucifer.

❦

From Lily's gasp, Andrew surmised the man standing before them was not there to wish them well. A closer look revealed him to resemble the description she'd given of Lucifer. "Lord Darlington," the man said with a smooth, deep voice. There was something ominous about his tone. "And the Countess of Charm." He gave Lily a nod. "I wondered why you were here, but your little conversation with the earl was enlightening."

He felt her hand tighten in his. If this Lucifer had overheard their conversation, he knew everything.

"I should have taken the opportunity to kill you when I first saw you arrive. I knew leaving you alive was a mistake." He lifted a pistol. "I won't make the same mistake twice."

Everything happened in a blur. Lily pulled her hand out of Andrew's and shoved him aside. Andrew protested, but his words were swallowed by the sound of the ball exploding from the pistol. He fell to the ground, realizing Lily had pushed him to safety. She'd pushed him out of the way, leaving herself in the path of danger. He rolled down an incline before he could catch himself and jump to his feet again. By then, Lily was wrestling with the man, her hands around his wrist, keeping the pistol pointed toward the sky.

He scrambled up the slick, leafy ground, wondering what the hell the woman thought she was doing. As he watched, she kicked Lucifer deftly between the legs, and when he doubled over, she yanked the pistol from his hand and smashed it over his head. Lucifer staggered back and down even as Andrew reached Lily.

She grabbed his hand, still holding Lucifer's pistol in the other. "Let's go!"

Andrew could see Lucifer was still conscious and struggling to his feet. He was going to want retribution. Still, if she had not been there, he would have stood his ground.

How had she learned to fight like that? Andrew didn't think he could have managed it any better. If he'd had any doubts as to what she was before, he did not doubt it now. He followed her back toward the stream, eventually passing her and clearing the way for the two of them. He didn't hear any signs of pursuit, but Lucifer would come after them, given half an opportunity.

When they reached the stream, he was dismayed by how high the water remained. It would still be a struggle to cross it and reach the waiting horses. But Lily, God love her, didn't even flinch. She threw off her boots and tied up the long skirts of her habit. Andrew removed his boots as well, knowing they would only weigh him down. He tossed his and hers to the other side of the stream, but his aim failed on the last of her boots, and the water caught it, causing it to rush away with the fast-moving current. He gave her a sheepish look. "Sorry."

"It's not important," she said, and stepped into the water. Her face betrayed nothing but determination as she started across, fighting the strong current. He stepped in behind her and gasped at the freezing water. He wanted to whimper, but he gritted his teeth and pushed on. He kept his gaze on Lily, determined to catch her if the stream should snatch her away. A rock landed beside his right shoulder, and he turned to see Lucifer standing behind them. The man was not fool enough to wade into the waist-high water, but he was lifting stones and hurling them into the stream. His next volley was more accurate, and Andrew cursed the blow to his back.

"Here." Lily thrust the pistol into Darlington's hand. "Throw this. Do not miss."

Andrew turned and ducked another incoming stone. Then he braced himself against the current and took aim with the pistol. Lucifer raised another rock, quite a large one, and Andrew hoped his weapon hit first. He launched the pistol and watched as it arced over the water. Lucifer deftly sidestepped it and threw his rock. His aim was slightly off, or Andrew's head would have been flattened. As it was, his shoulder exploded with pain.

He felt Lily's arms around him, pulling him toward the stream's bank even as he wanted to sink down and recover. But she dragged him across, fighting the undercurrent and his weight, until they finally reached the shallower waters. A stone missed him and hit her upper arm, but she just hissed in a breath and pulled him up beside her. Lucifer pitched another rock, and his aim was good—much better than Andrew's had been. But the distance was greater now. Still, Andrew did not relish waiting for the moment when Lucifer's aim improved, and he forced himself to his feet, and with Lily hobbling barefoot at his side, ran for the horses.

They danced and whinnied, obviously glad to see their humans after having been left in the cold and the rain for so long. Andrew took a moment to soothe his mount and then Lily's. "A dry stable and an extra ration of oats await you," he promised. The trees offered them some protection, but Andrew did not intend to wait around for Lucifer to find a way to reach them. He helped Lily mount and then climbed into his own saddle.

By the time they reached the stable, he was shivering so badly he could hardly hold onto the reins. Lily looked as though she fared little better. He gave his reins to a groom, jumped down, and caught her as she slid off her horse. "I'm fine," she said, her voice little more than a whisper.

"You're not fine. I'm taking you inside."

"There's no need to carry me." Even as she spoke the words, she turned her head into his coat, and he felt her body relax. She was exhausted and on the verge of collapse. He carried her across the lawns until he reached the doors of Ravenscroft Castle. The butler must have seen them coming, because he had the door open before they reached the steps. "My lord!"

Andrew shook his head, not wanting the man's sympathy at the moment. "Where is my father?"

"Dining with his guests. It is past the dinner hour."

Andrew ignored the censure in the man's voice. "Find Miss Dawson's maid and order her to tend to her mistress. Have footmen bring hot water and a tub to her room."

The butler frowned. "The footmen are serving at His Grace's table, and Cook is preparing the last courses."

"Then heat it and bring it yourself. If you need my help to carry it, I am at your service."

"My lord!" the butler said, shock in his voice. But Andrew ignored him, starting for the stairs and Lily's room. She was pale and cold, and if he didn't warm her soon, she would catch her death. His own weariness pressed upon him like a boulder by the time he reached her room. Though she was light, he was out of breath. He nudged the door open with his foot and carried her inside, laying her on the chaise longue instead of the bed so her wet garments would not dampen the sheets and coverlet. He grabbed the poker and stoked the fire in the hearth, taking an extra moment to warm his numb fingers, and then turned back to her. She stirred, opening her eyes.

"Did I fall asleep? Is Lucifer—?"

"We're back at the house, and we are safe." For now. "I've had the butler fetch your maid, but we must change you out of these wet things."

"I can do it." She struggled to her feet and pulled ineffectively at her fastenings, which were all in back. Of course, she could not reach them. Andrew turned her and began loosening the garment.

"My lord, you shouldn't—"

"This is no time for propriety, and you are a courtesan, for God's sake. I won't ruin your reputation."

"Yes, my lord, but your father would not like this."

"He can go to hell, and stop calling me *my lord*." He pulled the riding habit down over her shoulders, freeing her arms, and pushing the heavy material to the floor in a damp puddle. "If I am going to help you in this endeavor—and I am already in too deep, so do not argue—then you will at least have the common courtesy to call me *Andrew*."

"Is that common courtesy? And here I thought titles were all the crack." She sounded bemused, but he ignored it because she was also shivering. His cold fingers made untying her petticoats difficult, but he persisted, wondering, not for the first time, why women wore so many undergarments. Despite the gloom and chill in the air today, it was summer. Finally, she stood in her shift and stockings, which when he bent to remove them, he saw were ruined beyond repair.

"I can do the rest," she said.

He lifted the hem of her shift, looking for the fastening of her garter. "I'm almost finished. I—" He touched the bare flesh of her thigh, and she gasped. He realized his fingers were colder than her skin here. He also realized she was virtually nude before him, the wet shift concealing nothing, and he had his hand on her naked thigh.

He looked up at her, trying very hard not to allow his gaze to linger on the damp material clinging to her breasts, the dark aureoles of which were clearly visible. He rose, slowly, allowing her hem to drop, though he would have rather dragged the garment over her head. "I badly want to kiss you right now," he said, standing so close their bodies almost touched.

"I don't think that would be a wise idea." Her voice was breathless, her eyes large and dark.

"No one has ever accused me of possessing wisdom. Allow me to kiss you. Please." He felt a fool for begging, but he wanted her permission. He'd taken too much from her in the past, this woman who'd had so few choices of her own. He wanted her to choose him. He wanted her to come to him. He could make her forget the past. He knew he could. But it would have to be her decision and on her terms.

"Please?" She reached out and touched his face, her fingertips light and tender. "How silly that word sounds on your lips."

"Then do not make me beg."

"Andrew…"

His name on her tongue all but undid him. He stopped himself from wrapping his arms about her only by grasping her wrist and pulling it to his mouth. He kissed it gently, darting his tongue out to taste her skin; then with his gaze fastened on her face, he trailed his lips to her palm, opening her fingers and teasing the inside of her hand with his teeth and tongue. She stared at him, her face flushed and her breath rapid, and he stared back, wondering what she would say, what she would do. Praying she would allow him to kiss her, hold her, love her.

"Ahem."

Andrew spun around and saw Lily's maid in the doorway. She was looking at the floor, pretending she did not see what was happening.

"Anna!" Lily stepped away from him as though she were an errant child, not a notorious courtesan. "Do come in."

"Yes, madam. The servants are bringing a tub and water. Shall I find your robe?"

"Please."

Andrew backed away, feeling the dampness of his own garments now. "I will leave you to your ablutions."

Her gaze met his, and there was something in her eyes he didn't recognize. "An—my lord, perhaps we could speak later?"

He nodded. "I am at your disposal."

He stepped out as the hip bath was brought in, and made his way to the other wing of the house and his own rooms. This time he would wait for her to come to him.

He was still thinking of her, his mind back in her chambers, when another form stepped before him. "There you are."

Sixteen

"Emma?" Andrew frowned. "Is anything the matter?"

"No, but..." She wore a robe and a cap on her hair and looked as though she were ready for bed. "Would you come into my room for a moment? I want to say good-bye."

He searched his memory for details. She was leaving early in the morning for his sister Katherine's home, where she would stay for the remainder of the summer. His sister lived a relatively easy distance, and Andrew had sent a runner to her house with a letter explaining the situation. Katherine had agreed to take Emma in once she understood Andrew wanted their young sibling safely away from the Kwirleys of his father's acquaintance.

He stepped into her room, spotting several trunks and valises stacked to one side. Her governess was closing one of the trunks, but she nodded at him and wordlessly stepped into the dressing room to give them privacy.

"I did not know if I would see you in the morning," she said. "I leave quite early."

"I am glad you found me."

"You were gone most of the day. I would hug you, but…" She gestured to his damp, soiled clothing.

He smiled. "I was caught in the rain." As he spoke, he glanced about her room. He could not remember the last time he had been inside, but he thought it had changed very little. It was still the room of a child, adorned with ribbons and lace. Dolls and porcelain figures were scattered among books and texts. He looked at her again, suddenly feeling a pang of loss. "I will miss you."

Her brows rose. "Will you?"

"Of course. I only want you to be safe."

"I know."

"It is not safe for you here. His Grace is too busy with his fun to realize that."

"He never paid much attention to me, in any case. You were his heir. The rest of us were incidental."

Andrew stared at her. Was that how she had felt? Was that how Katherine felt? On impulse, he reached out and hugged Emma hard. He should have been a better friend. He should have been a better brother. He would make it up to her.

"Andrew?" she asked, her voice muffled against his coat. "Will I really be coming back?"

"Of course. This is temporary."

"How long will I stay with Katherine?"

He could not answer her. A fortnight if his father was innocent of Lily's accusations. The guests would be gone by then, and it would be safe for Emma to return. But if his father was guilty… "I do not know. But you will return."

She sighed. "I suppose I will have to trust you." She leaned back and gave his coat a grimace. "Did you roll in horse manure? You smell horrid."

"Are you certain you caught a good enough whiff?" He grabbed her neck and wrestled her face into his damp, and truth be told, smelly coat.

"Stop! No!"

"You should smell my boots."

She was fighting him and laughing, and he was laughing too. He felt once again like an older brother.

"You're disgusting!" she exclaimed, breaking free. "Go take a bath."

He did as she bade him, returning to his room and ordering his valet to secure a tub and water. Of course, he had to wait. All the hot water had been procured for Lily, and so it was several hours before he was able to dress in clean clothing. Dinner was long over, and he did not intend to make an appearance in the drawing room. Instead, he dressed in trousers and a loose shirt, forgoing a cravat or a coat. He nibbled a light supper of grapes, bread, and cheese, and drank from an expensive bottle of wine he'd pilfered from the cellar before the house party had begun. Several letters from acquaintances and associates in London had arrived, and he was thumbing through those, idly opening and reading any that caught his interest, when he heard a tap on the door.

He didn't even look up when it opened to admit his valet. "You can retire for the evening, Phibbs. I won't need you."

"I wasn't aware I needed your permission."

That was not Phibbs's voice. He looked up slowly,

hoping his ears had not tricked him. But no, she was standing there alone, dressed in a deep purple gown and lovely as the sunset on a clear summer night. He didn't invite her in, but neither did he protest when she stepped inside and closed his door. His heart was pounding, and his fingers had begun to tremble, making the letter he held shake. He set it down. "You look much recovered."

"I am. You look better as well."

He nodded and waited for her to speak, but she said nothing further. "Do you want—?" he began at the same time she said, "I came because—"

"Go ahead."

"No, you first, my lord."

"It's Andrew."

She smiled at that. "I came because everyone is in the drawing room, playing cards. Anna says the stakes are high tonight, and the company is quite engrossed. They should be at it a while. Now might be a good time to search your father's private chambers."

"You came to ask for my assistance?"

She shrugged. "You did offer it. If you want the truth, I am at a loss. I have searched the library and his bedroom and found nothing. I do not know where else to look."

"I do." He crossed to the window and parted the draperies. The long summer hours meant the sun set later, and though it was clearly evening, the sky was still streaked blue. "But I'll wait until full dark. The place I have in mind is not inside the house, and anyone in the drawing room who looked out a window would have a clear view of me."

"Where are we going?"

He glanced back at her. "You are staying in your room. Lucifer is out there. I don't want you in danger."

She pulled a small pistol inlaid with sapphires from a hidden pocket. He remembered it from the time he had rescued her outside London. "I am no fainting miss. And you are not leaving me behind."

He cocked a brow. "Do you even know how to work that toy?"

"It is not a toy."

"No?" He made a swift move and snatched it away from her. "It won't be when Lucifer takes it from you as I just have."

She moved so quickly, he didn't even see it coming. He heard a whistle of air next to his ear, and when he looked behind him, a jeweled dagger protruded from his bedpost. Andrew couldn't quite catch his breath.

"As I said, I am no fainting miss." She crossed to his bed and grasped the dagger's hilt, straining to pull it out. Andrew slid his hand over hers and easily dislodged it. When she turned, he didn't lower his hand, effectively pinning her against the bedpost, though she had a dagger in her hand and was far from defenseless.

"Have I told you I think you are amazing?" He reached up and stroked her cheek. Her eyes remained locked on his face, her fingers wrapped around the dagger at her side.

"No."

He laughed then lowered his forehead to hers. "Lily, I am dying. I'm like a giddy schoolboy. My hands are shaking, and my heart is thundering."

As though to test him, she put her hand on his

chest, which caused his lungs to constrict. He could scarcely breathe. "I want you," he whispered. "And you want me too."

She shook her head and allowed her hand to drop. He felt cold seep in where her warm flesh had been. "I cannot."

"You're afraid, but it will be different with me. You know it will. I care about you." He stroked a curl of her hair and tucked it behind her ear. "How can I prove it to you?" he whispered. "I will do anything."

She was silent for so long he thought she would not answer. If she did not answer, he could live with that as long as she stayed. As long as he could touch her, hold her in his arms. He did not want to be without her.

Finally, she looked up at him, her eyes as green as a cat's. He'd seen that look before, and it worried him.

"You once promised you would stand on your head."

"I did?"

"You did."

He shook his head. "That doesn't sound at all like something I would say."

She laughed, a lovely deep sound. "It is *exactly* the sort of thing you would say, and you said it to Juliette in Hyde Park. You said the Duke of Pelham would never attend the regent's ball, and if he did, you would stand on your head."

Andrew had a vague memory of that day. He'd been so angry at the gossip pairing Juliette and Pelham. And he'd been desperate to prove it was not true. He remembered the encounter with Juliette at Hyde Park, vaguely remembered Lily there. She'd always been there, but he had never noticed her.

"I was called away and did not attend the ball. I did not observe the duke at this ball."

She tapped his nose. "But you know he was there. That is where he and Juliette met. It was in all the papers."

"I don't read—"

"If you want to prove you care for me, then make good on your promise."

He narrowed his eyes. "You want me to stand on my head?"

"Yes."

What new foreplay was this? "And if I stand on my head…"

"Then you may kiss me."

Good God, he was a pathetic specimen of a man. At one time, he would not have made any more effort than to lift a finger to have a woman. This one asked for everything. And he would give it to her too. He would have given her anything. He would have jumped from his window, sang an opera, danced a ballet, if she'd but asked it. Andrew knelt and removed his boots then moved the small table holding his wine and his plate. He lifted the glass, drank a good quantity of the wine, then stood in the cleared space.

"Are you actually going to comply?" she asked, leaning down and returning the jeweled dagger to a hidden pocket.

"I made a promise," he said. Of course, he'd never stood on his head before. How did one accomplish such a thing?

She gave him a wary look and scooted onto his bed. He liked the look of her there. Keeping her there was motivation enough to at least try this ridiculous maneuver. He bent and kicked his legs up, and they came down again just as quickly. He heard her giggling, but he ignored it. If he amused her, that was fine. Women liked men who made them laugh. He tried again and failed, but thought he might have the idea now. He would kick one leg up and then slowly raise the other once his hands were solid and steady on the floor. His third attempt was better, but he moved too quickly, and his legs went over his head.

She gasped and moved to slide off the bed. "Are you hurt?"

"Stay there." He held up a hand. His back was going to hurt like the devil in the morning, but he was going to do this. "I think I have it."

"Do be careful."

"Your concern is touching." Considering it was her demand that would cause him to break his neck. He moved back into position, put his hands on the floor, and carefully lifted his legs. "I have it," he said through clenched teeth, concentrating to keep his balance. He wobbled, losing his balance, and quickly lowered his legs before he took another tumble. When he stood, he heard clapping.

"Bravo!" Lily was kneeling on his bed, clapping enthusiastically. "That was impressive."

He felt slightly dizzy and rather ill, but he made a sweeping bow nonetheless. "I have honored my word yet again. And the next time I see Pelham, he will hear about it."

"Then I suppose it's my turn." She slid off the bed and seemed to glide toward him. His breath caught, watching her. He did not know what she would do next, but he prayed she would touch him, kiss him… He had a rather long list of what he might pray for.

She put her hands in his, and her skin was incredibly soft and her hands sinfully warm. "Now I honor my promise." She stood on her tiptoes and brushed her lips against his.

❦

She was afraid he would feel her trembling. She did not know what to do next, only that there was nowhere she wanted to be besides in Andrew's arms. She giggled, and he pulled back. "Kissing me is amusing you?"

She shook her head and attempted to compose herself. "No. I was remembering the sight of you standing on your head. I still cannot believe you attempted such a thing."

His brow creased in what she now recognized as annoyance. "I did not merely attempt it. I was successful."

"Of course you were."

"I do care about you," he said, looking into her eyes in a way that made her heart clench and her belly flutter. "Whether that proves it or not."

She hadn't needed him to prove it. She knew he cared. She could see it in his eyes, in the way he touched her, in the way he took care of her, even when she didn't need it. Something had changed in him. Had he fallen in love with her?

She dared not hope. Possessing his love had always been a dream too lofty even for her. "I did not need you to prove it," she said, looking up at him. "I already knew."

"Then why…" He sputtered something incoherent, which made her laugh. To stop his babbling, she placed a finger over his mouth.

"I needed a moment to collect myself, because I knew what was going to happen."

"And what's that?" The poor man truly looked as though he did not know.

She wrapped her arms around him and pressed her body against his. "You are going to take me to bed."

"Am I?"

Her pulse kicked with sudden anxiety. Had she been presumptuous? "Will you?"

"Is that what you want?" His hands were on her waist, and they tightened slightly. "Lily, I can wait. I can wait as long as you need."

It was tempting to take him up on his offer. She rarely, if ever, admitted her fear. If she admitted it, then she had to face it, and it was hard enough to act the spy when one was not thinking about fear. So she'd learned to block it out. But she could feel it hovering like a black cloud on the edge of what should have been a beautiful moment. The old nausea rose in her belly when she thought of what would happen between them—the chance she could become with child, the chance that the intimacy would remind her of those awful events of the past—and that awful man.

She did not want to remember that time in her life. Thus far Andrew's touches and kisses had not made her think of anything but having more of him, but she had always stopped him when her fears began to bubble to the surface. And, admittedly, he was the first man who had ever touched her tenderly and with her pleasure in mind. Perhaps that was why being with Andrew did not remind her of the past. Or perhaps she was finally willing to let the past go—to forgive herself for her mistakes and to start a new chapter in her life.

"You are thinking long and hard," Andrew murmured.

"Impatient?" she said, arching a brow.

"For you?" His hand trailed up her back then down again, making her shiver with pleasure. "Always. I respect your wishes. Only, if I must wait, put me out of my misery and tell me. I grow more nervous the longer we stand here."

She gaped at him. "What have you to be nervous about? You've bedded a hundred women!"

"If that were true, I'd be the worst sort of lecher and probably suffering from the pox. It's barely a tenth of that, but, Lily, how can you think you are like any of those others? You are Lily. My Lily." He bent and kissed her temple, dragging his lips over her eyebrow and back again, down her cheek until his breath teased her ear. "Put me out of my misery one way or another."

She squeezed her eyes shut and attempted to control the way her body trembled with fear and shivered with delight. "I don't want to wait."

"Thank God." His mouth moved to her neck, and he pulled her hard against his chest. She could feel the solid strength of him under his shirt, the heat of him burning her up, while his lips tempted and teased her sensitive flesh just behind her earlobe.

"Andrew?" she whispered.

"I love how you say my name. Say it again and promise never to call me Darlington again as long as you live."

She almost laughed. "Andrew, I have a confession to make."

His forehead fell to her shoulder. "Right now? I am dying for you, Lily."

"But that's just the thing. I'm terrified. I haven't allowed a man to touch me like this since—"

He pulled back. "I have been a dolt, as usual. I didn't even think of what you must be feeling. Stop me at any time. You can trust me, Lily."

All the icy fear in her chest began to melt, and the heat slid low in her belly. This was desire, the desire she had always felt for him, though it had seemed so much safer when he'd been enamored of Juliette.

"No more delays." He scooped her into his arms, which made her laugh, until he carried her to his bed and set her gently on the soft velvet coverlet. The fabric was sapphire blue and so plush she could not stop herself from running her fingers over it. She expected him to come down on top of her, but instead he lowered himself beside her, propping his chin on his hand.

"I've dreamed of having you here," he said. He reached for her hair, tugging at the pins holding it in place and then spreading it out. His fingers were sure and skilled against her scalp, easing away the tension. And it felt good to have the heavy mass out of its confines. It was not quite dry from the bath she'd had earlier, which made it even heavier when pinned up.

When the pins were gone, his fingers moved to her gown. He slipped one finger under the puff of a sleeve and notched it down to reveal her shoulder. Then he bent and kissed it softly before he tugged on the sleeve of the opposite shoulder. She watched him as he undressed her, watched the play of light from the candles on his face, the curve of his lips when another sliver of flesh was revealed. He was so beautiful to her. She had never thought she would be in his bed, never thought he would look at her like this, touch her like this. She wanted to remember everything about the experience. She closed her eyes and inhaled the scent of the beeswax candles, the coal in the fire, and the unforgettable scent of him. It was leather and spice and something uniquely Andrew. She could smell it on her fingers after she'd touched him, in his hair when he bent to kiss her, and in the bedclothes where she lay.

The fire crackled, and despite its welcome heat, she felt the coolness of the air on her bare flesh. She opened her eyes and looked at the mural painted on his ceiling. It was done in the ancient Greek style, with musicians and soldiers and revelers all in a line, passing a jug of wine. It suited him. Finally, she was aware that he had not moved, and her gaze met his.

"There you are," he said quietly.

"I was trying to see everything, smell it, hear it. I want to remember this."

He stared at her, his expression unreadable. "You slay me, Lily. How will I resist falling in love with you?"

Before she could answer, even silently, he said, "Stay with me. Don't allow your thoughts to wander someplace safe. I'm safe. I want you, all of you."

She nodded and followed his gaze to where he'd loosened the bodice of her gown and her stays. Now his hands shook slightly as he parted the material, revealing her breasts. One hand brushed across the flesh, and she sucked in a breath at the contact. What he did not understand was that she went away in her mind to keep her longings under control. She ached for his touch. She wanted him with a frenzied abandon that would no doubt shock and appall him. He bent and kissed her flesh, the stubble on his cheeks chafing the sensitive skin. She could not stop a small moan, and she arched to press more firmly against him. His hands slid under her back, and he lifted her then stripped off her gown and her stays. She pulled his shirt over his head while he untied her chemise. It slid down her arms as she kicked off her slippers and reached for the fall of his trousers.

His hands locked on hers. She looked down at the chemise pooling where she knelt on his bed. "That is hardly fair. I'm completely undressed."

"Yes, but you are not going to ravish me."

"Don't be so certain." She pushed him, and he, not expecting the gesture, fell onto his back. She held him down with one hand and removed her chemise then straddled him. His hands locked on her bare hips as she bent to take his mouth. She kissed him with all the pent-up longing she'd felt for him for so many years. She took his mouth over and over, twining her tongue with his, exploring every inch of him. He tasted like sweet wine, and she could not taste enough of him, was drunk on the feel of his warm chest beneath her bare breasts, the way his hands held onto her as though he was afraid he would fall if he released her, the way his tongue met hers thrust for thrust.

Finally, he pulled away. "Are you trying to drive me mad?"

"I told you I want you," she said, voice breathless.

"We're supposed to go slow this first time."

She laughed. "I never was very good at following anyone else's plans." She kissed him again, nipping at his lips playfully until his hands slid up her waist and cupped her breasts. The feel of his thumbs brushing over her sensitive nipples made her gasp in surprised pleasure.

Andrew took advantage of her distraction to flip her over. She protested loudly until his mouth silenced hers. And really, she did not mind. He was warm and solid on top of her, his fingers caressing her tenderly, moving from her shoulder down to her waist and then... She groaned.

"You were serious, then," he murmured against her collarbone. "You are ready for me."

"Yes," was all she could say as his fingers delved between her legs and parted her. Her legs seemed to fall open of their own accord. She had no control over her body at this point. She was entirely at Andrew's mercy. He seemed to know what she needed, what she craved. His fingers played her body, stroking and plucking and gliding. And then his fingers were inside her, slick with the evidence of her desire. He pressed up, and the sensation heightened until she all but cried out from pleasure. Then he withdrew, and she wanted to scream.

"Shh." He soothed her with kisses. "I want to go with you this time."

She saw him reach down and open the fall on his trousers. He stood and peeled them off, and she stared at the evidence of his arousal. He was large and rigid and surprisingly beautiful. And yet she still felt a stab of panic at the thought of what was coming next. What if she could not breathe; what if he would not stop; what if he hurt her?

He must have seen something in her eyes, because he held up both hands. "Lily, it's still me, Andrew. I'll stop whenever you wish. We'll go no further now, if that is what you want."

She nodded. Disappointment flooded through her. She had thought she might be able to go through with it. She wanted him so badly, but all desire was quickly being eroded by her fear.

"I also have another idea," he said. He lay down beside her, leaving plenty of room between their bodies. "I'm at your disposal." He linked his fingers and put his hands behind his head. "You are in control."

She sat and frowned down at him. He did look much less intimidating this way. "I'm not sure what to do."

"Why not begin again? As I recall, you were threatening to ravish me?"

She shook her head at him. How could he speak so lightly at a time like this? How could he be so patient with her? She could see quite clearly he wanted her. Wasn't he annoyed at having to wait? Wasn't he angry that she, who was supposed to be a notorious courtesan, knew very little about the act for which she was famous? Her past experiences had been exercises in fear and submission and pain. She'd had virtually no control over what happened. And now he was offering her complete control. She had to admit, she was intrigued. She leaned down and kissed him, and though he kissed her back, he allowed her to lead. He did not unlink his hands or urge her to do what he desired. He seemed quite content to do whatever she wanted. She kissed his mouth, his neck, his chest. It was muscled and smooth, and gooseflesh appeared when she stroked him. She kissed him all the way to his navel, then reached to touch his hard member. He inhaled sharply but made no move to stop or encourage her.

"Did I hurt you?"

"No. This is a pleasant torture."

She laughed, because she knew what he meant. His own touch often seemed a most pleasant form of torture. Despite the fire in the hearth, she was cold, and she climbed on top of him, remembering the luscious feel of skin against skin. She saw his hands unlink, claw into the bedclothes, then link again behind his head. "You're struggling for control," she noted.

"Suffice it to say you do not realize the power of your allure. And this position…" He looked up at her, admiration in his gaze. "I do not think I have ever fully appreciated its merits before."

"Touch me," she said. "I want your hands on me."

Slowly, as though he didn't trust himself, he unlinked his fingers and held his hands out to her. She moved them to her waist and then guided them slowly upward so they caught the heaviness of her breasts. He teased her until she was all but breathless, and then his hands slid down, cupping her bottom. He lifted her slightly, and she felt him heavy and hard between her legs. He was showing her what to do, if she so chose. Her heart pounded, and she leaned down to kiss him, feeling safe in that act. His hands moved up and down her back, and she began to move with them, his hard length beneath her arousing her. Heat pooled between them as her need increased. She moved more quickly, trying to sate that need, and finally reared up and took him in her hands. She rose on her knees, which trembled with apprehension, but the need overwhelmed the fear this time, and she guided him inside her.

His hands left her back and gripped the bedclothes. His knuckles were white as she moved over him, taking him inch by inch. She tensed, expecting pain, but there was none, only the pleasant fullness of him. But now what was she to do? She had thought this would ease the yearning.

"Rock back and forth," he said, his jaw clenched. "Find the rhythm you like."

"Is this hurting you?" she asked.

"No!" His voice was emphatic.

She tried his suggestion, rocking slowly. Andrew groaned. "Are you certain you are not hurt?"

"You are killing me. Incredibly slowly," he said, eyes closed and jaw muscles straining. "But it's the kind of death I prefer."

She moved again, slowly, watching as he visibly held himself back from whatever it was he wanted. And then she felt her own desire pierce through her, and she could no longer hold herself back. She rode him, quickening her movements until they reflected the frenzied passion she had known would be between them. His hands were on her hips now, holding her as she took him. And then suddenly everything broke free, and she reared back and succumbed to pleasure. The sensation came upon her in waves, each stronger than the last, until she was all but weeping. She collapsed on top of him, out of breath and damp with perspiration.

He held her for a moment, his hand caressing her back, and then he gently flipped her over. He was still inside her, and she realized he was still quite hard and quite large. "I thought that went away when…"

"That was for you," he said. "With your permission, this is for me, though I might be able to last long enough to please you again."

"I don't understand."

"Do you trust me?"

How could she not? She nodded.

"Good." He bent and kissed her again, moving inside her with the same slowness she had used on him. The sensation was not unpleasant, and when she looked up, his gaze was locked on hers. She could not look away from his eyes. They were windows to his feelings—desire, need, tenderness… love?

She must have mistaken that last one.

His fingers moved between their bodies, stroking her where she was most sensitive. She gasped. "Andrew!"

"Let it happen," he told her. "I have you."

She arched up to meet him, and white-hot pleasure exploded around her, inside her. This time the feeling was sharp and fast and verged on ecstasy. He thrust deep, and she cried out again, wanting more and more of him. But just as quickly, he pulled away, and she felt warm, sticky liquid on her belly.

He collapsed beside her, breathing heavily. And then he grasped his shirt and wiped her off. She watched him, and burst into tears.

Seventeen

ANDREW STARED AT HER. HE WAS NO DON JUAN, BUT surely his performance did not merit tears. He tamped down the feeling of panic rising in his chest. "Lily, are you hurt? What did I do wrong?"

"Nothing!" She swiped at her wet eyes. "You did everything right." And then she gave him her back and burst into more sobs.

Andrew lay back and tried to catch his breath and think what he was supposed to do now. If he had done everything right, did that mean she was crying because she was happy? Why the devil did women do such things? It made a man's head spin.

And his head had already been spinning. Lily wasn't the only one affected by what they'd just shared. Andrew had never felt anything like that before. The physical aspects had been more than he could have hoped for or expected, but it was the warmth he felt in his chest—about where his heart might be—that concerned him. He was not the kind of man to spend hours in bed with a woman. He did not sleep in anyone's bed but his own.

It was full dark now. He should have been encouraging her to dress and make ready to go to the chapel. But he did not. Instead, he found he wanted to hold her. Just hold her.

Devil take it! There was something wrong with him. Next he'd be quoting Byron or some such nonsense.

And still Lily sobbed beside him. He was going to have to do something about that, and he did not think jumping up and dressing would help the matter.

"Lily." He touched her shoulder. Damn it. She was cold. He lifted the coverlet and wrapped it around her, covering himself as well. This was cozy. He did not want to like it. "Lily, don't cry. Tell me why you're crying."

She turned to him, and her nose was red and her cheeks tear-stained. And still he thought she looked beautiful.

She walks in beauty, like the night… his mind taunted him.

He was doomed. *Doomed.*

"You care about me," she sobbed.

He should have thought it obvious by this point, but he thought it might be wise to keep quiet.

"You knew I did not want to beget a child, and you took precautions."

Was that all? She'd probably cry for a week if he told her he was quoting poetry about her in his mind.

"And I really do believe you would have stopped if I'd asked."

"Of course. I wouldn't have been pleased, though," he added. He did not want to sound too saintly.

She laughed, which was better than the crying. "I

wouldn't have been pleased, either." She cupped his cheek. "You were wonderful. I'll never forget it."

"I had hoped to repeat it."

She smiled at him and tucked her head under his chin. He found he liked her there, curled up against him, and he enfolded her in his arms, pulling her closer. He did note she failed to reply when he'd mentioned their future together. If she'd been another woman, he would have attributed it to modesty; but though she might not be as experienced as she claimed, she'd lived the life of a courtesan. She was neither modest nor easily shocked.

Perhaps she saw no future for them.

And perhaps he was behaving like a ninny. These thoughts were better suited to his fifteen-year-old sister.

And so he held her and marveled at how much he enjoyed the simple act. How her hair smelled faintly of lemon, and how her breathing grew regular as she fell into a light sleep.

And then his thoughts turned to his father. He did not want to believe the duke was capable of all Lily claimed. What reason would the duke have for wanting the King's men dead? The duke might be a glutton for wine and women, but he was not a fool. Killing spies would not bring back the money he had lost in the war. And it was not as though the rubies Lily spoke of were a secret. They were not the sort of thing anyone in the family talked about, and the gems were not paraded about. The stones were whole, not broken into pieces and fashioned into jewels. The family had possessed the rubies for centuries, and their association to the duchy was well documented.

Which meant if the duke hoped to pay assassins using the rubies, he did not care about being caught. That made no sense. No peer of the realm could possibly want to sully his name or that of his family by going to prison as any common criminal might.

And yet, if Lily's claims were correct, a prison was his father's future residence. Once she had the evidence she sought, her superiors would act. There was no reason Andrew could not act now. He knew where the rubies were hidden. His mother had hidden them there and told him where they were because he was the heir. Might any other documents his father wished to hide be in the same location? There was no place safer or more secret. No one knew about it. Come to think of it, not even his father knew of it. In which case, the documents would not be there. And yet he had to see for himself. His sister's words came back quite suddenly.

You did not see what she was really like, Andrew. She could be cold and, well, frightening.

Andrew felt a chill. He shook his head, but he could not shake his unease.

Carefully, so as not to wake Lily, he climbed out of bed and began to dress. The lamp had gone out, and the fire had burned down, but he knew his way about the room in the dark. The shirt he'd been wearing was soiled, and he had to open his clothes press to search for another. He pulled on a fresh one and then donned his coat. No sense in running about in the night in a white shirt. He'd be a beacon for anyone who happened to look out the window.

"You are not planning to go without me, I hope," a voice said in the darkness.

He sighed as she sat up.

"I see that was your plan." Her tone was accusatory, and he could hardly fault her.

"I did not want you to put yourself at risk. I will go alone and bring back anything of importance."

"It is my duty to put myself at risk," she said, sliding off the bed and stumbling about in the dark. She did not know his room as well as he. "I should have never involved you."

He found his tinderbox and lit a taper. "You did not have much of a choice. Go ahead and dress. I'll wait for you."

"How accommodating."

He had to assist her with her purple gown. He could have acted like an insufferable ass and refused, but the truth was he rather liked dressing her. He liked any excuse to touch her. He gave her a black cape he'd bought one year when he particularly admired the dandies. It was a bit long for her, but it would conceal the pale skin of her neck and shoulders in the darkness. He led her out of the house through the servants' stairs. He did not want to meet his father or one of the other guests and have to answer questions. No doubt his father was already questioning the whereabouts of his fiancée. He was not a man to suffer inattention.

Finally, they stepped outside. The rains had passed, but the ground was soggy and muddy. They had picked their way carefully across the lawn, especially as it was a cloudy night and the moon was intermittently visible. At one point, Lily's boots tangled with her cape, and she had to pause and straighten her garments. Andrew waited for her, looking back toward the great house. He thought he saw the flash of a light in one of the windows, but he might have imagined it. Still, he felt a sense of urgency. Lucifer would strike soon. Possibly even tonight. Andrew wanted Lily back inside, where she was safe. Or at least safer.

When they reached the small family chapel, Andrew pushed the door open. In the daylight, the building was flooded with sunshine. Stained glass windows abounded, as did many of the regular sort, and they lit the floors with color and light. In the dark, it was a place of shadows. There was a central aisle with a single wooden pew, worn and shiny from centuries of use, on either side. At the front of the chapel stood a large white marble altar on a raised dais. Three steps led to the altar on which stood a gold cross and several candles. Pedestals dominated the corners of the chapel with their large candles poised on top. He'd slipped his tinder box into his pocket, and he drew it out now and lifted a lantern placed beside the entrance. When it was lit, he walked to the altar and lit a brace of candles. A warm light suffused the place, and he lifted the lantern, shining the light about.

In the lantern's light, he noticed the thin layer of dust all around. When his mother had been alive, there had never been any dust. She would not have allowed it. He felt his gaze pulled toward the stained glass window of Saint Peter, depicting the man with a halo and a key. That has been his mother's favorite window. She had liked to come here and look at the window and enjoy the solitude. Sometimes she invited him to come with her. They'd sit together, her arm around his small shoulders, and she'd whisper prayers, all of her hopes and dreams for him. Once he'd asked her about the key the apostle held, and she'd told him it was the key to heaven.

"It must be heavy," he'd said, thinking of the jingle their housekeeper made when she walked with all of the keys to Ravenscroft Castle in her hand.

"Or very light. It all depends on your heart." She'd squeezed his shoulders and left him to ponder those words. She was always making remarks he did not understand. But when he looked at Lily now, her red hair burnished by the candlelight, he thought he knew what his mother meant. His whole being felt light when he was with her, as though he could do anything, carry any burden as long as she was beside him.

"I feel as though I should pray," Lily said, meeting his gaze. They were the first words she'd uttered since they'd left his room. "I haven't been inside a church in years."

"Now you're just gloating."

She gave him a ghost of a smile. "Not at all. Courtesans and fallen women are not welcome in the house of God."

"That's strange. I would think your sort would need it all the more."

Her smile widened. "No one wants *my sort* tainting anyone else. Just the sight of me might spur a virtuous woman to take up a life of dissolution."

"One could only hope." He held out a hand. "Care to join me, my little Jezebel?"

"Where are we going?"

"I know a secret alcove. I suppose it was meant to be a crypt, but there aren't any remains inside. If there is something my family wished to hide, this alcove is the perfect place."

She nodded. "But if what I seek is not there, I will not stop looking. Too many lives are at stake."

"Which is as good a reason as any to let my father be and pursue the real culprit. Come, let's put this to rest."

She climbed the steps to the altar, and he offered his hand. She took it, her fingers cold in his. He led her to a room, a closet really, where vestments might be stored and where a visiting man of God might retreat to dress for a service. The room was barely large enough for two, and Andrew had to duck when he went through the arched wooden door. Inside it was dark and musty, and he held his lantern high. The gold chalice and plate set aside for communion glinted back at him, but he was more interested in the table upon which these items were laid. He moved toward the rectangular wooden furnishing and moved it aside. Behind it was a wall, but if he looked closely, he saw one of the large square stones in the wall could be removed.

"Is that it?" Lily asked. She'd seen it immediately.

"Yes. I think it was designed to hold remains—ashes, I suppose—or possibly to safeguard a valuable item." He set the lantern on the floor, knelt, and struggled to fit his fingers into the grooves on either side of the block. This had been easier when he was a boy with small hands. And, he thought, if he had been a woman with small, dainty hands, the chore would not have been difficult.

"And yet here sit gold communion pieces." She gestured to the chalice and tray.

"We've never had a problem with vandals or thieves," Andrew said, struggling with the weight of the stone. "Until recently."

"Lucifer is not after your gold and silver plate. What he seeks is far more valuable to him."

Andrew grunted and finally slid the stone out. He pushed it aside and shone the light into the small alcove. First he reached for a large black velvet bag. He loosed the drawstring and pulled out a smaller bag. "Hold out your hand."

Lily cupped both hands together, and he toppled the ruby into her palm. It was half the size of her palm and shone darkly in the weak light. "A ruby as big as your hand," she murmured.

"Not quite. That was a bit of an exaggeration."

"Close enough. Are the other rubies inside?" She shrugged off his cape and laid it on the floor, placing the ruby from her hand reverently on top. He poured the other two from their respective bags, but there was another velvet bag inside.

"Hmm. I don't know what this is." The bag was cinched tightly, but he managed to work a finger in and open the mouth. He shook it, and a handful of smaller gems fell onto the cape.

"Sapphires," Lily breathed.

"I've never seen these. Are you certain they're sapphires?" He lifted one. "This one is pink. This one is yellow."

"I'm not an expert, but I believe they come in different colors. Do you know when your father acquired these?"

"No." And it was troubling. He had never seen

them before. And this was where his mother had hidden the jewels.

"This in itself does not damn your father. The rubies were mentioned by several men involved in the assassination attempts. I can't think who else would possess such large rubies, but if the Crown is to accuse a duke of such loathsome behavior, more evidence is required." She was looking at the alcove, and Andrew knew that to put the matter at rest, he would have to ensure nothing else was inside.

A sense of dread filled his chest as he reached back inside.

And felt the papers.

No. Please, no.

He pulled them out and stared at them. They might be anything: baptism records, old documents pertaining to marriages, dowries, jointures. But they were not. The paper was not old or worn. He handed the stack to Lily. With practiced efficiency, she opened the first document and sighed. She turned it so he could see. On the paper were the names of five men, his friend Warrick Fitzhugh's among them.

But there was more. She handed him another sheet of parchment, and on it were lists of frigates and ships of the line, as well as an analysis of the weaknesses and strengths of each ship and its captain. More sheets detailed munitions and military orders, troop placements, vulnerabilities.

"Even with Napoleon out of the way, Lucifer could sell this information for a tidy profit. If this were to fall into the wrong hands, it could be devastating. But I am confused. Your father sent me several pieces of correspondence when we were in Town. This is not his hand. I wonder if it is Lucifer's."

Andrew swallowed. "That is not my father's hand." He knew it, though. He knew it very well.

He watched, wordless, as she opened another document. Her eyes widened when she'd scanned the contents. "Artemis," she whispered.

Had he misheard her? He peered at the missive and the next she opened. Both were addressed to Artemis. He looked into her face and saw her gaze on him. "I'm sorry," she said.

"Is this the Artemis—?"

"Yes. The assassin."

"Why would these papers be in our possession?"

"Your father is Artemis."

Andrew stared at the proof of his family's treason. Irrefutable proof. "I can't understand it," he murmured. "Why?" He shook his head. "I don't believe it. There must be some mistake."

"I applaud your faith in me, Son."

Lily jumped, dropping the papers, and Andrew jerked toward the doorway. His father filled the opening, making the tiny room seem that much smaller.

"Your Grace." Andrew stood. "You have found us."

The duke nodded. "I knew she'd hidden them. I did not know where. You knew all along." The duke glanced at Lily. "And you! I should have guessed you would be trouble. Something told me to stand clear of you, but I've always had a weakness for redheads. A weakness I see my son shares."

"If it wasn't me, it would have been someone else. The Crown has suspected you for weeks."

She rose, defiant and unafraid. "We but needed the proof."

"If you are looking to send someone to the gallows, you are too late. I am not Artemis."

Lily lifted the documents. "These suggest otherwise."

"They would if they were intended for me. I was not Artemis." He looked at Andrew. "Your mother was."

"You forced her into it. You gave her no choice!" Andrew dove for him, but the duke produced a pistol. Lily pulled Andrew back.

"Believe that if you want," the duke said, "but the evidence will prove my innocence."

Andrew tried to lunge again, and Lily held tightly. "He will use the pistol, Andrew," she whispered then looked at the duke. "If the Duchess of Ravenscroft was Artemis, why have the attacks on the Diamonds in the Rough continued after her death?"

"How was I to stop them?" the duke asked. "I went to London, but the plans were in motion."

"And you were in too deep. Better the Diamonds die, lest they discover your complicity."

Andrew shook his head. This was not true. It could not be true. His mother an assassin? His father a traitor? His head reeled, and he felt dizzy.

The duke spread his hands. "She gave me no choice but to do as she bade me."

"Is that why you killed her?"

"No!" Andrew protested. "It was an accident."

The duke kept his gaze on Lily, and Andrew's blood chilled. He did not want to believe it. He could not begin to comprehend any of this.

"I think you killed her because you were tired of living in her shadow," Lily said. "I think you wanted the money for yourself."

The duke clutched his chest in a mockery of innocence. "What would I gain from their deaths?"

"The loyalty and the gratitude, *lucrative* gratitude, of those who would rather the elite spies of England not stand in their way."

Andrew shook his head. "How could you?"

The duke stared at him, and Andrew felt as though a stranger were looking back. This man was not his father. Or perhaps it was his father, but he had never known the man. He had only created the man he wanted his father to be.

"What do you know about it, little brat? You, who have lived a life of ease and privilege? How do you think your life has been possible? Do you think our family so different from that of other peers? We are bleeding blunt. That monstrosity of a house leeches pounds by the moment. And I was not going to be the duke who lost it all."

"No," Lily said. "You would be the duke who turned traitor. A lovely story for your grandchildren. You must come with me."

The duke threw back his head and laughed. "Go back to the brothel you crawled out of, *Countess*. I'm here for the rubies and the rest of it." He lifted his pistol. "And I will have what I came for."

Andrew pushed Lily behind him, a gesture she did not seem to fully appreciate. "Step out of my way!"

But he stood firm, blocking her from skirting around him. In the small space, it was not difficult.

"My son, ever the knight in shining armor," his father said. "Your mother and I never understood you. You did not seem descended from either of us. Throw me the bag with the jewels. Put the documents in it as well," the duke said, gesturing to the cape on the floor, where the rubies lay glittering. "And you two can go back to bed."

"Where will you go?" Lily demanded, still pushing at Andrew.

"Somewhere your precious agents of the Crown will never touch me." He motioned with the pistol. "Throw me the gems."

"No."

His father's brows rose. "What?"

"Those rubies are mine as much as yours—Emma's and Katherine's too. You'll not take them for your own selfish means. If you want to run, run. I won't stop you—"

"Andrew!" Lily made another effort to push him out of the way.

"But you won't take what rightfully belongs to the duchy."

"You always were an arrogant little bastard." He aimed the pistol.

Andrew did not flinch. "You won't shoot me. I'm your son."

"Move out of my way, or you'll see just how deep my paternal affection runs."

Andrew saw the look in the duke's eye was not to be mistaken. He would shoot. Then so be it. There were some things worth fighting for, worth dying for. He would stand here and protect Lily and his family legacy until he was laid in his grave.

"No."

"Have it your way." The duke cocked the hammer, and Andrew flinched. *Misfire. Misfire.* He closed his eyes and heard the shot ring out. At the last second, he was shoved violently aside and hit his hip hard on the table. He went down on one knee then roared with anguish, "Lily!"

Eighteen

She was lying on the cold marble floor, and she was not quite certain how she had landed there. She heard Andrew calling her name, fear in his voice. She was shaking with fear too, but she did not feel any pain. That might be a bad sign. If she had been shot and felt nothing, did that mean she was dead?

But she couldn't be dead. Her eyes were open, and she was rising to her knees, and she was staring at—"No!"

The duke lay blocking the doorway, a pool of blood spreading from his skull. She crawled closer and saw the wound in the back of his head.

"What happened?" Andrew was yelling. "Are you injured?"

"I'm fine," Lily said calmly. She rose to her feet, looking straight ahead and into the chapel.

"Father!" He rushed to her side. He gasped when he saw his father and fell to his knees, cradling the man's body. "No, no! I don't understand."

But she did. She understood perfectly. And at that moment, Lucifer stepped into the doorway.

"Good evening. I believe you have something that is mine."

"How long have you been waiting here?" Lily asked.

"I've been watching the house, waiting for you to come to me."

"You might have been waiting all night."

Lucifer smiled. It was a charming smile on what would have been a handsome man—if his eyes were not so full of hatred and contempt. "Sometimes a man is lucky. Now listen very carefully, lord duke and lady slut. You will do exactly as I say. I want those documents and all the jewels. And then I want you to return to the house and bring me enough blunt to buy my passage to the Continent."

Andrew rose shakily to his feet. "You killed my father, you bastard!" His voice was full of anguish, and his clothes covered in blood, and yet he pushed forward and tried to move her out of harm's way again. Lily stepped to the side and evaded him. When would he realize she had been trained for this?

"Perhaps we ought to serve you a four-course meal as well, Lucifer," she said. "This is ridiculous. Nothing could persuade me to meet your demands. You will be charged in the murder of the Duke of Ravenscroft, as well as the other crimes you have committed here and elsewhere. And all of that is nothing compared to the punishment you will receive for your treason."

"You are quaint, Lily. That is your name, is it not? I did nothing treasonous except possess sensitive information. It was stolen and sold, and I have done the Crown a service by recovering it. But no matter, as I will not be here to stand trial for any murders, because you will arrange a carriage for me within the hour."

"Why would we do that?" Andrew asked.

Lucifer smiled, and Lily felt a chill run down her back. "Because if you do not, I will kill her son."

Lily blinked and felt herself stumble. Andrew was right behind her and caught her by the arm, steadying her. "That's not possible. I don't have a son," she heard herself say. But her head was throbbing, and the blood rushed so loudly in her ears, her voice made her sound as though she were trapped in a well.

"Lily." Lucifer shook his head. "My dear Lily. Do you really think I am that much of a fool? Come, see for yourself." He moved aside and gestured to the interior of the chapel. Lily swayed forward, but Andrew held her arm.

"It could be a trap."

"To what end?" she asked, despair filling her as the truth became more and more apparent. "He needs us to escape—or at least you." She was expendable, and so was her son. She would be kept alive only so long as she was needed to keep Andrew cooperative.

As if in a trance, she followed Lucifer to the outer door of the chapel. It was slightly ajar, and the darkness pooled outside. He swung the door wide for her, and she held the lantern aloft. And began shaking.

There was a small form on the grass, and the form was not moving. With a gasp, Lily rushed forward and knelt beside the boy. It was he. It was her son. Her hand hovered over his face, but she dared not touch him. His eyes were closed, and after a moment, she saw his small chest rise and fall.

She turned to Lucifer. "What did you do to him?"

"Nothing yet. He's asleep and unharmed. I pressed a handkerchief dipped in tonic from an apothecary to his nose. He is not aware of any of this and, if you cooperate, he can wake up in his bed tomorrow morning."

Lily wanted to thank God for small mercies, but she did not believe Lucifer would allow her son to go free. They were all damned now. The man's reputation and penchant for violence told her that much.

"You!" Lucifer pointed behind her, and she turned to see Andrew standing in the light of the chapel. She had almost forgotten about him, but Lucifer had his plans. "Fetch me the contents of that hiding spot, and be quick about it."

Andrew's gaze met hers, and he turned slowly to do the man's bidding. Lily looked away, back at her son. This might be the last time she ever saw him. She might be the reason he never grew into a man. "I'm sorry," she whispered. "So sorry. I never wanted this for you." She reached out and brushed back a wisp of his hair. It was so much like her own color, and his complexion was pale, similar to her own. She had not been this close to him since he was a newborn babe, so she had not known he had a smattering of freckles on his nose or that his eyelashes were pale red. She reached out and touched his face, smoothing away a bit of dirt marring his beautiful skin.

Lucifer had not lied. The boy was warm and unconscious. He was not dead. Under her fingertips, she could feel the life in him. And it seemed once she had touched him, she could not stop. She knew the night was cold and her knees wet where she knelt, but she felt nothing other than her child. Her son.

She lowered her head to his chest, listening to his heart, hugging him to her. He no longer smelled like the sweet baby she remembered. He smelled of fresh hay and churned butter and of something all his own. She buried her head against him and closed her eyes. For this one moment, he was hers again. Hers alone, as he had been so long ago.

"This is quite touching," she heard Lucifer's cutting voice. "But I really must be going."

Slowly, Lily rose from her son. It was an effort to tear herself away from him, but she reminded herself he was no longer hers. And only she could save him. She looked at Lucifer, noting Andrew had returned and handed the man the jewels and papers from the secret alcove. Andrew was watching her, his face drawn and haggard. He had lost both of his parents now, and he would very likely lose her as well before the night was over. But she could not let this end without telling him how she felt about him.

"Carry the boy toward the stables," Lucifer ordered Andrew. "Lily, my dear, you walk beside me."

They had little choice but to comply. For the moment. She would fight him, and she knew Andrew would never let the man who'd murdered his father leave the estate alive. She needed to think of a plan. Could they alert the grooms or someone in the house without putting a bystander in danger? Without endangering her son?

No, it was too dangerous to involve anyone else.

They would be lucky if none of the guests was wandering about the grounds, foxed and disoriented.

"When we reach the stables, Your Grace will go inside and secure a fresh horse for me—a blood horse, mind you. Then you will bring me no less than one hundred pounds from the house."

"What makes you think I have that kind of blunt lying around?" Andrew's voice sounded cold and angry. The shock of his father's death was wearing off. His anger might help them, but it could be a detriment if it led to impulsivity. "Use the jewels to finance your passage," he said with a sneer.

"Save your suggestions, boy. I want to travel inconspicuously. I suggest you find me enough blunt to make it to the Continent, or I will slit first the boy's throat, then your lover's." They had reached the side of the stable, and Lucifer gestured for them to pause in the shadows. "Put him down," he ordered.

Lily reached for her son, cradling him as Andrew lowered him to the ground. They were close enough now that she could whisper to him. "Bring back a weapon," she murmured as she took the boy.

"No!" he hissed. "We can't ri—"

"No talking!" Lucifer roared, and Lily jumped from surprise. "Fetch me what I want, or I will kill them both."

Andrew's gaze was riveted to her face. She kept her own gaze steady, willing him to follow her instructions. "I only wanted to say *I love you*," she said to Lucifer without breaking eye contact with Andrew. "I wish I had said it before. I wish I could tell you how much."

"Lily—"

"Oh, do shut up!" Lucifer ordered. "I feel as though I may vomit. Go!" He gestured to Andrew. "And not another word."

Andrew watched her for a long moment then moved along the wall of the stable until he disappeared inside. She watched him go from where she knelt on the grass and began to shiver. When she couldn't see him any longer, she looked up at Lucifer. "When are you going to kill me?"

"What?" he gasped melodramatically. "I'm not going to kill you!" He was mocking her.

"There's no need to kill the boy," she said. "He doesn't even know who I am. Kill me, but let him go."

"You break my heart, Lily. I shall weep when I slit your throat."

Not if I slit yours first. But she still needed a plan, and time was running out. When Andrew returned, they would need to act.

Her arms began to sag under the weight of her boy, and she lowered him slightly, until the backs of her hands touched the ground. Rough pieces of gravel scraped her knuckles. The drive was nearby, and the horses' hooves had probably scattered some of the small, sharp stones over this portion of the lawns. Her fist closed around the gravel and sand, the small jagged pieces biting into her flesh. Her actions were hidden by the sleeping form of her son, but the longer Andrew took to return, the more agitated Lucifer became.

"Stand," he ordered. "Leave the boy and stand beside me."

She moved slowly, keeping her fists hidden in the folds of Andrew's cape. The last thing she wanted was to give Lucifer an opportunity to put the pistol to her head. Then Andrew would never take a chance to attack the man.

"Move!" Lucifer ordered when she continued to drag her feet.

Hurry, Andrew. Hurry.

She heard footfalls, and prayed she had not imagined them. Lucifer looked in the direction of the sound as well, raising his pistol and readying it to fire. Andrew rounded the corner, leading a horse by the bridle. When he saw the pistol, he raised his hands to show he carried no weapon. Lily's heart sank. But this was not the end. Andrew still had to go to the house to gather the quid Lucifer wanted. She feared that was the moment Lucifer would kill her. He'd have no use for her once he had the horse and the money.

"What took you so long?" Lucifer demanded.

Andrew dropped the bridle and moved to the horse's flank, soothing the beast and pointing out the saddle. "I had to saddle him."

"You took your time."

Andrew shrugged. "It's not something I do every day, and he has spirit." His gaze flicked to hers, and there was something in it. Had she imagined it or…? Andrew's hand slipped inside one of the saddlebags. If he had a weapon secreted inside, this was her chance. She could trust Andrew. He'd proven that over and over. Lily held her breath, and when Lucifer moved forward to take the horse's reins, she loosed the mixture of sand and gravel into his face.

Lucifer yelled and brushed at the dirt and grime, and Andrew pulled some sort of metal implement from the saddlebag. He swung it at Lucifer, who still pawed at his eyes, and Lily realized it was a farrier's hammer. The hammer made a thud when it hit Lucifer's head, and he stumbled back. The horse, frightened by the commotion, danced to the side, and Lily ran to her son to move him away from the horse's hooves.

Her loyalty to her son cost her. She'd thought the blow to Lucifer's head harder than it was, and when she looked up from her small charge, Lucifer dove for Andrew's abdomen. The two men sprawled across the ground, with Lucifer having the edge in this sort of fight. But Lucifer wasn't fighting to win. He managed to roll Andrew over then jumped up and raced to the horse.

"No!" Lily screamed, but it was too late. She had only enough time to move the boy and herself out of Lucifer's path as he spurred the horse away.

❧

Andrew was damned if he was going to let that murderer escape now. Not only was his jaw throbbing where Lucifer had hit him, the man was on his best hunter. And then there was the small matter of Lucifer's having murdered his father. The duke was no saint, but he didn't deserve to be shot in the back in his own chapel.

And his mother.

Had he always known and just allowed himself to be deceived? He could not think of that now. He could not face it yet.

"Andrew!" Lily called. Sweet Lily. She loved him. And he loved her too. He didn't know when that had happened. He'd loved her without even knowing it. But when he saw her throw the gravel into Lucifer's face, that was the moment he knew for certain. That was the moment admiration and affection merged and he knew he would always love her. He knew he would do anything for her.

"I'm going after him!" Andrew called, racing into the stable. Several grooms, disturbed by the commotion, milled about, groggy and half-awake. "Out of my way." He tore into the stall of one of the more amenable mares and led her out. As soon as he was free of the stables, he mounted clumsily and followed Lucifer.

"What are you doing?" Lily cried.

He turned to her. "You said you wanted to be there when I was forced to grow up." If that time was not now, tonight, he did not know when else it could be. He raced away with the image of her shocked face in his mind. He knew which way Lucifer would go. If the man had any sense, and he did or he wouldn't have stayed alive so long, he would head for the coast. He was wanted in London, or he might have made the trek there. It was as good a place as any to lose oneself, but it was a long ride from Nottinghamshire, and the coast was closer. Andrew was still on the estate's grounds when he spotted Lucifer up ahead. Andrew wasn't used to riding without a saddle, so he hung on tightly to the horse's mane, leading her with his knees. Lucifer must have heard him coming, because he turned and spurred his horse forward.

But the man was a stranger to the beast, and the horse was not quick to obey. Andrew gained ground, his heart pounding as he neared Lucifer. Lucifer, sensing he was caught, raised the pistol and fired. Andrew ducked and turned the mare sharply left. And yet he still heard the shriek of the ball as it raced by him. Too close. His hands were clammy now and his heart pounding not from excitement but fear. And he was more determined than ever to kill this bastard who dared shoot at him.

He jabbed a knee into his mare's flank, guiding her after the hunter again. Lucifer had gained some ground, but Andrew would make it up. He ducked low, riding as fast as he could over the dark, uneven ground, and then he swore he heard hoofbeats.

He shook his head to clear it, but they did not disappear. He chanced a glance over his shoulder and gaped when he saw her.

Lily. On the back of one of his horses. And she was gaining on them.

Her hair flew out behind her, a ribbon of flame in the cloudy night. What the devil was she doing? She was going to fall and break her neck at that speed. The night sky was far too cloudy to make out obstacles, and she was riding as though she were racing on Rotten Row. As she gained speed, he could make out the horse she commanded. His fastest gelding, which explained how she had caught up to him. And the beast was saddled for a man. Her skirts were ruched up to her knees, and the look of determination on her face was more than a little bit scary. Truly, she surprised him at every turn.

"Go back!" he yelled. "You're going to break your neck."

She was abreast of him now, and she flashed him a grin. The woman was mad. That was the only explanation. "*You* go back. I'm trained for this sort of thing."

No one was trained for this sort of thing, though he would admit she'd had some experience riding horses. She handled her mount exceptionally well.

Andrew dug his heels in, urging his horse faster as Lily's mount began to outpace them. When he was beside her again, she glanced at him, then ahead to Lucifer. They would reach him in a matter of moments… that was if one or both of their horses didn't fall into a ravine or trip on a fallen log. They rose over a field, and Andrew estimated they were no longer on Ravenscroft property. If it had been morning, he would have noted landmarks and known where they were, but for the moment, nothing looked familiar. He was not even certain at this point that he could have found his way back.

"If you're going to stay with me," she was saying, looking alternately at him and ahead at the man they pursued, "cut him off on that side. We'll box him in!" she yelled over the thunder of the hooves.

It wasn't a bad plan—for a madwoman. He didn't have a better one, so he angled his horse to Lucifer's right, while Lily took the left. Lucifer's mount was finally flagging, and Andrew thought it was none too soon. His own horse would not last at this speed much longer. He spurred her one last time, wanting a final burst of speed, and then he was neck and neck with Lucifer. The man jogged his horse to the right, trying to collide with Andrew's mount, but Andrew's mare easily moved aside.

On Lucifer's left, Lily gained momentum. Lucifer must have heard her, but Andrew was attempting to keep Lucifer's attention to give Lily time to... he did not want to think about what she would do. She undoubtedly had a plan, and undoubtedly, he did not want to know it.

As Lily closed in and Lucifer turned to gauge her progress, Andrew reached for Lucifer's horse's bridle. Lucifer jerked the beast aside. Unfortunately, he all but ran into Lily. Andrew yelled to warn her, but he needn't have bothered. She was ready, and she dove from her horse onto Lucifer's.

Andrew felt his chest constrict. He watched in stunned silence as both she and Lucifer went over the horse's back and tumbled to the ground in a dizzying blur of dust and bodies. And then they were gone, and Andrew had to rein in his mount and reverse direction. The other two horses continued running. They would slow and return on their own. Andrew nudged his horse back, his gaze searching the ground for some movement among the various shapes.

And then he spotted them. He caught the glint of Lily's hair in a brief flash of moonlight. She lay in a heap on the ground, and neither she nor Lucifer moved.

Nineteen

For a moment, she didn't want to open her eyes. Everything hurt.

And then she remembered Lucifer, and she forced her eyes open and attempted to sit.

"Stay still." Andrew was kneeling beside her, his expression full of worry. "You took a nasty fall."

"I didn't fall." She struggled to sit, despite his injunction. "I jumped."

"I was trying to give you the benefit of the doubt. It was a suicidal maneuver." He seemed to realize she was not going to stay put. Reluctantly, he cupped her elbow and assisted her to her feet.

"It is only suicidal if I fail. Where is he?" A movement caught her attention, and she spun to find Lucifer gaining his feet. "Oh, no you don't."

She went after him, her body protesting the movement even as she pushed the limits of her endurance. Lucifer was limping himself, a dirty, crooked remnant of what he'd been. She caught up to him then ducked when he swung at her.

"I'll kill you yet," he rasped.

"You are welcome to try." She'd never been lauded for her talents at fisticuffs, but she had learned a thing or two living on the streets of London. When he lunged for her, she elegantly sidestepped then brought her foot up, slamming it into his breadbasket—that *was* what the pugilists called it, was it not?

He doubled over, and she rounded and kicked him in the flank. But he was ready for her, and he caught her ankle and tipped her backward. She fell and rolled before he could grab her. But he was quick and dove before she could move well away. He would have landed on her had Andrew not stepped in. She thought he had shown remarkable restraint in waiting this long. But now he caught Lucifer by the shoulder, swung the man around, and plowed his fist into Lucifer's face. Even if she could not see the blood spatter in the dark, she could hear the sickening smack of flesh crushing into bone.

Lucifer wheeled back and fell on his belly. But Andrew grabbed him, yanking him up and slamming his fist into the man over and over again. Lily was too shocked for a moment to do anything but stare, and then she blinked. Andrew was going to kill him. "Stop!" She rose to her knees, wobbled to her feet, and stumbled to the two men, one limp and one unrelenting in his assault. "Andrew! No!"

The new duke did not seem to hear her. Lucifer had collapsed to the ground, and Andrew fell to his knees beside the unconscious man, pummeling him. Lily took a risk and jumped in front of Lucifer. She winced as Andrew's fist slammed down, but he pulled the punch at the last moment.

"Move."

"No. You are killing him. Enough." The wind had kicked up now, sending the clouds racing above them. The moon's light shone intermittently, and she caught a flash of the anger and determination set as though in stone on Andrew's face.

"Move!"

"No!" she screamed up at him. "I cannot allow you to kill him. Justice—"

"What justice?" Behind him, the wind whipped his hair about his face, making him look like some sort of madman. But she could not give up now. She had promised the Crown answers, and she would deliver. Lucifer would stand trial for his crimes. If Andrew continued in this manner, he would be the one on trial. "Did my father receive justice?" Andrew yelled. He stood rigid, his fists balled. "My father is dead. Where's the justice in that? My mother is dead too. Both traitors. How do I live with that knowledge? There's no *justice*!" He spat the word, and then he bent slightly. It was enough of a capitulation that Lily rose and went to him.

She wrapped her arms around him, and he stiffened, resisting for a moment. And then he crumpled against her. "There's no justice," he said, voice full of anguish.

"Shh." She stroked his back, and together they went to their knees. "You are not a murderer, Andrew. A quick death is not justice. Justice is a lifetime in prison or the agony of waiting for an appointment at the gallows."

His arms came around her, and she knew the rage inside him was ebbing away. The sound of hooves drew her attention, and she spotted several grooms riding toward them. When they neared, she held up a hand, giving them the signal to stand back and respect their lord's privacy.

"I cannot believe he is gone," Andrew murmured against her shoulder. "She is gone. Is it wrong to miss her?"

"No, no. Never. I understand, Andrew. I do. You know I do." She missed her own parents. She did not even know if they still lived, but no matter. She had been dead to them years ago. "Killing Lucifer will not bring your mother or your father back. Nothing can do that."

His body relaxed, and he pulled back from her, holding her lightly about the waist. She saw his gaze land on the grooms and then flick to Lucifer's motionless form. She began to rise, expecting him to do the same. It would be a long night of explanations and details to be seen to. Her son must be tended. The duke's body retrieved.

But Andrew held her in place, his hands moving from her waist to cup her face. "How is it you are so wise, Lily Dawson?"

"I'm a courtesan." She smiled at him. "We know everything."

He kissed her lightly. "Yes. You do."

He rose then and went to the grooms, but throughout the remainder of the night and the long day that followed, she was never far from his side. She tried, a dozen times, to give him a moment alone, but he would catch her hand and draw her to his side. When his sister departed in the morning, the decision having been made that the trip to her elder sister's should not be put off, Andrew kept Lily by his side throughout the tearful farewell. Like her brother, Emma had two parents to mourn now.

The broken man she had held briefly in her arms on the cold, windy field the night before did not return. Andrew was every inch the duke now. He had taken the mantle and wore it as though it had always been his. Several times, throughout the ordeal, she found herself watching him, amazed at how serious, how efficient he was. This was the man who had a quip for everyone and every situation. This was the man who recited bawdy verses he'd spent hours composing himself. This was the man who danced at balls until the sun rose.

This was the man who had never given her a second glance. Now he would not allow her out of his sight.

She'd had to reveal something of her role in the Foreign Office during the investigation that followed. Her first priority had been ensuring her son was safely back in the arms of his parents. After a doctor had examined the lad and assured her he would be fine, she had escorted him home herself in the carriage. The Ravenscroft steward had accompanied her, and she'd left it to him to explain to the boy's distraught parents. The less involvement she had, the better. She had already put him in danger. She would never do so again.

When she'd returned, she'd written to Fitzhugh, asking him or his superior to come at once. Lucifer would need to be collected, and the documents the duke had hidden away would be taken into possession by the Crown. She would lobby to keep the identity of his mother secret, but she could not guarantee such a thing.

For all intents and purposes, her work here was done. And yet she was in no hurry to leave. Andrew needed her—or at least he wanted her beside him. She would stay until the official from the Foreign Office arrived, and then she would return to…

To London?

To the demimonde?

To the Countess of Charm?

She could. Her engagement to Ravenscroft had not been revealed—only Lady Emma and Andrew knew, and they had bigger secrets. She could return to being the last of The Three Diamonds.

Except masquerading as an Impure held no appeal. Even her work for the Crown had lost much of its luster. She was bruised and weary after this mission. The Duke of Ravenscroft was dead, killed before her eyes. She would never erase that horrible sight from her memory. Lucifer had almost killed her, and if he hadn't been stopped, he might have gone on to ensure Fitzhugh and the other Diamonds in the Rough were assassinated.

But the Diamonds were safe now. Lucifer was locked away in a sturdy gaol in the nearby town. Her son was safely home, and from what she understood, had no memory of the events of the night before.

She watched through the windows of the front parlor as the last of Ravenscroft's guests departed, looking somewhat less gay than they had when she'd arrived. Only Kwirley had asked questions and pried into Andrew's affairs. Everyone else had gone without fuss.

Andrew had not seen the lot off, and as the last carriage pulled away, she turned to see him standing behind her. She was not surprised. He would not have been far. She studied him, the haggardness of his features, the strain about his eyes. His bearing was still rigid and ducal, but he was fraying at the edges.

"You need sleep," she said at last, going to him. "I know it's barely time for dinner, but you have been up all night."

"So have you." He pulled her into his arms, and she was surprised by how easy and comfortable she felt there, pressed against his chest. She inhaled deeply and could not resist resting her head against him. She would miss this when she returned to London. The security she felt when he held her, the warm, masculine scent of him, the tender way he held her. There had never really been a chance for them. She had only wished it so. If he were still the "Darling of the *Ton*," they might have been happy together. For a little while.

But those days were over. He was the Duke of Ravenscroft now. He had responsibilities and a title to pass on to his heirs. He would no longer be allowed the luxury of trifling with a courtesan. Even one who loved him.

Even one she suspected he cared for very much.

"We're the last ones left," he said.

She almost laughed. Ravenscroft Castle employed a staff that numbered in the hundreds. They were not alone by any means.

"The funeral?" she asked.

"Will be small and without fanfare."

That was probably best. While no one would make an effort to brand the duke as a traitor, the truth would come out when Lucifer was tried. He took her hand. "Come. Let's to bed."

She followed him, too weary to protest much, but they passed several maids and footmen, each of whom raised their brows as they passed. At his bedchamber door, she drew back. "I should retreat to my own chamber."

He shook his head, opened his door, and drew her inside. "Now that I have you, I am not letting you go."

"But the servants!" she protested as he dragged her inside and closed the door behind her. He reached around her, locked it, and bent to kiss her. "Andrew, do think what you are doing."

"I know exactly what I am doing." He gave her a wicked grin.

"You are the Duke of Ravenscroft now," she reminded him. "You need an heir."

He arched a brow. "Are you offering?"

"What? No!" She tried to push him away, but he would not release her. And his wandering hands were beginning to distract her. "I am a courtesan. Dukes do not beget legitimate heirs via courtesans."

"You are not a courtesan." He bent to kiss her neck.

She closed her eyes and struggled to focus. "I am, for all intents and purposes."

"Not a very good one. We shall have to work on that."

"No." This time she succeeded in breaking free. "I care too much for you, Andrew. I think the sooner I leave, the better." She started for the door, wishing he would stop her, wishing he would sweep her into his arms, carry her to the bed and make her stay. But that was a fantasy. Even if he had attempted it, she would have resisted. There was nothing he could say or do to make her stay. She had to protect his reputation and her own heart now.

"I was going to do this after the funeral, but I suppose I do not have the luxury of time. Lily Dawson, will you do me the honor of becoming my wife?"

There was nothing he could have said or done to make her stay, except this.

She spun around and stared at him. He was kneeling. "Stand up," she demanded.

He shook his head. "I do not think so. I have studied the form, and this is correct. I am supposed to entreat you on bended knee."

"You will not…" She gestured helplessly. She could not even say aloud what he was doing. "You will not do this. Stand up."

"But I am doing it, Lily. And I am a duke. You do not order me about. If I wish to propose, if I wish to make you my wife, I will do so."

She shook her head. "Oh, no, you will not. I will not do you the *dis*honor of becoming your wife."

Anger flashed across his features, and he rose. "It's no dishonor. You were born to be a duchess, Lily. Look where you have been. Look what you have overcome."

"Exactly. I will cause you nothing but scandal. You know who I am. You know what I have done." Tears threatened to spill onto her cheeks, and she wanted to turn and run, but he had locked the door, and when she attempted to turn the key, it fell to the floor. She went to her knees, trying to retrieve it, but he was beside her, his hands on her face, raising her gaze to his.

"You did what you had to in order to survive. You thought of your child more than yourself. You made mistakes, and you learned from them. Neither of us are saints, Lily, but if one of us is a devil, it is certainly not you."

"And you are? The sins of the parents are not passed on to the children."

Andrew ran a hand through his hair. "I was always so proud of our family honor. I thought my mother walked on water. But it was all a lie." He took her hand. "What I feel for you is the only truth I know."

"I'm sorry. I can't. Not when I know Juliette will always be your first choice."

He was shaking his head. "No—"

"How can you deny it? I loved you for so long." She rose, clutching her hands into fists. "And you never saw it. You never saw *me*. I was invisible whenever Juliette was nearby."

"Lily, believe me when I say I do not want Juliette. I don't even remember what I admired in her. This has nothing to do with Pelham or Juliette or anyone but you and me. I want you for my bride." He took her fists, unclenched them. "Marry me."

"I cannot. You will regret it within a year. When everyone talks—"

"Let them talk!" His tone was vehement, and he tightened his fingers on her hands. "I don't give a bloody farthing what they say. I *need* you, Lily. I *love* you."

She stared at him, her jaw dropping open. "You don't know what you're saying."

"I know exactly what I'm saying. I *see* you, Lily. I see all of you—the good and the bad—and I love you. Exactly as you are. I love *you*—Lily Dawson. Only you."

A tear escaped one eye and made its way down her cheek, where Andrew reached out and caught it. His hand lingered on her cheek, caressing it, and then he leaned close and kissed first one eye and then the other. He pulled back, his gaze locked with hers. "What must I do? Stand on my head again? Say the word, Lily. I will do anything for you." He released her suddenly and bent.

"What are you doing?"

"A handstand."

She laughed and tugged at his waist. "No! Not again. It was awful enough the first time."

He straightened. "Then tell me."

"Yes."

His brow furrowed. He looked so young and confused and utterly adorable.

"I said, yes. I will do you the *honor* of becoming your wife."

He blinked, and then he let out a loud holler of joy and swept her off her feet and into his arms. She laughed and kicked her feet, but he spun her in a circle then dropped her on the bed. She laughed harder.

"You are not hoaxing me, are you? You mean it?"

"I mean it, though I think you should change your mind."

"Never." He fell on his knees beside the bed. "I do not want to be here without you, Lily. I want you as my duchess."

"Is that the reason? I thought you wanted to tumble me again."

He grinned. "Well, there's that too." And then he was beside her, his body warm against hers, his hands in her hair, freeing it of the pins she'd stuck here and there at some point to keep it out of her face. It felt so good to let it fall down onto the pillows, to let him work his hands through it, to look into his eyes and to see passion and admiration and, yes, love in them.

"I cannot believe this is happening to me," she whispered.

He brushed his lips against hers. "Give me a few moments, love."

She laughed again. He was always making her laugh. "I meant I cannot believe I am going to marry you. I cannot believe you love me. Do you know how long I have dreamed of this?"

"Years and years, I imagine."

She swatted his shoulder. "You are horribly arrogant."

"No. I am horribly obtuse. How is it I did not fall in love with you the first moment I saw you?" He would have gone on, but she put her finger over his lips.

"Stop talking, or I shall begin to weep again."

"God forbid. No more weeping."

"Then kiss me." She ran her fingers through his hair and pulled his mouth to hers. "And do not ever stop."

❧

He had no intention of stopping, not now that she had agreed to be his. The past day had been the worst of his life. The only reason he made it through the ordeal was that Lily stood beside him. Every time he thought he could not go on, every time he thought he was at his limit of endurance or grief or anger or frustration, every time he began to seriously consider spending the rest of his life wallowing in abject humiliation rather than face the truth of who his father and mother were and what they had done, Andrew would raise his eyes and see Lily.

There was no pity for him in her eyes. There was no condemnation. He saw only love and admiration. He'd known she loved him before she ever said the words. He could look into her eyes and see that she thought he was the most wonderful creature to ever walk the earth. Had she always looked at him thus? If so, no wonder he avoided her. He knew his faults better than anyone. How could anyone truly love him if they knew all of his faults? Better that he disguise himself with false smiles and exaggerated wit. The entirety of Society adored the Darling of the *Ton*. But the Earl of Darlington—a man who did not always feel jovial, who made bad decisions, who at times felt at a loss as to how to manage his estates. That man was ever so tedious.

But Lily had not found him so, even though she'd known him as the Darling of the *Ton*. And there was more. He knew her faults too, and he thought he probably loved her more for them.

He linked his fingers with hers, twining their hands as he twined his body with hers. This was why he needed her. When he touched her, he felt he was sinking into another world—a world where farmer tenants, a leaky roof, and a father accused of treason faded away for a brief respite. He sank into the scent of her, the feel of her silky skin, the sound of her breathing. Her breathing matched his, and both of them were all but panting as clothes fell away and hands and mouths began to explore in earnest.

He would never tire of this. Never tire of the pleasure of her curves or the soft sounds she made when he stroked the dent of her waist or the swell of her breast. He was not a man who felt he could never be happy with one woman. He had always known when he married, he would be faithful. But he had never found the woman who could inspire such lofty thoughts of fidelity.

Until now.

Lily was all he needed. All he wanted.

He slid down her body, tasting and touching, listening to her gasps of breath and her sweet moans of urging. He kissed the back of her knee and the inside of her thigh, his kisses trailing upward until she was writhing and bucking against him. When she shattered, he wanted nothing more than to be inside her, to bury himself deep, but she looked up at him and said, "Your turn."

Andrew's eyes widened. "Lily, as much as I appreciate your eagerness to... ah... play the blanket flute, there are a few things you might improve in that endeavor."

He expected indignity, but she merely cocked a brow. "Do go on. I feel as though my education as a courtesan is finally to commence."

"This may not be the time." He eased her back down. "I will prepare a tutorial later..." Her cheeks were flushed and rosy, her body so warm and inviting. He really could not wait much longer.

But she pushed him back and sat. "I'm ready now. If I'm going to become your wife, I should learn how to please you."

"You *do* please me," he protested, knowing it was all in vain.

"I swear to reward you by acting the attentive pupil." She pushed him down. "I promise you, Your Grace, I am a quick learner."

And hours later, as they both dozed off to sleep, wrapped in each other's arms, Andrew mused that she was indeed an admirable pupil. Either that or he was a particularly gifted instructor.

Her elbow landed in his midsection, and he coughed. "What was that for?"

"Practice," she said with a yawn. "I imagine it will take a great deal of effort to keep you in line."

That had been his thought regarding her exactly. And for it, he was rewarded with another elbow to the gut.

Read on for a preview of the next in Shana Galen's
Lord and Lady Spy series

Love and Let Spy

Available August 2014
from Sourcebooks Casablanca

One

Somewhere in Europe, 1816

SHE CREPT DOWN THE CORRIDOR, BACK TO THE WALL, straining to place the voices of the men. Somewhere a woman was crying, a dog barked, and a horse-drawn cart rattled by. The stench of urine and blood burned her nostrils, but she moved forward.

Two men. Speaking French, though only one was a native speaker. The other, the accent sounded… Turkish? She turned her head from side to side to locate the voices.

Closed door.

Room at the end of the hall.

Three steps. Two. One.

She paused outside, drawing her knife. She didn't want to risk her pistol misfiring and left it tucked inside her coat, along with a stash of balls and powder. She was dressed as a man because the clothing was more practical and attracted less attention, although she wouldn't fool anyone who looked closely. And she didn't care.

A man inside the room—the Frenchman—spoke again, and her hand stilled on the door's latch.

"Reaper is dead," she translated silently. "He took his life in prison."

News traveled quickly, though not accurately. The report she'd seen claimed Foncé had gained access to Reaper and slit his throat. The leader of the Maîtriser group didn't tolerate failure. When Foncé realized she, an agent of his hated Barbican group, had tracked two of his men to this ramshackle safe house, their lives would be forfeit as well. Perhaps that cold fact would be incentive for them to assist her in locating their leader.

Or perhaps it would only make them more eager to kill her.

Either way, the games were about to begin.

She pulled her hand away from the door, stepped back, raised a booted foot, and kicked. The thin wooden door splintered and shot open with a loud *crack*. The men jumped up, but they didn't move quickly enough. Her knife flew from her fingers, catching one man in the shoulder and pinning him to the wall behind him. He screamed while the other man fumbled for his pistol. She obligingly reached for hers. "I'll kill you before you even pack your powder," she said in French. "Do us both a favor and lower your pistol before I'm forced to shoot you."

"I don't owe you any favors, Bonde," the man holding the pistol sneered. He was called Tueur, and he was an assassin—one of Foncé's best now that Reaper was dead. She wished she'd thrown the knife at him. They'd met before and, since he had been trying to kill her at the time, had not parted amicably.

But she could let bygones... and all of that rubbish. "That's *Miss* Bonde to you. Shall we have a little chat?"

"No time today," he said and threw the pistol. She ducked, and the weapon clattered to the floor behind her. She reached for it, tucked it in her waistband, then whirled back around. Tueur had wasted no time. He waved as he raced across the room and climbed out the window.

Bonde uttered a most unladylike expletive, her body pulled between Tueur and the Turk. She couldn't split in half—that was the disadvantage of working alone. Working with another agent—that was the disadvantage of a partner.

She headed for the window, glancing at the Turk over her shoulder. A knife protruded from his neck. Tueur had made certain the other man wouldn't talk. He'd also made her decision easy. She leaned out the window and spotted Tueur hanging from the faded awning of the shop below. He dropped to the ground and made a rude gesture.

Bygones were, apparently, not bygones in Tueur's opinion.

She did a quick calculation, then dove out the window, pulling her knees in so when she landed on the awning she would roll easily to the edge. She held her breath for the free fall and felt the air whoosh out of her when she hit the fabric.

But she didn't roll.

She heard an awful ripping sound and reached out

just in time to catch the edge of the awning before she fell through. Her feet dangled above the hard cobble-stones as the material slipped through her fingers. With a sigh, she let go, dropped and tumbled. The ground was hard, bruising her hip and shoulder. She hobbled to her feet and wiped her bloody hands on her trousers. Where was the dashed man? She glared left and then right.

Unfortunately, he'd seen her and took off at a fast clip.

She went after him, her hip protesting the move-ment. Red clouded her vision, and she realized her forehead was bleeding. She swiped the blood away and rounded a corner, emerging onto a busy avenue lined with carts and vendors. Men and women walked leisurely along the avenue, shopping on the lovely spring day. Bollocks! Again she'd lost him. And on a crowded street, no less.

Bonde noted a statue and raised fountain standing in a nearby esplanade and dodged horses and carriages to reach the monument. She climbed up, hanging on by one arm, and peered down the busy street. He was gone... no... wait.

There! He'd climbed into a Bath chair, which two men were hastily pulling away. She jumped down, searching for another chair for hire and realized Tueur had taken the last. She glanced about, her attention landing on a sporty gig. A footman waited beside the horse, presumably while the vehicle's owner shopped for produce. Bonde ran for it, hopping up before the footman could protest. He stared at her dumbly for a moment, but when she snapped the reins, he grabbed for the horse's bridle.

"Sorry!" she said, straining to control the skittish animal. The horse tried to rear and then shot off. Fortunately the beast chose the direction she wanted. Unfortunately, he was going much too fast for the crowded avenue. Men and women jumped out of the way as she struggled to gain the upper hand. The Bath chair was just ahead, but the horse bolted to the side before she could jerk him back. The gig's wheel caught on the edge of a fruit stand, sending the vendor's cart toppling over. Oranges and lemons tumbled into the street, and apples bounced in every direction. One bounced into the conveyance, and she caught it with one hand, took a bite, and snapped the reins.

She was grinning. She had Tueur now. He yelled furiously for the men pulling his chair to go faster, but they couldn't compete in a race with a horse. She gained ground until she finally pulled alongside the chair. "Ready for our chat now?" she yelled.

"Go to the devil, Bonde!"

"You first," she muttered, steering the horse closer to the chair so the men pulling it were forced to move aside. Tueur didn't wait for the inevitable. He rose and jumped from the chair, smashing onto the ground. She reined in the horse and jumped nimbly down, landing on her feet and running to grab Tueur before he could rise. She collided with a woman carrying an armful of flowers, and the woman tripped and went sprawling to the ground. Bonde spit a daffodil from her mouth and kept running. But the delay cost her. Tueur was up again and moving quickly toward a busy alleyway, where artists sold jewelry, paintings, and mementos. She pictured the city map in her mind. At the end of the alley was a canal. If Tueur reached the canal, he could jump on a vessel and she'd never catch him.

She pushed two men out of the way and raced forward. Tueur saw her coming and began to jog. Some of the crowd saw them coming and parted, but others had to be thrust out of the way. Bonde jumped lithely over a stack of crates, wobbled, and regained her balance.

Tueur was definitely headed for the canal. If she lost him, M would have her head. She sped up just as a young mother holding a little girl's hand stepped out from behind a stall. With a yell, Bonde narrowly avoided them and crashed into a flower cart. Everything went dark and floral for a moment, and when she surfaced, this time spitting tulip petals from her mouth, the flower girl screamed obscenities. At least Bonde *thought* they were obscenities. Amidst the haze of petals and stems, she could hardly remember in which country she'd landed and the native language spoken. She pulled a rose from her hair, handed it to the woman and arrowed for the canal.

Tueur was already there, and she saw his dilemma immediately. No vessels. Bonde reached for her pistol. She had him.

He saw her coming, then looked back at the water. Then back at her. He took a step forward.

"No!"

But it was already too late. He took two more steps back and fell. When she reached the edge of the canal the water was splashing back down, mud from below churning up and darkening the already filthy waterway.

"Come up. Swim, damn you," she muttered. The ripples grew larger and the water stilled. She stared at the place he'd gone under for a long moment, her gaze scanning the rest of the canal.

Nothing moved.

"Bollocks," she said.

"Hey!"

Bonde turned to see a crowd of angry merchants and shoppers approaching. Some waved damaged goods, some waved fists, some didn't have the courtesy to wave.

"Bollocks," she said again. There was nothing for it. She pulled off her cap, allowing her golden hair to spill down her back, and smiled prettily.

Two

London Season, 1816

"I DON'T CARE HOW BEAUTIFUL OR RICH OR BLOODY socially acceptable she is," Dominic said, turning fiercely from the drawing room mantel. "I am not marrying her."

"Sir, need I remind you that your mother is present?"

The marchioness waved a dismissive hand. In her pale blue muslin morning gown, she seemed almost one of the furnishings of the drawing room, which had been done in blue and cream and a panoply of gilt and ormolu. "I have heard it all before," his mother said. "One does not raise four sons without hearing a bit of the vulgar tongue."

Dominic gestured as if to say, *See?*

"I do not give a bloody farthing," the marquis said, standing and pointing at Dominic. "You *will* show your mother some respect."

Dominic refrained, just barely, from mentioning the contradiction inherent in his stepfather's curse. The man had no sense of humor and would not appreciate the irony. He also had a selective memory. At the moment, he chose to forget that his wife possessed a somewhat less than savory past.

Dominic wished he could forget.

"My lord," Dominic said, tamping his fury down from long habit, "I do not wish to marry. I have no obligation to produce an heir as I have no lands or titles to pass on. There is no need—"

"There is every need!" Lord Edgeberry boomed. Dominic clenched his fists to keep from using them. He was a grown man and did not enjoy being treated like a child. But he would tolerate it for his mother's sake. "Your behavior is scandalous, and I'll be damned if I will stand by while you produce a passel of bastards who show up on my door, begging for money."

Dominic cut his gaze to his mother, and the marchioness hissed in a breath and shook her head at her eldest son, her eyes pleading for forbearance. "My lord," she said, rising and taking her husband's arm. "Might we speak in private for a moment?"

Dominic turned his back on the room and faced the mantel, staring at the figure of a small porcelain shepherdess. She was a typical English beauty with flaxen hair, rosy cheeks, and huge blue eyes. Dominic hated the type. Behind him he heard his mother's rapid whispers. Every few moments, he was able to discern one of her words. "Fatherless… Pride… Careful."

The door opened, and Carlisle, one of Dominic's half-brothers, entered. "Oops! Sorry." He stepped back out just as quickly, but not before catching Dominic's eye and giving his older brother a grimace.

"No, no, Carlisle," their mother said. "Your father

and I will speak in the parlor. You go ahead." And she tugged the marquis out of the room, leaving Carlisle little choice but to enter.

"I'm not going to ask what that was about," Carlisle said, "so you'll have to volunteer the information."

Dominic couldn't stop a smile. Carlisle was his youngest half-brother and just out of school. At nineteen, he was not yet jaded by the world. But then again, why should he be? He was the son of a marquis, he was handsome, with blond hair and brown eyes, and he was wealthy. Nothing could touch him.

"I'll give you one guess," Dominic said, lifting his teacup from the drawing room side table. He'd always liked his youngest brother. With thirteen years between them, they were too far apart to be rivals.

"The woman who showed up with the babe last week?"

"Your father wants me to marry before I bring more shame on the family name." He sipped the tepid tea. He'd not had a chance to even taste it before his stepfather had launched into his tirade.

Carlisle popped a teacake into his mouth and reached for another. "Is marriage so bad?"

"I don't see you rushing into the parson's mousetrap."

Carlisle held the teacake in front of his chest like a shield. "I'm far too young. You're an old man."

"Charming to the last," Dominic retorted.

"Was the babe yours?" Carlisle asked, his mouth full. Dominic rolled his eyes. The boy had no sense of decorum.

"No."

"Who do they want you to marry?"

"Does it matter?"

He seemed to consider as he reached for a dainty sandwich. "It might."

"A Miss Jane Bonde."

Carlisle dropped the sandwich, and it rolled under a chair. The boy ignored it. "And you *refused*?"

"I don't want to marry, and I certainly won't marry some chit I haven't even met."

"But you've seen her?"

"I don't think so." Dominic avoided social events. He had nothing to say to the *ton*. He was well aware they looked down on him. He did not need to be reminded of it nightly.

"That explains it, then." Carlisle reached for another sandwich.

Dominic drank his tea. "You imply if I laid eyes on her, I would change my mind."

"Maybe not," Carlisle mumbled around the bread. "But you'd think twice."

Dominic set his teacup down. He was beginning to think it a good idea to escape while he had the chance. "I doubt we have the same taste in women."

"She is every man's taste, I assure you. Are you leaving?"

Dominic was halfway across the room. "Yes, but I must say, Carlisle, you have intrigued me. I might have to see this Miss Bonde for myself."

"There is a long line of men ahead of you."

Dominic opened the door. "Give Lord Edgeberry my regards."

"That ought to be a pleasant task," Carlisle muttered. Dominic closed the door and started for the stairs. He hadn't made it far before his mother stepped in front of him. She was petite, dark and exotic with her gypsy coloring. As far as Dominic knew, she was not of gypsy blood, but she did nothing to dispel the rumors. He was a great deal taller than she. His father must have been a man of some height, for Dominic was a head taller than his stepfather and his three half-brothers. But woe to the man or woman who equated height with power. Titania Griffyn—now Titania Houghton-Cleveborne, Marchioness of Edgeberry—was a force to be reckoned with.

"A word, my darling son." She gestured toward her boudoir, where she met with her closest friends, and set off, not waiting to see if he would follow.

Dominic sighed and followed.

Want more of Lily and Andrew?

They appear in the other titles in Shana Galen's Jewels of the Ton series

WHEN YOU GIVE A DUKE A DIAMOND

IF YOU GIVE A RAKE A RUBY

And don't forget to stop by Shana Galen's website, shanagalen.com, for a special series epilogue featuring all of your favorite characters.

Acknowledgments

It's an amazing feeling when a book is complete, and as I sit at my laptop in the wee hours of the morning and contemplate typing *The End*, I am thankful for those who have helped me in some small way with Lily's story.

First of all, I want to thank my readers, who encourage and inspire me.

I also owe a debt of gratitude to my agents, Joanna and Danielle, who are my biggest cheerleaders.

I would sleep a lot less if not for my awesome assistant Gayle, who takes all the tedious administrative tasks off my plate. Jen and Maddee at xuni.com are also indispensable.

When I get stuck, I can always turn to the Brainstorm Troopers for ideas or suggestions. Thanks, Margo, Robyn, Anne, and Emily. When I need a boost, the Peanut Butter on the Keyboard Moms can always make me feel better. Thanks to Kieran, Maisey, Ellie, Robyn, and Emily.

When I'm stressed, Emily and Amy are only a text away and always "ready to rock" at 5 a.m.

Thank you to Grace Burrowes, who answered my horse-related questions. Any mistakes in the manuscript are my own.

As an author, it's a gift to have an editor who loves my work and allows me to take risks. Thanks to my wonderful editor Deb Werksman. And thank you as well to the team at Sourcebooks who works so hard on my behalf—Rachel Edwards, Susie Benton, my cover designers and copy editors. Danielle Dresser, you are a rock star.

And finally, thank you to my family for their support and sacrifices.

About the Author

Shana Galen is the bestselling author of fast-paced, adventurous Regency historicals, including the RT Reviewers' Choice *The Making of a Gentleman*. She taught English at the middle and high school level off and on for eleven years. Most of those years were spent working in Houston's inner city. Now she writes full time. She's happily married to a man she calls Ultimate Sportsfan and has a daughter who is most definitely a romance heroine in the making. Shana loves to hear from readers: visit her website at www.shanagalen.com, download her free author app for exclusive content and first looks, or see what she's up to daily on Facebook and Twitter.